Also by Thomas Rayfiel

SPLIT-LEVELS

colony
GIRL

colony GIRL

by

THOMAS RAYFIEL

Farrar Straus Giroux / New York

Farrar, Straus and Giroux
19 Union Square West, New York 10003

Copyright ©1999 by Thomas Rayfiel
Distributed in Canada by Douglas & McIntyre Ltd.
Printed in the United States of America
Designed by Nick Burkett
First edition, 1999

Library of Congress Cataloging-in-Publication Data
Rayfiel, Thomas, 1958-
    Colony Girl / Thomas Rayfiel.
        p.   cm.
        ISBN 0-374-12644-5 (alk. paper)
        I. Title.
        PS3568.A9257C65   1999
        813'.54—DC21   99-20042

for Ann Weissberg (1934–97)

colony
GIRL

1

I used to take those tests in teen
magazines. "Would You Invite Yourself to Your Own Party?" That
kind of thing. "In a room full of people, do you (a) act strong and
assertive, monopolizing the conversation? (b) listen to what others
have to say and respond intelligently? or (c) withdraw to the corner
and sulk?" I was more like (d) drink too much cheap wine and go
outside and vomit. That's how I met my first serious date, behind a
suburban house in a small Iowa town, as I held on to a tree trunk
like it was the center pole of a merry-go-round. He wasn't another
kid, though. He was our "host's" father.

"Had too much to drink?" he asked.

I didn't answer. I had this theory that if you didn't talk to people
they would go away. It had worked pretty well so far. Besides, I
couldn't lift my head. All I could focus on was the ground, this
rolling ocean of dirt and twigs and tufts of grass. It was a very bad
lawn for Iowa, where people said you could just toss a handful of
seeds out your window and watch them grow.

"I'm Joey's dad," he tried again.

I found his shoes, big brown clodhoppers, then blue Sears work pants. With an effort, I raised my eyes as far as his white button-down shirt, so pale in the summer evening it glowed. He was big, almost fat, with graying hair and thick glasses. He had a squashed nose and ears that stuck out. A friendly face. Very safe and unthreatening.

"Herb." He held out his hand. "Herb Biswanger."

"Eve," I answered, and substituted him for the tree trunk, falling against his soft side.

He braced himself to take me on, but didn't actually touch or hold me. He just stood his ground while I slid down his shirtfront. Finally I found his belt buckle and hung there.

"You OK?" he asked.

"I'm fine," I said into his belly.

"You want me to call someone? Have them help you home?"

"No telephones in the Bible."

"Oh, you're from the Colony?"

He tried stepping away, but I had found his shoe tops and was standing on them. They had steel tips under the leather. Construction shoes. I moved back with him, as if we were dancing.

"I'm going to be sick," I warned.

He just kind of scooped me with his arms, like a forklift. Then he staggered and tossed me in the air to get a better grip. I settled against his chest and breathed in aftershave. The moon and stars bounced as we walked. There was a looming darkness behind the house. He kicked open its door and stepped over the piece of wood that ran along the bottom.

"This is the toolshed," he announced.

It had been a barn once. A wide bank of fluorescent lights hung level with the hayloft. The floor was poured concrete. Tools were hung on the wall, every kind you could imagine, screwdrivers, saws, planes, old-fashioned drills and bits, everything a hand tool, nothing electric. There was a big workbench with a vise built into it. And one stool, high, with no back.

"There you go," he said, setting me down gently on the floor.

He walked away. I had this moment of sheer terror. But before I could imagine something really horrible—my arms and legs caught in all that cold steel—he turned and smiled. The feeling of rightness flooded back.

"Where's he got it?" he asked, fiddling with something in the corner.

"Who?"

"Joey. Where's he got the wine hidden? At least it smells like wine."

"Nowhere," I answered, then added, as if it wasn't a contradiction. "In the cellar."

He shook his head, coming back at me with a green tank, the kind scuba divers wear, and holding a clear plastic mask.

"Take a deep breath. It'll clear your head."

"What is it?"

"Oxygen."

Even though I'd hugged him as he'd carried me, this was our first real touch. He held out the mask. A tube connected it to the tank. Our fingertips met.

"I get short of breath sometimes," he explained, turning the squeaky knob. He sat opposite me on the floor and watched. His eyes did that thing men's do, traveled up and down my body, stopping, then going on, coming back to my face and smiling as if nothing had happened. "They let you dress like that at the Colony?"

I gave the same sort of look to his place. Women have bodies, men have places. It was very neat, but with a layer of dust. All these tools, the blades gleaming, the handles soft and stained with sweat.

There was no sign of work, nothing on the bench or in the vise. No sawdust or scrap. Nothing on the floor either, but me, sprawling, propped on one elbow, holding a gas mask to my mouth. The fluorescent lights somehow made things darker. I squinted, trying to penetrate the mystery. What mystery? That was a mystery, too. Mysteries within mysteries within— Hands blotted out the picture. Big soft fingers brushed my eyelashes, made me shiver. He had a gold wedding band with a deep scratch in it. I wondered what it would be like to be married to him and live here on this concrete floor, surrounded by woodworking tools, sucking down oxygen. He took the mask away. My lips made a wet parting sound, they were so dazed. My mouth stayed open. Unresisting. As if I had just been kissed.

"There." His voice came from far away. "Better?"

Everything snapped into focus. My head was right on top of my body. Perfectly centered. I looked down and saw how the rest of me all led up to it, tapering to this one precious moment of being. I was a freshly sharpened pencil.

"Wow," I breathed.

He was already pressing on his knees, getting up off the floor.

"They don't," I called, not moving, staring at where he had just been, willing him to sit back down.

"Huh?"

"They don't let me dress like this at the Colony. They don't know I'm here."

I was wearing an incredibly short black dress, purple stockings, and pillowy boots of soft leather that only came up to my ankles. I had never used makeup before and could feel it flaking on top of my face like a crust.

"Well, isn't that kind of dangerous?" he asked.

"Only if I get caught."

He sat back down. I blinked. It was the first time anyone had ever done exactly what I wanted. I felt as if I had used my thoughts to bend a spoon.

"I could stay here," I suggested.

"Oh, I don't think so."

"Why not?"

He smiled. "You'd get bored."

"No, I wouldn't." I looked around, surveying his place from the strange low angle of the floor. "What do you make here?"

"Well, this was going to be a wood shop, you see. I was going to make antique-type carvings, furniture and stuff, using the actual tools of the period. Some of these are collector's items." He motioned vaguely. "But I kind of got caught up in the planning. In the setting up. Haven't done much actual work. None at all, in fact."

"It's beautiful." The words escaped my mouth like a hiccup. "Can I have more? Of that oxygen, I mean."

"I think you've had enough . . ." He frowned, trying to remember my name.

"Eve."

". . . Eve. Eve what? If you don't mind my asking."

"Just Eve. No last names in the Bible."

"But you must've had one to start out with. On your birth certificate, I mean."

I shook my head. He was probably fifty. By the time the divorce came through I would be sixteen. We would have to start having children right away.

"You work at the playground factory?" I asked.

"Well, now how did you know that?"

"Your belt buckle." It was gold-plated, with a raised picture of a jungle gym on it. It meant he'd been working there at least ten years. Five was a tie clip. I forget what fifteen was. Then, at twenty-five years, I think, or maybe when you retired, you got a special clock you never had to wind. It ran off the motion of the earth somehow.

"You're a very observant girl."

All this time there had been music, the kind that floats on the summer air. It jumped now, as the back door to the house opened and voices spilled out onto the lawn.

"I am going to kick that boy's ass," he sighed.

"He's OK. Joey."

"Because he invited you to his party?"

"I think he did *that* on a dare."

"What do you mean?"

"Just talking to us is apparently a major ordeal." I don't know if it was the oxygen or the alcohol, but suddenly I was leaning forward, confiding in this man whose name I had forgotten. "Once, in the bathroom at school, I caught two girls spying on me over the top of the stall. Because there's this rumor we're forced to wear some special kind of underwear. And my friend Serena heard even weirder stuff, people saying that we all had this operation to keep us pure. For until we're married. They think we're these . . . freaks!"

"And that's why my son invited you to his party?"

"Well, why else?" I mumbled, suddenly wanting to take the words back. "I mean, it's not like I know him or anything."

He was holding the soft plastic mask in his hand. He frowned down at it as if it was a face.

"Joey's mom died last year."

I could see myself in his glasses, two of me, small, persistent.

So that means . . . you're available? I wanted to ask.

He cocked his head at someone screaming, another boy, not Joey, about ten feet away from us, just on the other side of the wall. It took me a while to realize it was laughter.

"They're not going to come in here, are they?"

"No. No one's allowed in here." He smiled. "In fact, I haven't been in here myself since—"

A bottle smashed on a rock.

"Hell!"

He got up and hauled his dad act on, his armor of authority. It made him look old and tired.

"I'm sorry," he apologized.

"For what?"

". . . for saying Hell."

"Just a place." I shrugged. "Like Iowa."

"Once I chase these clowns away, I'll drive you home."

"I walked," I said, getting up to join him.

"Walked? It's six miles to the Colony."

"I cut through the woods."

"Well, take a flashlight, at least. I know"—he caught himself—"no flashlights in the Bible. What *is* in the Bible, anyway? I seem to have forgotten."

"Salvation," I answered automatically.

The woods beginning past the last ring of new houses were fields they had let grow over. Instead of prairie, they had become a patch of tangled, skinny trees, not spooky like a real forest, except when you came face-to-face with the ghost of an old scarecrow. I kept some mystical straightness in front of me and walked with my head down for twenty minutes before pushing out into the cool night air, down the steep side of a drainage ditch, and then up onto the shoulder of the county highway. I was exactly where I had expected to be. It was impossible to get lost in Arhat, Iowa, no matter how hard you tried. There was an overpass where the Interstate ran. They were experimenting with a new hi-tech sign that read your speed as you approached. I walked down the middle of the road, the heels of my boots making solid striking sounds against the pavement, sending reassuring shock waves up each leg. I was still a little wobbly. The sign flashed 0 MILES PER HOUR.

After a while the ground actually rose. Millions of years ago, our science teacher had told us, a glacier screeched to a halt here, right in front of town. I liked Gordon's explanation better, that God had been asleep, flattening all that was under His body, and reached back to scratch Himself, tearing up the ground, digging out the lake, giving our little corner of the world character, while leaving the prime farmland that began on the other side of the Interstate bland and featureless.

The cemetery was as far as people from town went. Sometimes you'd see them bringing flowers or clipping the grass around a stone. One family had picnics, which I thought was nice. Most just glared when they saw us. Past the graves, up the beginning of what was almost a hill, the highway stopped. Suddenly the road was dirt. Trees crowded in. Instead of my heels banging against the asphalt there was just the scratch and shuffle of my toes feeling their way along. The sky got smaller, then disappeared. I thought of Joey's father—what was his name again?—offering me a ride. I would never let anyone drive me here. To reach the Colony was a journey. Each time. It reminded you, with every step, of what Gordon had created, made you appreciate and fear it more. At the top of the hill, the road plunged. You had to watch yourself, almost crouch, it was so unexpected to find a drop that steep. Everywhere else was flat. It was easy to slide on the loose round stones. Then you got your bearings and your eyes adjusted. You looked up and you saw the lake.

And the lake saw you, because Gordon's house sat high above the water. A light was on. It reflected in the still circle like an unblinking eye. It had been a farm years ago, and then a summerhouse. After that, it had been where the head counselor slept, when there had been a camp here, a big log cabin with a wraparound porch, all enclosed in screen, brown with red trim, dark and gloomy. There was some sort of dried-out putty or gum stuffed in every seam where two logs met. You couldn't see in the windows, the porch screening was so old and black, but people said Gordon could see out. I stayed to the side of the road, which was eroded by rainfall and neglect. Sometimes we dumped a load of gravel, but it never seemed to help. To be watching me, Gordon would have needed nighttime and X-ray vision, but the power of his personality was so strong that I didn't doubt for a second it was possible. I shrank into myself. Where I'd been held, caressed, just two hours before, burned. I brushed my fingers to my lips, wishing I could suck out the poison. Undo events.

The lake had a bad reputation. People in town told stories about accidents and outbreaks of fever. Even a murder. Gordon said it was envy, that there had been all these failed attempts to develop the place, to make money off it. The Rotarians and Chamber of Commerce types saw what they had dreamed of as a country club or a casino turned into a tax-exempt religious community. Of course, to us it was just home, a bunch of cabins scattered around a large pond. Not a good place for swimming, because it was always cold and there was no beach, just a sudden solid six feet of freezing water. It was easy to see why people drowned. It was very beautiful and very harsh. Our cabins didn't have electricity or insulation. There was the Meeting Hall, which was our church, where we could go love God anytime, and Gordon's house, the castle, unattainable, a source of pride and mystery, but most important of all there were the sixty-two of us, twelve families, refugees from a world that was out of control, trying to lead Christian lives.

Our cabin door never closed completely. It was easy to get in without making noise. I took off my boots and held them, squeezing the raw planks of wood with purple-stockinged toes as I pulled my tired body down the hall. From the safety of familiar surroundings, the whole evening suddenly seemed ridiculous. I took a deep breath and tried not to giggle.

"Eve?"

In my room, grateful for the darkness, I took off my clothes and pushed them behind the bottom drawer of my dresser.

"Eve, is that you?"

"Yes, Mother."

"How was it?"

For a minute, I thought she knew. For a minute, I *wished* she knew. I didn't feel guilty, I felt . . . bursting with my little adventure. And Mother could be a great person to talk to, more like an older sister sometimes. I put on my pajamas and appeared in her doorway. She was in bed, staring at the ceiling. She never used the oil lamp. We had a good cabin, right near the lake, across from Gordon's. His light bounced off the water and shone up through her window, making shifting shapes on the ceiling. That's what she looked at most nights, until she fell asleep. She watched the bubbles and flaws and streaks of the old-fashioned pane dance.

"How was it?" she asked again, not even looking at me, tranced out.

She didn't suspect anything, I realized.

Mother accepted the world. She wanted nothing from it. She was a true mystic. The women of the Colony called her "spacey," and much worse, because she had the ability to stare past people, past events, past her own emotions even, to some deeper truth. But I knew exactly how much it cost her to keep things together, to keep that calm, blue-eyed gaze so clear. Her stillness was the stillness of a hummingbird. Her blank expression was a drum skin, stretched tight. I think they hated her for her body, too, the women, because she was still so petite and perfect and unmarked. Only her face had aged. Her frazzle of golden hair had thinned, her fine cheekbones and straight nose had been stranded by some receding tide, the corners of her mouth had turned down. I had found a picture—the only one that existed from before she joined the Colony—and knew how beautiful she had been. Now she was something else, an unapproachable ideal of femininity, delicate and ageless. All the time I was growing up, her looks had been the most important thing in my life. I stared at her for hours. The way she lost herself in the whorls and dots of the antique glass, that's the way I lost myself in her.

"It was good," I said, standing there in my ratty old pajamas. "Serena's smart."

"Serena . . . ?" she murmured.

"I was studying with Serena, remember?" It annoyed me she couldn't even keep track of the lies I told her. I mean, then what was the point of my having made them up in the first place?

"You're smart," she objected.

"No, I'm not. Serena knows all the answers."

"The answers. And she tells them to you?"

"Well no, not exactly. I mean we study," I lied. "Together."

"And what do you tell her?"

She frowned. The pattern on the ceiling had changed. The shapes had gotten sharper and began to jump crazily. They were blue now, instead of white, coming from Gordon's big-screen TV, what he called the Perpetual Flame, because he left it on all night. He's up there now, I pictured, drinking Diet Coke, slumped in front of the tube, half-asleep, mumbling some prophecy that, more likely than not, would come true, would "come to pass," as he put it.

"What?" I asked, finding that I had been staring along with her.

"Serena tells you the answers," my mother summarized calmly, "and what do you tell her?"

"Oh, I make her laugh, I guess."

She turned to me. Her eyes narrowed a moment, zoomed in on my very soul, then flicked it aside with distaste, pulled back and widened, returned to that pitying, forgiving tenderness, leaving me exhausted.

"He was here tonight," she said.

"For how long?"

"An hour."

Bastard. Just long enough to make every fat cow in the Colony jealous. They were all supposed to be equal in his eyes, but she was the one he spent time with, whose cabin he graced with visits, and I was the only Colony child he seemed able to tolerate. Mother continued to smile at me.

"He's concerned about you," she said gently.

"Me? Why?"

"He feels you're unhappy."

I laughed. I couldn't believe Gordon knew or cared how I felt. I couldn't believe anyone did. I had gone to such lengths to hide my feelings. I had never even asked myself the question: Are you happy? It was as irrelevant to me as my missing last name, the one Outsiders were always getting so hung up on.

"I'm happy," I protested.

"Your . . . grades?" She pronounced the word like it was some strange concept. "He says you're not doing well in school."

"My grades are OK. I get B's. And C's."

She looked me up and down, not the way men did; it was more brutal and professional, a cold, appraising look. I don't think beautiful women ever lose a certain contempt for those of us who are not.

I think it was physically painful for her to see me. I was taller than her already. Bulkier. My eyes were too small and my nose was too big. I was awkward. I was gauche. People hated me on sight. It was something chemical, I had decided. Not my fault. I was this terrible mistake she had made, and she loved me anyway.

"I told him you'd be at Morning Prayer," she concluded, shifting in bed to refocus her gaze on the ceiling. "He feels it might help."

"Morning Prayer?"

Morning Prayer was at five. Five a.m. Kids my age didn't have to go. It could be very beautiful. Sometimes it left you with peace, a glowing silence you took with you the rest of the day, sheltering it inside you like an ember. But I hadn't been in over a year, ever since Gordon had stopped leading the services personally.

"Sure," I heard myself say. "I'll go. If you want."

She didn't even nod. She had taken my obedience for granted. I still stood there, even though I knew it was time for me to go, especially if I had to get up again in a few hours. But since Mother had just given me this order and since I had unquestioningly followed it, I felt I had to be . . . dismissed, and so I waited. I watched her frown and move her lips as she tried to make sense of the constellations of her universe. After a while, she sensed my presence. With an effort, coming back from some faraway place, she said, "Good night, Eve," and continued to stare up at the ceiling.

"Night," I said.

My room was just a closet. The mattress took up almost the whole floor. A plant, something between a bush and a tree, with thick, oily leaves, scratched its back against my window, shutting out the sun and moon alike. I had an old dresser, with a mirror on top, wedged against one wall, and a wardrobe with one leg missing tilted against the other. They towered over me when I lay down at night. Gordon was paranoid about fire. Even so, Mother let me have a candle. I looked in the mirror and almost died. My makeup! I had forgotten to take it off. In pajamas especially I looked like a complete idiot, a child who'd been playing with paints. So that's what she'd seen, in her rapid, repulsed gaze, and chosen not to say anything about. I wished she had. I wished we could have talked. But when she was angry she didn't really believe in talking. She believed in silence, in having me find out a minute later that she knew where I'd been. That was punishment enough.

It was the first time I'd ever used mascara. I didn't know about cold cream. I just sucked on a rag and kept rubbing my face, for hours, it felt like, staring anxiously in the mirror. If only I could have kept going. Mother's face was sanded down to its essence. Mine was animal and alive. It could have been a boy's or a horse's. I blew out the candle and got undressed in the dark. I lay on my stomach, then on my side, then on my back, then on my stomach again, like I was being turned on a giant spit. I had forgotten to pray, but it didn't matter. I'd be at that stupid Morning Service pretty soon. Besides, I didn't want to pray that night. What I was feeling, even though I was bouncing around on the thin, worn-out mattress like a crazy girl, had nothing to do with God's Grace, or Jesus, or the Holy Spirit. What I wanted was to be cradled forever—his name finally came to me—in the loving arms of Herbert Biswanger.

"It's a natural perfume."

"It is not," Angela said. "Besides, it's disgusting."

"Well, it's just something I heard," Jewell yawned. "You don't have to have a conniption over it."

"Besides, if it's perfume, it's forbidden."

"Don't be silly," Serena said. "It's us. How can *we* be forbidden?"

Jewell had heard some girls say that if you put your finger between your legs and then behind each ear it would "drive boys wild." I liked that picture, a thundering herd of boys, like bison, kicking up a big dust cloud on the plain.

We were quiet a moment, clacking our way down the road. From time to time a school bus roared by. Some of the more energetic kids hung out the windows and hooted at us.

Jewell, Angela, Serena, and I were the oldest children in the Colony, the only ones who went to school. The younger ones were taught at home. The walk was too long for them, and Gordon wouldn't allow any other form of transportation. Besides, they were "impressionable," he said, while we, supposedly, were immune to the sins and temptations of Grover Putnam High. We all dressed the same. Gordon had picked out our clothes. A white blouse, a tan skirt ending just above the knee, black shoes with a modest heel. No makeup or, God forbid, perfume. But because we were so different, and because there were only four of us, we never thought of ourselves as wearing uniforms.

Angela was tall and thin, like a whip, not just how she looked but the way she talked and acted. Her father, Richard, was an Elder. They had come here the most recently, only four or five years ago, so she was much more careful about following the rules and being a good girl than the rest of us. It made her a little crazy. She was always egging us on, enjoying whatever slightly daring thing we did, all while miming disapproval and standing off to one side, in case there was trouble. She had a long, twitchy nose and a little mouth. She was smart. Richard hadn't beaten that out of her yet. And she could be very nice. But when she was scared or nervous she would get just like him. She had a mean streak, which she mostly turned on herself.

Jewell drove her crazy. She was a big girl with a luxurious, unrestrained body, a friendly, freckled face, and eyes that closed up when she laughed. She said and did whatever she wanted. People thought she was outrageous, but really she was just content. Jewell didn't have any doubts about her future. Of all of us, I thought, she would turn out to be the most perfect wife. I could already see her with kids and cookies and a couch, and some dim, shadowy husband in the background, coming home at night and leaving again in the morning, totally irrelevant. She was a hard worker, didn't care about how she looked, didn't care about school, and she got away with things. That's what Angela couldn't stand. In all the years we had grown up together, I never saw Jewell get punished, while the rest of us had been bashed around too many times to count.

But it was Serena I loved, my best and truest friend. She seemed untouched by what we were going through. It didn't exist for her, the way we'd find ourselves saying and doing and, in my case, wearing things that were so totally wrong. She had just stepped over that part of her life. She was already a person, so sure of herself. But she wasn't slow and dead to things the way the adults were.

"Here," she said quietly, lagging behind, handing me the sheet of homework we had pretended to be doing together last night.

"Thanks," I breathed, slipping it into my notebook.

I'm sure I idealized her. She had problems, just like the rest of us. She only had her mother, which was another reason for our special bond, and at times there was a kind of bleakness to her vision. She was too practical, too clear-eyed to have any goofy, sustaining hope. I don't know if she dreamed enough. Or at all. But I loved her. And she found something to like in me, which was her most amazing quality. She would be beautiful one day, but no one else could see it. Nobody bothered her, gave her that kind of nasty fake attention "pretty" girls got. She was quiet, with chestnut hair, grave brown eyes that really saw you, took you in unquestioningly, and this very full mouth from which came the most unusual, unexpected wisdom. She was our oracle, our priestess in touch with the world's Hidden Powers.

"Guess who was at Morning Prayer today," Angela said.

I was the clown of the gang, the daredevil, the scuttling weirdo they made fun of. I made them laugh. I scared them, too. I scared myself. The bad things I saw about adolescence, the demonic possession, the fear and self-hatred, the awful future—more awful the longer you looked at it—I was all that carried to some horrible extreme. I banged into things. I didn't know where I was, where I began and ended, from one day to the next. It was like I had been chosen for some lab experiment in total humiliation. I still felt dirty from last night, even though I'd scrubbed my face till it was raw. My hand compulsively clawed at my cheek, my eyes, my lips.

"Who?" Jewell asked.

"Guess," Angela insisted.

"Your father," Jewell said promptly.

"Well yes, Einstein. He was leading, of course. That's how I know."

"Know what?"

"Who else was there. I didn't go."

I yawned. I was so tired, not just from getting up early, but at the thought of the whole day now stretching out in front of me. First this, which I hadn't anticipated, their finding out so soon, then the stares of the kids at school, the boring classes and ugly teachers, then the same long walk home, ending up right back where I had started from, only even more tired and more deeply ashamed. And of course there was Joey, who I couldn't face, even in my imagination. The highway was chewing up my feet. I closed my eyes, listened to the clatter of our shoes, all of us perched on hooves, so vulnerable, like a herd of gazelle or antelope, traveling in a pack for protection. When I woke up again, the others were staring. Angela must have pointed.

"OK," I said. "So it was me."

"You went to Morning Prayer?" Jewell grinned.

"She was in front."

My mother made me, I wanted to say. But didn't. If it got back that Gordon had taken any special interest, even a negative one, like telling her I should go to Morning Prayer, it would be bad for her. The other women in the Colony would talk.

"I just felt like it," I mumbled. "I couldn't sleep anyway, so—"

"She sang," Angela concluded. You could tell it was the end of her store of information, what her dried-up stick of a dad had reported later, over his corn flakes. She gave a horrible little self-satisfied snicker.

"I prayed," I said steadily, putting one foot in front of the other. "What's wrong with that?"

"Nothing," Serena said gently. "They let you be in front?"

I had gone there, bleary-eyed, at five, mist rushing off the lake, the Elders already assembled. When the weather was good we held services outside. There was always some kind of order, who stood where, unspoken but observed even more strictly for being unspoken: Leader, Elders, men, women, children. Mother always stood off to the side, in her own little pocket of space. Gordon, when he was more involved in the day-to-day running of the Colony, used to lead. He'd stand with his back to the lake, sing a hymn, then begin the Prayer, something spontaneous, and topical, about what had happened yesterday or what was supposed to happen today. It was like getting the morning newspaper, except it was all about God and Jesus and our own personal, crucially personal, salvation, which made it much more interesting than any newspaper could ever be, more like a cliffhanger. He would turn around and kneel. We would pray, communing, both within ourselves and together, the group, all sinners, struggling. For a long time we'd pray. The only sound would be a mosquito buzzing in your ear or a fish twisting out of the lake, slapping its side back against the sheet of sky. "Amen," Gordon's voice would come, calling us. And in the meantime, something would have floated free.

But with Gordon secluded in his house, wrestling with the Devil, it wasn't the same. Richard didn't even try to inspire us. It was more an exercise in remembering, for me at least, because I hadn't been there in so long. But I went through the motions, both external and internal, and was surprised to feel the same things I had felt before, maybe muted a bit, but still real enough that I felt good afterward. Until now.

"Did you ask to be in front?" Jewell wanted to know. "Or did they invite you?"

"Neither."

The last time any of us had been to Morning Prayer, we stood with the kids. We weren't really expected to participate. We were supposed to be quiet, the older ones taking care of the babies, and watch. Then, at a certain age, thirteen or fourteen, we didn't have to go at all. In fact, we were encouraged not to. Because Gordon said our thoughts were too confused, too undisciplined to submit to communal prayer. We would only muddy the waters, he explained. This morning, when I had gone, I just automatically joined the women, without thinking, and they had just as naturally moved aside to accept me.

Serena gave me a private smile.

Angela straightened her immature body and self-consciously walked on ahead. Despite whatever malicious pleasure she might have taken in embarrassing me, I could tell she was upset.

Was it a race to womanhood we were on, I wondered, as the four of us continued down the road. Or some inescapable fate we saw ourselves doomed to?

Joey caught up with me in the hallway, just before the end of school.

"What happened to you?" he asked.

"What do you mean?"

"Last night. I saw you go outside. So I went to look for you. But you were gone. It's like you disappeared."

"I wish," I said defensively. "Anyway, I didn't disappear. I'm right here."

He was my height and had muscles on his upper body that made his arms stick out from his sides. Just a little, not like he was deformed. On the contrary, he was perfect. Town girls talked about him like he was this ideal guy. It wasn't just that his skin was clear and that he had shiny black hair, or that his teeth were white and his eyes were blue. It wasn't even that he was so flawless and we were all so misshapen. It had more to do with him being comfortable. He never looked nervous or uncertain. He didn't seem, like the rest of us, embarrassed just to *be*. If Serena had somehow skipped being a teenager, Joey embodied it, all the good points, at least.

"So then I tried to look you up in the phone book," he went on. "But I don't know your last name."

"No phones in the Bible. No last names, either."

"What about Jesus Christ?"

"Well, yeah. Him."

We were both quiet. I held my books in front of my chest, as if History could save me.

"How's your dad?" I asked.

He had opened his mouth to say something else and just stood there.

"Who?"

"Your father." I was blushing. When I blushed, these spots appeared on my face, little black holes of shame eating into my skin.

He stepped aside to let people pass. I went against the lockers with him, so we were standing next to each other, shoulder to shoulder, staring at everyone as they shuffled by.

"You know my dad?" he asked.

"No."

He nodded, as if that made sense.

"I hate those things," I said. "They're just like all you town kids, all these upright, faceless, little square-shouldered boxes, each with a breathing hole and combination lock. I swear, when I first saw them, I thought they were where you all slept at night. You know, like vampires?"

"What are you talking about?"

"You know . . . the lockers."

"Oh."

"Hello, Eve."

Angela was passing. She saw Joey and gave me a nasty little tattletale smile. I smiled back and took his hand in my own, which was just the kind of rule she would never break. Physical Contact. I held both our hands up so she could see. We had just gotten engaged and were showing off the ring. Angela was kind of bug-eyed anyway, but that made them pop out so wide she looked super-ugly and I immediately felt bad. Then the traffic in the hall carried her away.

"So what are you going to do this summer?" I asked with sudden boldness. I had never held hands with a boy before. I was clearly insane. I'd read about me in books. My knees were weak, but out-wardly I knew I looked absolutely calm. I was psychotic, that was the word.

"Work at Duffy's."

"The garage? You're going to be an auto mechanic?"

"Grease monkey." He smiled.

The bell rang. He looked down at his hand, as if he'd just noticed it was in mine. He worked his fingers free. I just stood there. After that sudden burst of confidence I couldn't think of a thing to say. My feet had put down roots.

"Well," he said, like that was a complete sentence, and left.

Well, I thought, watching him go down the hall. His muscles were more expressive than his face, the way they . . . sat on him, as if he had the weight of the world on his shoulders. Why else would you make your back so broad unless you had some load to bear? He turned once and caught me staring, but I didn't acknowledge him. I was seeing past him, down the long hall, as he headed toward his future, a cinder-block wall, unaware. And he is Herbert's son, I reminded myself. Which meant, if we married, he would be my stepson. That would be awkward at first, of course. But manageable. I could give him baths.

Coming late to class was one of the small freedoms that went along with being a freak. Teachers never questioned me. They prob-ably thought I was praying or adjusting my chastity belt. School would be over in three days. I kept staring.

Just because none of us went to Morning Prayer anymore didn't mean we'd stopped being Christians. Gordon was smart. At the age when we would have rebelled and started questioning his authority, he dropped all the requirements. Suddenly no services were manda-

tory. The chores that had been such a big part of our growing up—
helping to gather wood, do laundry, memorize Scripture—all fell to
younger members of the Colony. We were set free. Naturally, the
first thing we tried to do was find our own way home, to carve out a
new place for ourselves in the order of things. I had prayed, in private, learned how, really, to pray; and instead of the Meeting Hall's
Evening Service we had gathered, the four of us, and unconsciously
mimicked what we so gleefully thought we were escaping, just a few
hundred yards off. The willow was our church, a strange combination of height and hiddenness. It grew on a hilltop overlooking the
lake. Even Gordon's house, from there, was mostly roof. The willow
must have been planted by a farmer when his fields extended to the
very limits of where you could grow. It hung down over the top of
the slope, its tender branches flipping and flicking in the wind,
almost touching the ground. We would push them aside like a bead
curtain and huddle together, invisible, the space for just us, inti-
macy and green giving it a holy, stained-glass feeling. You could
hear the hymns rising from the Meeting Hall and hear the silence,
even louder, as Gordon knelt.

"Highway crew?" I suggested.

They looked at me.

"You know, the road crew. There's always a guy with a flag who
waves the cars around. And he wears this jersey." I tried to indicate,
helplessly, with my hands. "Orange and white stripes, sort of . . . fluorescent. It pays ten dollars an hour."

Jewell was chewing on a long blade of grass. She had daisies in
her hair. School was over. We were celebrating.

"Well, I filled out an application," I concluded defiantly. "Down
at the Town Supervisor's office."

"And?" she asked.

"Haven't heard from them yet."

Angela snorted. We all wanted summer jobs, but no one would hire us. Jewell had put up signs for babysitting and gotten only one response, from a man who admitted he didn't have any children.

"Why work at all?"

Serena was lying on her stomach, stripping the bark from a twig. It lay in curls all around. Her fingernails were green.

"To get money?" Angela said tentatively.

"And what would you do with the money?"

"Buy things?" she guessed, even less sure.

"What things?" Serena persisted, not looking up.

"Bus ticket," Jewell said.

I looked at her.

"To where?" Serena asked.

We heard the scraping of shoes and freeing of long-suppressed coughs as people got up from prayer.

"AMEN!" sounded, on a deeper level than hearing, a bell tolling through our bodies, through our souls. We felt cut off, which was kind of thrilling, but also sad. It was romantic.

Jewell was lounging, lying on her side, her frowning face obviously running through every city she'd ever heard of or imagined, and coming up blank. Where to go? And once you got there, what would you do? Who would you call? Her body was draped in young willow branches.

"It's not to make money," I said.

"Then why?" Serena went on, maddeningly simple, gouging the soft wood.

"I want a job . . ." I recited, hoping I would find the answer in the saying. But I didn't. The words hung there and fell to the ground.

"Eve wants to meet someone," Angela supplied.

"I do not."

"Because she already has. Eve's in love."

"Shut up."

"What's it like to be in love, Eve? Do you dream about him every night?"

"Angela sleeps with her father," I announced.

"You're sick! Take that back."

"No." Serena was finally finished with the twig. Its essence scented our space. "It's not to make money or to meet people. You all want jobs so you won't have to go down there."

Evening meal would be starting soon. Everyone ate together, the women serving the men. It was an orgy of eating. We watched Serena, waiting for her to go on.

"You all know the emptiness inside you is just going to grow. But what can you fill it with? Babysitting? The 'highway crew'? And even if you got one of those jobs, even if you left here and lived somewhere else and met someone and . . . everything! It would never be enough. You'd get tired of it. You'd give up and come back. You'd kneel in front of the whole Colony and ask for His blessing. You'd beg His forgiveness. You know you would. So why fight it?"

We heard the big doors to the Meeting Hall creak open. You had to walk them out, like the doors to a barn.

Serena smiled. She dug into her pockets and came out with four small, slightly crushed boxes of maple sugar, each in the shape of an impossibly thick leaf.

"Where'd you get those?" I asked.

"From the Candy Barn, out on the highway. I stole them."

We stared at her a moment, then began to laugh, high, hysterical girls' laughter, as much to erase what she had just said, to drown out the sound of those people she predicted we would soon join (our "family," sawing meat, tearing bread, talking, yelling, their coarse, gross voices rising higher and higher), as from it being so funny that Serena, Miss Perfect, had stolen candy. It was the kind of laughter you couldn't stop, scary, with a mind of its own, but purging, too. We rolled on our backs, gasping, breaking out in giggles again, until our lungs ached. Finally we put the pieces of leaf-shaped sugar on our tongues and let their sweet melting soothe us. Even Angela lost her tight little scrunched-up expression and smiled at me. Jewell sighed and wiped tears from her cheeks. They glistened, smeared on her fuzzy skin. The daisies had fallen from her hair. She picked them up now and scattered them over us. I tried to look up through the millions of green branches. I tried to look past everything. I tried to look without seeing, pure sight, not fixing on any object, just striving, searching, and felt my body go limp, as if the vision itself were flowing out of me, leaving me empty.

"Let's run!" Serena said, and led us out of the willow. She and Angela and Jewell ran off down the hillside. I tried to follow, but they were going too fast. I couldn't catch up. I couldn't even get started. I had lost that weightless, nimble feeling. I heard them scream at the magic moment when they overcame gravity, when their feet left the ground. Laughter floated back to me, and a voice (which? I couldn't tell, they were all one) sang, warned, celebrated. "I can't stop!" . . . faint as the light from the evening sky.

But I was going someplace else.

From behind, without the big porch and black screens, Gordon's house looked smaller, more like a home. There was a back door that led into the kitchen. Inside, slick piles of catalogues spilled off the tabletop. I looked for the latest copy of my teen magazine. Cases of Diet Coke were stacked from the floor almost to the ceiling. I nudged one with my toe. All empty.

Giant state-of-the-art speakers had been set up in the living room. They were wide but so thin you couldn't believe there was anything inside them. They made the room even darker. He had been on this buying jag lately, ordering things over the phone. He loved that you could order "twenty-four hours a day," and used to call at two or three in the morning, just to chat with the operators. He had gotten this electronic mirror that was supposed to show your "true reflection." I couldn't figure out if it was occult or scientific. Anyway, it didn't work. There was a switch on it. Who ever heard of a mirror with a switch? It was set on the mantel, over the TV, part of a home entertainment center that blocked off the fireplace. He had moved his BarcaLounger. It was about six inches from the tube. Lots of the gadgets lay scattered on the floor and on the couch. A super-fancy Walkman, a radio that "could get Mars," a metal detector, a radon detector, a carbon monoxide detector, two electrodes you could stick in your food to see if it was poisoned. Some of them were still in their boxes, half-unwrapped, like chicks that hadn't made it out of their eggs.

But the bar was the same. It wasn't like all the tacky junk he'd bought with his credit cards. It was still just a wooden packing crate set on its side, with three or four bottles and some thick glasses. It had always been there, despite looking temporary, while the expensive toys that Gordon's manic moods demanded came and went. I didn't know what to drink. I chose the fullest bottle, figuring he'd miss it the least, and raised it high to my mouth. It came out faster than I thought and splashed down the sides of my face. I was so busy trying to wipe it away that I didn't even notice the taste. I must have taken a big swallow. Someone laughed. I whirled around and saw Gordon, buried in the armchair, his whole body shaking.

"That's poison," he said. "Look at the label."

It had a big burning Iowa sun on it, with two ears of corn underneath, like a skull and crossbones.

"'Danger. Flammable,'" I read. "So what?"

"That's Everclear. It's 180 proof. And you just swigged it down like it was a cup of your mamma's lemonade."

"I don't feel a thing."

"You'd better sit, honeypie."

I cleared a space on the couch. I was still holding the bottle.

"If it's poison," I reasoned slowly, "then why do you have it?"

He laughed again. I hadn't seen him in the chair because he'd kept so still. Only his eyes moved, like a lizard's, and a vein that pulsed in his temple. Gordon was either hair or not-hair. His skull wasn't just bald but . . . naked, really, this oily white dome with a moonscape of moles and craters. His face had a thick beard, so bad he had to shave twice a day. And his arms were incredibly hairy. But once I'd seen him with his shirt off, and his chest was bare, like there'd been a forest fire, all red and singed. He had sunken cheeks and tiny black eyes. He wasn't your idea of a preacher, "a charismatic," as he called himself, but the thing was: he knew what you were thinking before you did. He got there first, somehow, and was always waiting, until you weren't sure if you were thinking at all but maybe just carrying out instructions.

"I didn't expect you'd be here," I said. "I thought—"

"Yeah, yeah. Thought I'd be down there breaking the bread and pressing the flesh." He still didn't move, just grinned at me with his bad teeth. "Go ahead, have some more, if that's what you want."

"You said it was poison."

He nodded. I raised the bottle and took a much smaller sip, just to show him I wasn't afraid. Just to wet my lips, really. But that one hit me like lightning.

"To what do I owe the pleasure?" he asked. "Haven't seen you since you picked up your party dress. How did that go, anyway? Your big night out?"

They'd started singing, down the hill. It was a big barbecue. They'd get drunk on all the food and sociability. Everyone was stuffed and tired, and night was coming on, but they were joyful, full of the Holy

Spirit. Songs would break out, gain strength, then falter. "Nearer, My God, to Thee." "Amazing Grace." Babies cried. They'd light the lanterns and swat at the flies.

Gordon had a big remote control on his lap. He pointed it behind his shoulder, like a sharpshooter making a trick shot. The singing stopped.

"White noise," he explained, seeing me try and follow what he'd done. He'd silenced the Colony just by pushing a button. "I can play it through the speakers. It's like anti-sound."

I listened for it, the sound of the universe: a distant roaring. Or maybe that was the Everclear. I lifted the bottle again, just to see what he would do. He was watching me. Nobody could watch you like Gordon. You were stripped bare. He gave a little nod. Permission. That was enough for me to stop. I put the bottle down.

"Been expecting you," he said.

"I told you, I didn't think you were going to be here."

"Oh, I'm always here now. The place pretty much runs itself. Hadn't you noticed?"

He got out of his chair. He was on the other side of his mood. I could tell because he wasn't paying attention to his clothes. His pants didn't have a crease in them, and his shirt had stains from eating and drinking in the recliner.

"*Eve,*" he read off a piece of paper he'd retrieved. "Just *Eve*. And for address: *The Colony*. Do you know that by that simple act of honesty you caused several of the state's supercomputers to have nervous breakdowns?"

"That's my application," I said. "How did you get it?"

"Because I am your Lord and Savior." He yawned, scanning the rest of the form. "Politically speaking, that is. *Flagman*. You want to be a flagman, Eve? You even know what that is?"

"Are you sleeping with my mother again?" I asked.

"What do you mean 'again'?"

"He wears this jersey." I don't know why I was so obsessed with what I would wear. I guess just because it was clothes. I had a hunger for clothes, after years of full-length pioneer-girl dresses, and then that little receptionist's outfit Gordon made us wear to school. A shirt like a highway sign seemed really cool and exotic.

"He? He wears a jersey?"

"Or she," I said weakly.

He laughed and made his way back to the recliner. I watched it take him, the leg rest flipping out until it held him like a body cast. He stared at the blank TV.

"Life-size," he said.

"What?"

"The picture I get. The people are life-size. Sometimes, at night, they actually seem to be coming out of the screen."

"Gordon—"

"Never mind. Forget I said that."

"You should do Evening Service. I mean, I can understand why you don't do Morning Prayer anymore, I guess . . . but Evening Service, that's important, isn't it? Besides, it might make you feel better."

"The Healer cannot lay hands on himself," he intoned, mocking how he sounded when he preached. "Besides, I am up here on your behalf."

"I know."

"I am fighting for you, all of you. Filtering the world clean at my own expense. I am the shepherd, patrolling the perimeter of his flock with a burning brand, while out there in the darkness there are wolves! Wolves, I say!"

"I know, Gordon. I know."

"Go on." He didn't turn from the empty picture tube. "Take another swig. It feels good to have you drinking here. I've been lonely."

"If it's poison, how come you have it?" I asked again, reaching down for the bottle.

"Mithridates," he pronounced carefully. "You know him? An ancient king. Took poison every day, a little bit, so he would become immune."

"Immune to what?"

"Immune to *poison*, of course. What else would you want to be immune to?" It was dark now. He was dying to watch TV. His finger was playing with the remote control, prying at the buttons, caressing them, twitching. "You know, with these work crews I send out, I've become quite a source of cheap labor around here. Very important in the power structure of the county. That's why, when Supervisor Olney got your application, he damn near shat in his pants. Question is: Are you ready?"

"Ready for what?"

"Ready to leave. You'd be the first."

"The men leave. Every day."

"The men are different. They leave only in body."

"I go to school."

"That place was designed to send you running back here." He smiled. "Screaming. Place is a goddamned recruitment center."

"I don't care," I said. "I shouldn't even be here. You decide."

I got up to go. I must have been drunk, but I didn't feel it. Not like the other time, at Joey's. I felt great. I was a knife cutting through space.

"You got it all wrong, Eve," he called, when I was almost out of the room. "About your mother and me. She's a fine woman. I enjoy spending time with her. I admire her. Hell, I respect her."

"And those are the reasons you *don't* sleep with her?"

". . . got to work on your social skills," he sighed. "That is priority number one. You start Thursday."

I waited, holding on to the door frame.

"Highway crew assembles outside the Road Commission garage. You know where that is? Seven a.m. That'll just about give you time for Morning Prayer first. You hearing me, girl?"

"I hear you."

"Now scoot. I got serious business to attend to."

I didn't thank him. I left before he changed his mind. Nobody was down at the lake. People went to their cabins after sundown. It wore them out, the praying and the eating and the singing. I took off my clothes. They lay lifeless at my feet, all sweaty and used up. Before that moment I had hated being naked. Now I looked at my reflection. It was taller than I remembered and rippled in the water. I took a step and almost passed out, the lake was so cold. It paralyzed me, but I forced my way deeper. My toes felt frantically for the bottom, got used to it not being there, and began to kick. The cold found me, kissed me, made me feel streamlined. It licked every pore in my skin. I was all goose bumps and taut muscles, hard nipples and hoarse, heavy breathing. In the center of the lake I lay on my back and let starlight bathe my new body. I stretched my arms and legs as far as they would go. I pretended I was an astrological phenomenon seen only by the very lucky, visible only at certain times of the year and in certain parts of the sky: the Floating Girl.

2

"Nothing changes," Gillie said.

"What do you mean?" I asked.

We were standing in the bed of the cargo truck, with slats going up each side and piles of orange highway cones stacked in the middle. There wasn't room to sit, so we held on to the wood and swayed, the six of us.

"All this happened before," Gillie went on.

I looked around to see if anyone else understood what he was talking about.

"In Africa, during the war. See, I worked for the quartermaster. We had to find food for a whole regiment. These . . . tribesmen offered to take me across the desert along with some sheep the army was purchasing. Now this desert was called the Sahara. It's in Africa."

"You said that already," Walt called.

"Shut up. Anyway, I'd ride in the back of their truck. Nothing to hang on to but these sheep. So I'd steady myself by digging my hands into their wool. We'd ride eight, nine, ten hours a day that way, without stopping. Nothing but sand and rocks. The most god-forsaken country you've ever seen in your life. Then, at night, they'd stop, build a fire, pick out one of those sheep, and slaughter it. Butcher it right there on the spot. You should've seen the blood. Then they'd roast it over the fire. With tea," he added wonderingly, like that was the most interesting part. "Mint tea."

"Anyone see the game last night?" Walt yawned.

"You'd eat the whole sheep?" I asked.

"Whole sheep," Gillie confirmed. "There were five of these tribesmen. Black as the ace of spades. And me."

"Dumb as shit," someone mumbled.

"So this went on for three, four days. The desert is . . . vast!" He made a sweeping motion with his arm and almost fell. I helped push him up. "Me and these sheep would ride in the back. After a few hours, I'd start talking to them. They had their own habits, their own personalities! I named them, like I would a farm animal back here. Then, at night, I'd climb down off the truck, walk a few yards out into the desert, keep my back turned, while one of the tribes-men slit their throats. I could tell, just from the sound it made, which sheep it was."

"Lucky it wasn't you, old man," Walt said.

The other guys giggled.

"Nothing changes," Gillie repeated, glaring out at the highway. "I could tell which sheep it was just from the sound it made. Didn't even have to look."

Gillie must have been at least seventy. He had a purple nose and withered cheeks. He was the other flagman. I didn't know who had gotten him the job. It turned out flagman was this political favor you could offer to somebody if you were well connected. The rest of the guys, the backhoe operator, the ones who jackhammered the old pavement and raked out the hot tar, made fun of him. "Hey, old man. I'm going to run over your goddamned foot if you don't move." They never said anything like that to me. They barely acknowledged I was there. Walt, this fat lech-type with a little mustache, said that Supervisor Olney himself had come out to the site the day before I started and told them I was to be returned "in mint condition."

"I'm not a mint."

"Not a mint." He choked. He was eating a sandwich. "Not a mint!"

But for a sweetheart job it was hard work. The flag was heavy, especially after you'd been waving it for six hours. And it was hot. Clouds of pulverized gravel coated your face, gritted up your teeth. You'd breathe in lungfuls of hot tar. Jackhammers pounded in your ears. The first day, I staggered to the shade of the truck for a break and found out everyone else had brought lunch. Victor, the foreman, offered to drive me into town to buy something.

"No pickup trucks in the Bible," I said.

"Well, you rode out here."

"I had a dispensation."

"A what?" one of them asked, under his breath.

I closed my eyes and tried not to faint.

The jersey was great, though. It was everything I hoped for. It both hid me (it was big enough for some potbellied construction worker) and yet singled me out. I held up my flag and the cars stopped. I waved them forward, making sure the backhoe, or the dump truck, or the steamroller was out of the way, then whisked them through the opening. And it was all because of the jersey. I had never fallen in love with a piece of clothing before. It had magic properties. It also had adjustable Velcro tabs on each side, so I could cinch it in at the waist and then let it flow out again, like a dress. I had gotten the rest of my new clothes at the Salvation Army: a pair of threadbare jeans, work boots, and a bunch of T-shirts with the names of different sports teams on them.

"Who are . . . the Argonauts?" Walt read, squinting at me that first day.

"I have no idea," I said.

Gillie was the only one who really talked to me. He would talk to anybody. I don't think he had many friends. After, when the truck dropped us back at the Road Commission garage and the rest of the guys went off together, Gillie would just stand there, light up a cigarette, and look out over the empty parking spaces.

"Where are they going?" I asked.

"Number," he said.

"Number? What's that?"

"*The* Number," he corrected. "It's a bar."

"Oh."

That made sense. I didn't want to go home either. Bars were forbidden, of course, but I felt the need to celebrate, too. Back at the Colony no one would understand. The men usually came home from the work crews looking dead.

"What do you do?" I asked hopefully. "After, I mean."

He coughed up a big bloodstained ball of phlegm.

"You're looking at it."

He poked at it clumsily with his boot, like a horse touching something with its hoof. When I looked back, he was carefully grinding it into the blacktop, trying to make it disappear.

I didn't know what to do with my first paycheck. It wasn't much. They had taken out for all kinds of things, and it wasn't even made out to me, but to the Tabernacle of the American Christ, Inc. I walked to the bank. It was open late but I didn't go in. The thought of trying to explain, of having people stare, wearied me in advance.

I was tired of answering questions. I wanted something to be easy for a change. I walked a little farther, crossed the railroad tracks, and came to a low brick building with two open garages.

He was working on a black car. It must have been old, it was so wide and beat up. The seats were like the padded booths in the Luncheonette. One was patched with duct tape. He wore a red jumpsuit, a little grease-stained, but still new, with DUFFY'S AUTOMOTIVE embroidered in block letters above one pocket and *Joe* in script above the other. He bent over the engine. I moved closer. A light hung from the hood so I could see the fine hairs of his neck, their pattern, how they led my eye downward, past where I could actually see, to his broad back, his narrow waist, his tight little butt . . .

"How's your dad?" I asked.

His head jerked up and banged against the hood.

"Sorry."

"How long have you been standing there?" He was rubbing his skull.

I reached out, then stopped. Since my hand was in midair I pretended to be interested in some tool.

"What's this?"

"A socket wrench."

I hadn't expected him to be wearing a jumpsuit. I don't know why that threw me so much. It zipped straight down the front, but instead of a flat metal tongue the zipper had a dangling loop, like an earring.

"Doesn't that get caught on things?"

He looked down with me.

"No."

It was mesmerizing. I forced myself to look at the garage and saw how messy it was, with oil spills covered in kitty litter, loose parts, piles of old cardboard boxes that looked as if they'd been chewed up by mice or maybe rats. Still, with millions of things hanging off the walls or stacked on shelves, it reminded me of Herbert's toolshed. Very male. Especially the deep smell of gasoline.

"Like it?" Joey asked, patting the side of the car.

"It's yours?"

"Duffy lets me work on it after hours."

"You mean there really is a Duffy?"

"He owns the garage."

"I thought it was just a name."

"Well, it is."

"I didn't think it was a person."

He shrugged. He was wiping his hands on a rag. The loop twinkled and tinkled against the teeth of the zipper. He's not naked under that, I reminded myself. And even if he was, so what? Then I saw he was looking at me just as hard.

"You wear that all the time?"

He meant the orange-and-white-striped jersey.

"No," I said. "It's just that I walk home after, on the highway, so I figure I might as well keep it on. For protection."

He nodded. I didn't know why I should feel so awkward about wearing my jersey when he was still in his . . . advertisement, really, for this broken-down garage. At least mine didn't have writing on it.

"What's that?" He nodded to the paycheck.

"Oh, I don't know what to do with this. I don't have a bank account. It's not even made out to me. I thought maybe we could take it to your father or someone."

He held the check by the edges, so he wouldn't mark it up.

"What's the Tabernacle of the American Christ?"

"It's a holding company," I remembered.

"What's that?"

"I don't know. It's church-related. We don't own money."

He gave me back the check and closed the hood of the car. Quietly. He didn't slam it. He pressed down with the magic force of his muscles and the latch clicked.

"Want to go for a ride?"

"In that thing? You mean it runs?"

It was the first time I'd ever seen him look hurt, that I might be insulting his car. His eyes squinted and his lower lip stuck out. I could imagine him, a little boy, crying, or not crying, rather. Keeping it in. Just trembling a bit, as if something was passing through him.

"Sure," I said. "I'll go for a ride."

. . . and risk Eternal Damnation. Why not?

The seat was a big bench. When the car turned, the whole world tilted. I looked for something to hold on to, but there was nothing. I finally planted my hands flat on either side and pushed as hard as I could. Since he seemed totally occupied by the road, I figured it was my job to make conversation. Begin light and casual, I thought.

"So what did your mother die of?"

He was a very careful driver. He'd slow to a stop and look both ways. Then the car would take forever to get moving again. But when it did, it was so heavy it felt as if we were on a rocket ship. Soon we were outside of town. My hands relaxed, now that we weren't turning. I was still nervous, though. I sat back, rigid. The loop on his jumpsuit was going tink, tink, tink, in rhythm.

"How did you know about my mother?"

"I don't know. But she did, didn't she? Die?"

"Where do you want to go?"

"Anywhere."

He nodded, like that was a real possibility. A place. There was a little vinyl tab coming out of the seat between us. I pulled it and a cushioned armrest came down. He pushed it back up.

"She just got sick, that's all."

"Sick from what?"

"What does it matter?"

I looked at him. It was good we were driving. Our eyes didn't skitter away from each other like at school or in the garage. I could watch him, watch the way he was handling his car. The wheel, everything inside, was so big. His feet barely reached the pedals. I could feel the road under us.

"I like your jumpsuit," I said.

"I had to pay for it." He touched it. "What about your dad?"

"Who?"

"Your dad. People say that none of you out there have real fathers. That you're all the children of . . . that guy."

We were coming up on Angela. I could tell it was her by the way the long cotton-print dress whipped around her legs, how her shoulders hunched and her arms folded across her chest. Her whole body was an inward thing. I turned and watched as we passed, then followed her reflection in the round mirror that stuck out from the passenger side of the car. She hadn't seen me. Her head was down. I wondered what she was doing, where she was coming from, now that school was over.

"Gordon's our spiritual father," I said. "It's a religious community. Not a harem. Anyway, I don't want to talk about him."

"Then who's your real father?" he persisted. "I've seen your mom."

"You have?"

"Once. When all the women came into town to buy food."

"How did you know it was her?"

"Well, she looks just like you."

"That wasn't her. Where are we going?"

"I don't know. Just relax, Eve." He reached over, without looking, and touched my jersey, its shiny strips and tough plastic netting. "I like this. I mean, it's really weird."

I had never been this far out into farm country. There were all these back roads with abandoned barns and closed-up churches. Whole clusters of buildings that were just wrecks now, towns that didn't make it. But someone was still working the land. Companies, probably. The big agribusinesses everyone complained about. The fields were the intense deep green of soy. The sun was slanting low and the plants just drank it in. You could see them growing.

We talked a little more, enough to confirm that we had nothing in common. It got to be a joke. Everything he mentioned I wasn't interested in, and everything I brought up just made him frown.

"What do you mean, God scratched Himself and made the lake?"

"Never mind. It's just a story. It's actually a parable, I think."

"Then that would make this place the Asshole of the Universe, wouldn't it?"

Is there any way we can stop *talking*? I wondered.

He must have been thinking the same thing, because he started slowing down, even though there was no sign or intersection. He did it very gently, so we weren't thrown forward. We veered onto the shoulder and stopped. The loop went tink, tink, *tink*.

"Thank God," I said. "That zipper was driving me crazy."

He turned in his seat and put his hands on my hips. Suddenly the inside of the car didn't seem big at all. I reached out, hooked my finger through the little metal loop, and pulled. The top half of the jumpsuit came apart. He was wearing a snowy white T-shirt. He kissed me and I had no idea about tongues. It was this glaring gap in my education. I had never been so surprised in my life. Suddenly a million things made sense and about a million more didn't. I screamed, in a muffled sort of way, and he stopped, for just a second, like I might be saying no, before I grabbed his arms and pulled him closer. His shoulders were like stone. We kissed some more and his hands found their way inside my shirt, which I didn't mind at all, much to my surprise. I had thought this was going to be full of things I didn't like, but so far I had no complaints. I let this friendly dizziness take over and clung to him. He was so solid. Looking past his neck, I saw that I was still holding on to my paycheck. I must have been clutching it the whole ride, without even realizing.

"So . . . isn't there some way we can sign this over to your dad and then have him pay me in money?" I breathed into his ear. I was trying to act cool, I guess. Like I wasn't losing my mind. Whispering sweet nothings.

He broke away from me and sat back.

"Why do you keep asking about my father?" he yelled. "I hate him! Don't you know that?"

I stared at him a minute and began to cry.

He shook his head.

"I'm sorry," I choked. "It's just that I've never been in a car before."

He started looking for his keys, patting his pockets, glaring along the top of the dashboard, really angry.

Wait! I wanted to say. Don't stop! Go back to what you were doing.

The keys were still in the ignition, where he'd left them. He gunned the engine and took off, leaving a big cloud of dust behind.

For a while we drove in silence, not getting any closer to home. His taste was still in my mouth. The sun was going down. There were colors like the end of the world. I couldn't stop crying.

"What do you mean you've never been in a car before?" he complained. "You ride out with that highway crew every morning, don't you?"

"That's different," I said. "I stand in the bed of a cargo truck. Besides, I have permission."

"You don't have permission for this?"

"Are you kidding?"

"You want me to take you back?"

"Just drive," I sobbed helplessly; I couldn't stop.

He got us onto a paved road and went more slowly than before. I figured out how to roll down my window. The air speeding by dried my face. Then I rolled it back up again. I could see him, his pale reflection, in the glass.

"How do you know that?" I called.

"Know what?"

"That I ride out with the highway crew."

"I see you."

"You see a lot of things."

"I notice things," he corrected. "I notice you. Because you're different. I mean . . . you're special."

"No, I'm not. I'm absolutely ordinary. You just think I'm different because I live in the Colony. You're just curious."

He looked at his watch. "It's almost nine. Won't your mother be wondering where you are?"

"My mother won't even know I'm gone."

He nodded. He seemed content to drive. It calmed him. Me too, actually. We almost smiled at each other, and then remembered we were mad.

"My dad's just the opposite," Joey said. "He always wants to know where I've been. What I'm doing. Why I'm not studying." He patted the dashboard. "He thinks I'm stupid."

"Are you kidding? I think you're"— I was going to say, I think you're gorgeous, but then realized that wasn't really the opposite of stupid—"smart. Really smart."

But because I had hesitated, it came out wrong.

"Maybe I am just curious," he admitted. "I mean curious about you. But what's so wrong about that? Aren't you curious about me?"

"No."

He smiled, like I was lying. Like he was winning some argument, just by doing nothing.

"Why should I care about you?" I went on. "You're just some town kid."

He nodded, turning it into a compliment.

We didn't talk the rest of the way home. It got dark fast. We came to Arhat from a different direction. I recognized things in reverse. I was sneaking up on them, catching them by surprise: grain elevators, the state liquor store, the feed lot, the fast-food place off the Interstate. We came to the overpass. The sign that told your speed. He floored the gas pedal. The engine threw me back against my seat. The car began to drift across the road. I reached out for something to hold on to, found his arm, and grabbed it, hard. With my eyes wide open I read 80 MILES PER HOUR as we tore by.

"It only goes in tens," he explained. "They say if you get to a hundred, you break the sign. But I'll never get to a hundred in this thing."

I was kind of wishing I had snapped his elbow in half, but he didn't even seem to notice. I had to pry my fingers off one by one.

He stopped just where the road to the Colony began.

"I could take you farther," he offered. "Right to your house, if you want. If you have houses out there."

"What do you mean, if we have houses?"

"Some people say you all live in a giant beehive."

"Are you serious?"

He grinned.

"Very funny. So was this a date?"

"I don't know."

"Because I'm not allowed on dates," I said.

The car was still running. It sent a gentle rhythm through us, a rocking, like we were on a boat. The moment stretched out. I looked at him. I took him all in. He didn't know it, but in that moment I possessed him. It was better than kissing. Well, different. But we kissed, too. Just to make sure.

"My mother died of cancer," he said. "My dad and I clean her grave on Sundays. I saw you once. Walking by."

She wouldn't tell me anything. Not what he did or how they met. Not what he was like or why she left. Not even what he looked like. "Did you fall in love with someone else?" I asked. "Or did you never love him to begin with?" It didn't occur to me that *he* had fooled around or stopped loving her, because that seemed impossible. The picture was the only proof my father even existed. He had taken it. I was sure of that. It was his shadow that lay across the garden of cactus and rock formations. She stood there, a little out of focus, with her hands on her hips. It was the sixties and she had on a purple-and-red robe, what a queen would wear. Her hair was long and she was smiling, a wide-open unguarded smile I had never seen on her in real life. She was smiling at him. His shadow ended at her bare feet, so it was a circuit, light and dark, going back and forth, a closed circuit, because you could tell they lived only for each other and would never fight or be unhappy, and would reign forever in a magic kingdom of the heart. It was my model of Love. "What *happened?*" I wanted to scream. But appeals never worked with my mother. She would only tell you things when you didn't want to hear them. The rock formations were these red sandstone towers. Some were as tall as she was. One cactus had a flower. The way the picture had aged, the thin, cracked paper it was printed on, made it all seem like a distant time, hundreds of years ago.

After, we lived in San Francisco. I remember a man named Mike took care of me, took care of us both, really. He made sandwiches out of peanut butter, honey, and powdered milk. He said you could live on them forever, because they were "a complete protein." Then we moved to a house and there were more people, ten or twelve at least. I was aware of being the mascot to this whole group, even though most of them couldn't have been that old themselves, probably in their early twenties. But deep down it was really just the two of us, Mother and me against the world. Then she met Gordon. He was a street preacher. He still had hair. He gave sermons on corners. People would gather. Mother would wait for him, in back of the little crowd. Sometimes it was only us, at first. Then other people would come. Guys mostly, because she was so beautiful. Gordon pretended not to know us. He'd shoot a secret smile over their heads, even a quick wink. I was only five, but I remembered those looks, like they were meant for me, too. Like we were all in on this . . . scam, together. Mother and Gordon were definitely a couple in those days. They took me places, places for kids, and watched me ride the Ferris wheel or feed the ducks, holding hands the whole time. They walked down the street together and I ran between them, bouncing off one to the other.

Then they had a fight. I don't know about what. Gordon left San Francisco, to find himself, he said. After that, everything turned bad. We moved out of the house. There were still guys—there had always been guys—but now the sound of them climbing the dark wooden staircase was ominous, not exciting. We shared a bed, but there were more and more nights when I slept on the couch. I woke up once, forgot where I was, and found her with two men. It wasn't so unusual. I should have just backed out again, but for some reason I couldn't stop staring. She saw me, saw the look I had, and slapped me, hard, for not knocking. The next day we left. I knew it was my fault, that we had to go because I hadn't knocked, because of what I'd seen. My cheek still burned. Her open palm had branded me. I doubt now she even remembered, in the morning, what she had done. She used to get pretty high. We took all her incredible clothes—the Indian prints, the dress that was feathers, the boots that laced up a million times—to a shop and sold them. She stuffed the money in this ugly vinyl bag she was carrying. It was funny to see her dress so plain, because I noticed guys on the street still stared at her, as if the dull checked dress she wore was even more of a sexy costume than her silver tights. She dragged me to a diner and made me drink a milk shake. She stared at the tall glass, watching the level go down like it was medicine she had to make sure I swallowed. Then she told me we were going to take a bus ride across the country to meet Gordon. "Gordon!" I said, really excited. But she wasn't. She went right on, as if it was this bad news she had to get out all at once: We were going to become different people. We had no last name now. I was Eve.

"But that's my name anyway," I argued.

"No," she said. "This is different. From now on you're just *Eve*."

I squirmed in my seat. I remember pressing my legs together. Everything I ever felt, I felt because of her. And now I felt fear. She had been resisting him, his call, for a long time. It meant renouncing everything. Her very self. Who she was. And now, by going to him, she was giving up. Submitting. For both of us.

They were there when I got home, Gordon and Mother, sitting with a lamp between them, like old people waiting up.

"'Home is the sailor, home from sea / And the hunter home from the hill,'" he proclaimed. "Robert Louis Stevenson."

"How come you never quote from the Bible anymore?" I asked.

"I have internalized Scripture." He looked down and touched his chest in a certain place, like the Old and New Testaments were really right there, next to each other. "The words are now inherent in my actions, whereas before they were just a crust, something I exuded that dried on my skin and cracked and peeled. A kind of spiritual eczema."

I shot a glance at Mother like, Are you getting this? He's crazier than ever. But she was rocking contentedly, with that little hypnotized smile that made me want to strangle her.

I still held the paycheck. By now, I felt like I'd spent it all. My big night out. I handed it to Gordon.

"This is yours, I guess."

He scanned the deductions.

"Man, did you get taken for a ride!"

"What do you know about sex, Eve?" Mother asked.

"I know it's not for me," I answered promptly.

"State and federal? But the Tabernacle is tax-exempt. I'm going to have to talk to Olney about this."

"You're fifteen," she said. "Soon boys are going to start noticing you."

". . . sniffing around like dogs," Gordon murmured, still reading off the paycheck. His lips were moving. He was adding numbers.

"I'm not interested," I insisted.

I meant in having this discussion, especially now, especially with Gordon right there. But I also let it mean the other thing, that I wasn't interested in sex itself, because maybe that was true, too. What I mostly wanted was to get away from them and go to bed so I could examine every moment of what had just happened, so I could relive it all and try to figure out what it was. Because I had no idea. I didn't even know if it qualified as a date or not. I didn't even know if it was real. I wanted to think about Joey. But these two boring grownups wanted to talk to me about sex instead, which was some totally other topic.

"See?" Gordon smiled at my mother. "I told you."

"Told her what?"

"You're really disgusted by all this, aren't you? Boys, your changing body . . ." He started picking at one of the moles on his scalp, trying to pry it loose with his nail, as if it was another button on the remote control. "And that's a good thing, believe me. Disgust is a healthy reaction to something you're not ready for. See, despite your pipsqueak rebellion here, I believe you are truly on the side of the angels. In fact, you may have a calling. I've always suspected it. You may be destined for the ministry, Eve."

"Me?" I asked.

"The boy puts his penis in your vagina," Mother recited. "He moves it in and out, until he ejaculates. That releases the sperm."

"Does it hurt?"

"No," Gordon said.

"Yes," Mother said.

"Oh, does it hurt *you*?" He laughed.

"At first," Mother explained, trying to ignore him.

"What about after?"

"After?" Her eyes had clouded over, as if she was trying to remember, or relive, or forget, some time far back. The Summer of Love.

Gordon reached across and patted her knee.

"What your mother's trying to say, Eve, is: Don't let anything enter you but the Holy Spirit. Because Man, despite his best efforts, is a filthy, loathsome creature, and instead of Grace, all you will find is misery and damnation. Does that make it more clear?"

"So, do I get anything?" I asked. "I mean, my name isn't even on the check. But I did all the work."

He looked at me. I could have sworn that, unlike Mother, he knew exactly what was going on. With Gordon, whatever you were thinking was printed on your forehead. He held me with his eyes.

"Do not engage in fornication of any kind," he ordered slowly. "Don't mess around. You understand, young lady? Or you will answer not just to me, not just to your mother, but to your Colony and to your God."

"I know," I mumbled.

"I know you *know*. My fear is that you will fall into corruption anyway. In full knowledge. And so lose your Eternal Rest."

"That's a hideous top," Mother added. "Where did you get it?"

"It's what I work in."

"Work?"

"Out on the highway. The road crew. Remember? I told you."

"Now, what about your friends?" Gordon asked.

I looked up.

"A Colony girl was seen outside town the other day. In a place she shouldn't have been, doing things she shouldn't have done. You know anything about that?"

"No," I answered.

"You sure, Eve? Think now. People are talking."

"When was it? I was probably working . . . for no pay, it turns out."

"You'll be paid. Now, you know I'm going to find out who it was. I mean, there aren't that many possibilities. All I'm asking is that you save me some time and, if you need to, unburden your troubled conscience."

"When I was your age," Mother said helpfully, "when I think of the things I was doing, the terrible situations I was getting into, I would have wanted someone to stop me. I needed a strong hand. I never got one."

Right. Instead you got me, I thought.

"I don't know what you're talking about. Can I go to my room now? I'm really tired."

"A calling, Eve," Gordon reminded, as I left. "Bring sinners to Jesus. Preach the Gospel in word *and* deed. Remember, the soul you save may be your own. Think about it."

I began having this fantasy every morning, lying facedown in bed, feeling footsteps pound over the ground outside my window. A man would crawl on top of me and cover me like a rough blanket. His hands would reach under my arms and spread themselves over my breasts. I would purr like a cat. His hot breath made me shiver. Together, we snuggled deeper into the thin mattress. That was all. Just a feeling of comfort. And mystery. After, I would go down to the lake, always a little late. The children moved aside now to let me pass. He stayed. That was the nicest part, the way he lingered on into reality. My mystery man. Even though he was invisible, I could feel his delicious weight bearing down, this pressure all over my body. And somehow his hands were still splayed across my chest, pressing my breasts back into me.

"Eve?"

I looked up and saw I had almost walked off the road into a drainage ditch.

"Are you all right?" Serena asked.

"Of course."

"Can I see it?"

Even though school was over, she still went with me part of the way into town. She had nothing else to do. She hadn't gotten a job, and all that waited for her back at the Colony was a Bible class for children she had volunteered to teach.

"Here."

"Where?" She squinted.

I lifted my jersey and shirt, and thrust out the pale skin that sloped away from my hip.

"Oh."

"You see it?"

"I see it."

But I could tell from her tone of disappointment that it was gone. It had lasted for days, Joey's mark, where he had held me. One hand must have had grease or motor oil on it, because it left this perfect thumbprint I found the next morning. I hadn't bathed for as long as I could. I caressed it at night, imagining I could feel its ridges, tracing the beautiful whorl it made. Then I tried washing around it. But two weeks had gone by, and now it was just a square of dirt on my pelvis. I hadn't heard from him in all that time. It was all I had left of him, all that meant I was still his. Or ever had been.

"Maybe you left a mark on him, too."

"No. He's very clean. He probably takes showers."

"Maybe you left a mark on his heart."

We both giggled.

But it was sad. I was going off and she was going to turn around soon. I couldn't imagine her day. The thought of teaching the Bible to a bunch of five-year-olds made me sick. Now that school was over she had gone back to wearing her long Colony dress. It was too small for her. I could see a daisy chain knotted around her ankle.

"What's that?"

"Jewell." She frowned, looking down. "She made them for all of us."

"Not for me."

"Well, you're not here anymore."

We were coming to the invisible line where she would stop.

"Do you think God could ever have a daughter?" I proposed. I thought if I could get her chatting, the way we used to, she wouldn't notice how far she'd come and we could walk all the way into town together. I missed her. "I mean, if He had a son, why not a daughter? It makes sense."

"They want me to marry," Serena said.

I stopped. She was looking down at the road, embarrassed, smiling. "Who?"

"My mom. And Gordon, I guess."

"No. I mean, who do they want you to marry?"

"Oh. A man." She was blushing. I'd never seen Serena blush. Her hand kept going to her face, to push back some imaginary strand of hair. "I mean, obviously a man. I can pretty much pick. I mean, that's what they said. Except I said they should pick for me, because what do I know? Gordon's going to decide. I think it's going to be either Ethan or Gerald."

"Ethan *or* Gerald. You mean you don't know?"

"It hasn't reached that stage. I told you: Gordon hasn't decided yet. He said he has to pray."

Right, I thought. He has to pray . . . in front of *Mod Squad*. Lately he'd been watching these really ancient reruns.

"Ethan and Gerald are both *old*."

"No, they're not. They're the youngest unmarried men in the Colony."

"But they must be thirty, at least."

"I know that, Eve." She was staring at where the highway crumbled off into dust. "I'm not blind. But there are so many more women than men. It's really a great honor. That's how you have to look at it."

"You just turned sixteen!"

"I'm a woman," she said quietly. "In biblical times—"

"These aren't biblical times."

She looked up at me sharply. "Well, isn't that the point? To make these biblical times again? To make the New Testament come to life?"

"There should be a Newer Testament," I complained, kicking at a stone. "For how to live today. One where you don't get married just because you start getting your period."

"One where you drive around in a car with some boy you hardly know? Kissing him? You think that's so much better?"

"Yes," I decided. "It was fantastic, kissing him. I'd do it again, if he ever came back. In fact, I'd probably *give* myself to him, if he'd ever have me, which he won't, because he finds me physically repulsive."

"Shut up!" She looked around, as if everyone we ever knew was there, listening, hiding in the cornfields.

"But I wouldn't get married."

"I thought you wanted to. To his father."

"Well, that's different," I said, not knowing quite why. "He has his own place. And . . . a toolshed out back."

She tried smoothing the fabric of her dress. She pulled her sleeves down to where they no longer reached and looked at her wrists as if they'd betrayed her. She had changed. There was no doubt about it. I didn't know if it was that her body had grown or if it was just the way she held herself. But she was different.

"God's daughter. That's an interesting idea, Eve," she went on politely, as if I were one of the idiot children in her Bible class.

"Why do you think they want you to get married? I mean, why you in particular?"

"I don't know," she sighed. "I got straight A's on my report card. Maybe they're afraid I'll want to go to college."

"Well, if that's the reason, then I don't have anything to worry about."

"I like the idea of marriage," she admitted. "Of sanctifying our physical love in the sight of God. Is that so bad?"

"No," I mumbled. "I mean, I like it too, the *idea*. It's just, Ethan or Gerald . . ."

"I don't even know them." She shrugged. "Not really."

Neither did I. Men and women kept pretty separate in the Colony. All relationships ran through Gordon. The men respected him. The women loved him. We all feared and craved him. Alone, one-on-one, we were just a bunch of cripples, the same cripples who had come here in the first place, looking to be healed.

"Are you coming?" I asked.

"I can't," she said.

I had to go. I was already a few feet ahead of her. She was standing there, looking smaller and smaller.

"Is there still time for you to change your mind?"

"I guess. Once they actually tell me who it is."

"Well then, promise me you won't say yes yet. OK?"

"Jealous!" she teased.

"Promise?"

"I promise." She put her hand on her heart.

"What's so funny?"

"You." She smiled. "Trying to act all grown up."

I couldn't keep up with the corn. Just a few weeks ago the stalks that lined the highway had come up to my knee, then to my shoulder. Now they grew straight into the sky. Lately I had started to cut across the fields, discovering this green maze, these private streets, so rigid and geometrical. Once inside, I lost any sense of where I was going. All I knew was that they would get me to town, but I didn't know where I would come out. I wandered, squeezing from one row to the next, wishing I was a plant, walking along the black earth. White pellets of undissolved fertilizer stuck to my boots. What Serena had told me was terrible, but all I could think about was how I had answered her, because it was so completely unexpected and untrue, that I would "give myself" to Joey if he asked. I mean, it was not something I had even considered. I had only the vaguest idea, despite Mother's little talk, what it meant! But the expression itself was so seductive and thrilling. Just to say it gave me goose bumps.

And now Serena was getting *married*? Could she ever *give herself* to some guy?

The cornfield let me out behind the Road Commission garage, right where I was supposed to be. Like I said, it was hard to get lost in Arhat, Iowa. God knows I tried. The rest of the road crew was already there, drinking coffee, eating doughnuts. I spied on them from inside the last row. They looked so hopeless: Walt with his paunch, this clinging little boy he had never stopped being; Gillie, smoking a cigarette, the mark of death so clearly upon him; and Big

John, this huge sweet guy who had no clue, who kept looking down at his hands as if they could tell him what to do next. I remembered Gordon's advice that I become a preacher. Save souls. Suddenly it didn't seem so crazy. I could save people. Save them from their fate. Starting with Serena.

3

"Are you out of your mind?"
Angela asked.

We were sitting in the Luncheonette, Jewell, Angela, and me, in a booth all the way in back, right before the purple curtain. There were dirty magazines behind the curtain. Men paid a dollar just to go in and look. You could see their shoes.

"I thought we could talk to a lawyer," I said.

"A lawyer!"

Angela looked terrible. There were circles under her eyes and she trembled, drinking her Pepsi. She kept biting the straw and jabbing the ice with it. She looked like an anteater.

"Why not? I've got money now. Some."

"And what exactly would a lawyer do?" Jewell yawned.

"I don't know. Stop the whole thing. Take her away. Isn't it illegal? Couldn't we get her declared a ward of the state?"

We had all heard that phrase. It was what social workers threatened, whenever they showed up at the Colony and asked about a kid. Gordon would smile, act reasonable and friendly, put his arm around their shoulders, and take them up to the cabin for a chat. Then they would leave.

I was drinking a Pepsi, too. Angela and I had gotten them with lemon slices, which we thought was very adult. Jewell carefully spooned the ice cream off her root-beer float.

"All a lawyer's going to do is tell Gordon."

"And then you're going to *fry*." Angela's eyes shone, like she would enjoy seeing that.

I don't know why I had invited her. I don't know why I had gotten either of them to come, except that I really didn't know what to do. And I was lonely. I hadn't seen them that much since I started work. Jewell had ended up volunteering at the old folks' home. She served meals and helped the worse-off residents clean up after themselves. Angela wasn't doing anything. "Just walking," she said. Walking where, I wondered. She was even thinner than before. When she laughed, it was like glass breaking.

The curtain opened. We looked away. I don't know why it shamed us, that some guy was back there making a fool of himself. But it did. After his footsteps passed we looked up again.

"What I don't understand," Angela went on, "is, why Serena?"

"Why not?" I shrugged.

"Why not you, for instance?"

"No one would want to marry me."

"Those guys would marry a muskrat if Gordon told them to," Jewell said calmly.

"Well, thank you very much."

"Why not me?" Angela complained. That was what she really meant.

"Did Serena *say* she didn't want to get married?" Jewell took another bite of ice cream and stared at me while she ate.

"Not exactly," I mumbled.

It was Sunday. There was a farm family in the front, which was also the newsroom. It was a local hangout. I watched them like they were from another planet. A father and mother, two boys and a girl, happy, dressed for church, eating burgers and fries. Probably they were going bankrupt and had all kinds of other problems, but still, I would have given anything in the world to be them, all of them at once, somehow.

"I mean, I'm twenty-six days older than Serena," Angela was saying. "I'm the oldest one here. If anyone's going to—"

She broke off with a sob. Jewell, who was sitting next to her, banged sideways with her whole body, trying to nudge her out of hysteria.

"Ow!"

I could see how good she would be, working at the Senior Center, telling some guy to finish his mush.

"You want to get married to some fat slob with a beard growing halfway down his neck?" she demanded.

That was Ethan. Gerald was more normal, which made it even creepier that a seemingly normal guy would want to spend his life at the Colony. The men got up before five, prayed, went off to work in these "details" Gordon assigned, to nearby farms. They walked, trooped miles along the highway in their overalls, never talking, came back at night, exhausted, with just enough energy to sit through Evening Service, eat like pigs, and then fall into bed. They were "working off their debt to Satan," Gordon said. "Sweating their way to Jesus."

"Of course I don't." Angela sat up straight and tried to look regal. "It's just the principle of the thing, that's all. It's not fair."

"What you want to do," Jewell told me, "is buy a bus ticket."

"To where?"

"To where Serena could go. Talk to her. Find out where her relatives are, what she remembers from before she came here. Try and convince her to find them. If she says yes, then give her the bus ticket. That's all you can do. The rest is up to her."

"But then she won't be here anymore. I don't want her to leave."

"Things are never going to be the way they were. Do you think she can just say no and go back to being Serena?"

"Why not?"

"Do you think it's because they saw her doing something?" Angela wondered.

We both looked at her.

"Doing what? What would Serena do?"

"I don't know. She stole that candy, remember?"

"I don't think they marry you off because you've been shoplifting."

"Maybe she did something else, something that made them think they better get her settled down quick, taken care of before . . ."

"Before what?"

She shook her head and went back to sucking ice.

"Serena thinks it's because she got all A's on her report card," I said slowly.

"Well, then what about me?" Angela giggled, with the straw still in her mouth. "My grades were perfect, too, and all my dad gave me was a piece of gingerbread."

"I got F's." Jewell belched.

"Ladies."

Gordon was standing in front of us, standing over us, really. He had come out from behind the curtain.

"Gordon," Jewell drawled. "What were you doing back there?"

"Well, I just decided to mark the Sabbath by looking at some of these glorious representations of the female form, Jewell." He held up a bunch of magazines. "Have you girls ever been back there? I suppose not."

"It costs a dollar," I said.

"But that's deducted from the amount of your total purchase. It's just to discourage browsing."

He was dressed for town, neater than when I had seen him last, with cowboy boots that almost made him look tall and a Stetson hat. And dark glasses. He always wore dark glasses in the daytime. It was for a condition. I asked him once, What condition? and he said, "The condition of being able to *see*."

"Having a hen party? A little gender-bonding? Consciousness-raising? Mind if I join you?"

I was the one with space next to me. I worked my way over, rocking the table. Gordon waited until I was far enough away, then sat. He was fastidious. He didn't touch people except on his own terms. Never by accident. He gave us a wide, sweeping glance. With those glasses, you couldn't tell who he was staring at. He smiled at Angela.

"Angela honey, what are you doing with yourself these days?"

"Nothing," she said.

"Your daddy sometimes gets worried about you. But I told him not to be."

She nodded uncertainly. She wasn't sure if she was supposed to thank him or not.

"I told him, whatever it was that might be troubling him would turn out all right in the end," he assured her confidentially, and waited, watching her squirm. "It will, won't it? Turn out all right?"

She nodded a few times. She was scared to death. Of what? I frowned. Him? Or what she'd done? Then he addressed us as a group: "You know, I couldn't help overhearing some of what you were saying back there. Not the specific words so much as your general tone of anxiety. Is something troubling you girls? Something I should know about? There's no point in keeping secrets from me. That's like keeping a secret from yourself."

Jewell lifted her float and hid her face behind a big swallow of root beer.

"We were talking about marriage," I said.

"Ah, every girl's fantasy. A big church wedding."

"We were wondering," I went on, staring hard at Angela, "when do you think is the right time. The right age, I mean."

"To get married? Well, each one of you is already a bride of Christ," he pointed out. "Hell, that sounds like Bride of Frankenstein, doesn't it? What you girls have to understand is, you may think you're intelligent, functioning creatures, but really, viewed from the outside, right now you are all victims of hormonal poisoning. The world you see around you isn't the world the rest of us see. It's all . . . distended and nauseatingly illuminated, like the work of the painter El Greco." He looked at us expectantly, but didn't get any response. "That's why, ideally, you should all be kept in cages until you're twenty-one."

"Cages?" Jewell asked.

"I have tried to supply you with a moral framework. That's a kind of cage, you might say. A voice that says No! when you're about to cross the line. An inner voice. Because I can't always be here for you."

"So you think it's too soon," I said. "I mean, if we're still kids."

"You're not kids anymore. You're some grotesque hybrid. But yes, Eve, in your case I would definitely not worry too much about marriage. The only person I'd hook you up with"—he looked me over—

"is one of those color consultants. You know, the people who tell you how to dress?"

"What about other girls?" Jewell asked carefully.

"Each of you will ripen in your own sweet time. And you'll have to depend on me, Jewell honey, to decide when that time is. To decide when you're to be plucked from the tree, so to speak, and by whom. Do I make myself clear?"

We nodded. He unrolled one of the magazines he'd been holding in his fist.

"It's different with men," he sighed sadly. "Men will stick it any-where. As you see."

If what he'd said hadn't completely cowed us into submission, then the picture before our eyes certainly did. It was . . . I can't even describe it, it was so disgusting, but it left each of us feeling that we weren't ready yet. Not for that. Not even for a world where some-thing like that was possible. I wanted to throw up all over his stupid magazine. He took it back, got up out of the booth, and hitched his pants.

"What about Serena?" I asked. "Is she ready?"

"Serena's not here." He smiled. Gordon had repulsive teeth, and when he showed them it was a bad sign, like a cat's claws com-ing out.

"I know she's not here."

"Well, doesn't that tell you something?"

"Yes!" Angela cried, waking from her trance. She was back to being teacher's pet. I thought she was going to raise her hand and start waving. "It means she's different from us now."

"You are 110 percent correct, Angela. See? It's just like I told your daddy. You're going to turn out just fine." He touched the brim of his Stetson. "Adios, muchachas."

After he left, we started breathing again.

"You think he heard?" I asked.

"No," Jewell said, gauging the distance from the booth to behind the purple curtain. "He just plays mind games. He makes you think he knows everything. So you act as if he really does."

Angela looked over her shoulder.

"What did he mean, things were going to turn out fine for you?" I demanded. "What's your dad worried about?"

She got all stiff. "Nothing."

"He said—"

"I'm not pretty, OK?" She edged her way across the seat, mad. "I'm not pretty like you."

"Us?" Jewell laughed. I don't think anyone had ever called her pretty before. Or me, either.

"And I don't like it the way you guys are always getting me in trouble." She was standing now. You could see she had no idea where she wanted to go. She kept shifting from foot to foot. "Let Serena do what she wants. I mean, look at you. Is your life so great? Is your future so great? Who are you to judge?"

Then she left.

Jewell finished her float and wiped her mouth with a napkin. She did one thing at a time, very thoroughly, then moved on to the next. But I had no idea what was going on behind her face. I couldn't tell if she was happy or sad.

"What a nutcase," I said, watching Angela look both ways, to see if Gordon was still on the street, before letting go of the Luncheonette door. A bell tinkled as it closed.

"She's right, actually."

"No, she isn't."

"If Serena doesn't care about getting married, why should you?"

I had no answer to that question, except that I loved her. She was the only thing in the Colony worth saving. If Gordon's revelation of a community based on the New Testament and Old-Fashioned Values could produce a Serena, well, then it couldn't be all bad. But now they wanted to turn her into another drudge who would scrub the Meeting Hall floor on her hands and knees, serve men coleslaw and hamburgers, wash their clothes, and pump out their babies. And the worst thing was that if she went along with it, if she said yes, then it meant I'd been wrong from the start, that she wasn't so great to begin with. It meant she would be leaving me behind, turning back, just at the beginning of this adventure, an adventure I thought we were going to share, and that I would be left all alone. It would mean that I loved her, but that she didn't love me. Not enough.

"You wouldn't care if tomorrow morning Gordon picked out a husband for you?" I challenged.

"But he won't. That's the point. Because he knows I don't want him to."

"But what if he *did?*"

"It's His will," Jewell said placidly.

It got so hot my feet began to feel for the ground, like it might have disappeared in the middle of each step. There was a dip in the part of the highway we were working on. A mirage shimmered there, this stretch where the fabric of things broke down into what you saw before your mind put a name to it, just a bubbling puddle of matter. Cars came out of it, outrageous creations, weightless and noiseless, aiming themselves right at you. One day I almost flagged someone into the back of a Cadillac.

"I'm sorry," I said.

Victor opened his mouth to yell, but then stopped.

"See that sign over there?"

"Sign?" I asked, thinking he meant . . . a Sign.

He took me by the shoulders and pointed me to the exit ramp. There was a sign that listed Arhat's two motels. It was late afternoon. The metal threw a patch of shadow all the way past the shoulder, almost to the drainage ditch.

"Sit," he said. "Put your head between your legs."

I started to stagger across the wedge of grass that separated me from the spot.

"Eve," he called, and nodded to my side.

I was still holding the flag. When I gave it to him, my arm flew up, relieved of the weight.

With my eyes closed, I tried to think. But it was impossible. That was my problem. I couldn't think. All I could understand was a thing and its opposite. I could never build an argument from A to B to C. Cars passing on the highway, for example. I couldn't picture where they had come from or where they were going. All I could imagine was that, as they approached, they got more and more real. The slow tightness they made in my stomach was the feel of them coming into existence. And then, for one instant, they actually *were*, whizzing past, taking a little bit of me with them. After, there was that long, slow fade, that melting back into the steady hum of the world, until it was as if they had never been. My sweat dried. My muscles stiffened. Dust was layering me over. Soon I would be a shapeless mound by the side of the road. The next car was coming. I listened to it get more and more real, then waited for it to pass, like all the rest. But it didn't. Instead, its tires popped on a few loose stones as it stopped in front of me. The smell of exhaust wrinkled my nose and made me look up.

"So it's true," a voice said. "I didn't believe them."

"Didn't believe who?" I called back.

"People who said you were working on the highway crew. I told them it must be someone else. Some other Colony girl."

Why is it, I asked, that every time I see this man I am at my absolute worst? Both physically and mentally?

I had learned more about cars since I saw about a million of them a day. They were the major topic of conversation with the guys. Herbert Biswanger's was a little foreign hatchback, way too small for him, one of those "Japanese shitboxes" Walt said were ruining our economy. You didn't see many of them in Iowa, and most of the ones you did had out-of-state license plates. Herbert's was yellow, like a lemon pie.

"You in trouble?" he asked.

I wondered how he knew. Was it that obvious?

"About going to Joey's party, I mean. Wearing that dress."

"Oh, that. No." By now I was up, leaning in over the passenger-side window. Except my balance wasn't right, so I almost tipped into his lap. "That was a million years ago, wasn't it?"

"Less than a month, actually. I've been wondering about you."

"Have you? Have you been thinking about me?"

"Uh-huh."

I could see Victor, curious, crossing the grass to find out what was going on.

"Are you going somewhere?" I asked.

"Right now? Town. Then home." He looked the same, except he had a tie, loosened, and a plastic pocket protector with pens and a calculator in it. "I'm amazed I recognized you. It's Eve, isn't it? 'Just Eve'? You're so different."

"It's the jersey." I stepped back to model it a little. "It's reflective."

Victor was coming.

"Well," he said, getting ready to go.

I fainted. I mean, I pretended to faint. I mean, if you're weak enough from the sun and the smell of cars to fake fainting, isn't that the same thing as really fainting? The result was certainly the same. I fell face-up and kept my eyes closed while I heard the scrabble of heavy boots and the slam of a car door.

"I'm OK," I said, when they were close enough to hear.

"Eve!"

"I'm OK," I said again, louder, keeping my eyes closed. I couldn't tell which one was talking. They were both men. I had the greatest feeling of power, just lying there, with them hovering over me, being all concerned.

"It's the heat," Victor said. "That's why I told her to sit."

"Probably dehydrated." One put his palm on my forehead. It must have been Herbert. I could feel his wedding ring. I even imagined I could feel the scratch. "She's burning up."

"There's water in the truck."

"I'll get her into town. Here, help me lift her."

His hands were already under my arms. The same as when he picked me up the night of Joey's party. He was made to lift me and hold me close. To rescue me. That's why he was put on this earth. After all these years, he had finally found his calling. I felt so happy for him.

"She can't ride in a car," Victor was arguing. "It's some religious thing."

Oh great. So now, of all times, he was defending my Right to Worship.

"I *know* her," Herbert insisted. "She's a friend of my son's. I'll take her in to Dr. Carney's."

"I'm allowed," I moaned. ". . . medical emergency."

"Well, I guess," Victor said dubiously.

"Just get me inside." I was fighting the urge to yawn. I think it came out like a whimper.

They put the seat all the way back and laid me on top of it.

"You take care of her," Victor warned. I fluttered my eyes enough to see his look of fear, and felt bad. I could hear the guys yelling, asking him what was wrong.

"I'll be fine," I said weakly. "I feel better already."

". . . get you right into town," Herbert assured me.

I waited until I felt the surface of the road change, from the smooth blacktop of the ramp to the oatmeal of Route 6. Then I opened my eyes and looked up. Herbert was trying to drive and watch me at the same time.

"Don't have an accident," I said in my normal voice.

"How you feeling?"

"Thirsty."

"I'll get you over to the doc's. They'll rehydrate you. Maybe give you some salt tablets."

"No doctors in the Bible."

It took him a minute. Then he slowed the car.

"What's that supposed to mean?"

"Couldn't we go someplace cool and get something to drink? You know, like a beer? That's all I really need."

He shook his head. "Every time I see you, you're hurting, Eve."

"I just told you, I'm not. All I need is—"

"If that was a show you were putting on back there, then you're hurting far more than you think."

It was when he got angry that I saw he was Joey's father. His jaw stuck out and he got the same hard look in his eyes. His hands were so big on the steering wheel.

"Do you know a place called the Number?" I asked.

"The Number? That's a bar!"

"Walt and some of the guys go there after work. But they won't be there now. It's too early."

"Who's Walt?"

"He's on the road crew."

"Oh, Christ. Walt Connerly? He's a complete asshole, pardon my French."

"Can we go there?"

I got him to do it, even though he kept grumbling all the way into town. I didn't put the seat back up. I just lay there, stretched out. There were no clouds, but I could see the sky moving over us as we drove. A million different blues, one after another, each exactly the same and yet somehow different. If you squinted hard enough you could catch them passing. I was still light-headed. We stopped and I didn't feel it. I kept staring straight up, wondering why the edge of a power line cut across my vision without changing. Herbert had half-turned and was looking down at me. The engine ticked in the heat. He still had his seat belt on, this awkward harness that went over his shoulder and kept him from moving, kept him from landing completely on top of me. I could hear the metal hinge knock as he tried to shift his shoulder around more. His eyes were doing that same thing they had done in the toolshed, taking a cool inventory of every inch of me. I didn't have to look over. I could feel it happening. It wasn't sexual. Well, not completely. There was something else to it. It was mesmerizing, his interest in me. It was crazy, too. Why was he staring so hard? If he wanted me, he could just reach out. I didn't know what I would do. But I wasn't afraid.

"We're here," he finally said. "I think you might've slept."

"No," I answered softly.

"Shouldn't do this, you know. Go in there, I mean. It's no place for a young Christian."

"Technically, I'm a Tertiary Baptist."

"Oh, I don't want to hear about it."

"Then buy me a beer."

"The girl knows what she wants," he announced.

I lay there, listening to his footsteps come around to open the door.

The Number was right in the middle of town, but I would never have found it on my own. It was behind a bunch of buildings, through an alley, back where the employees' cars were parked. There was no sign. You just went down some stairs. I was still in my jersey. And my hard hat, which felt funny, because I usually left the hat in the truck at the end of the day. Herbert said I should keep it on, though.

"Why? Because it makes me look old enough to drink?"

"This isn't the kind of place where they check."

"Because it makes me look like a guy?"

"You don't look much like a boy, Eve," he sighed.

It was dark and cool, just like I imagined. There were rugs on the floor, all different kinds, overlapping, so some spots were thicker than others. It was easy to stumble. The tables and chairs were the kind that stacked and folded up. Only the bar looked attached to anything. It was a long length of stained, curving wood, with shelves of glasses behind it.

"Liquor's underneath," Herbert explained. "So it's not in plain sight. That's some legal term. Plain sight. The place doesn't have a license."

"So you've been here before?"

"Once or twice. 'Lo, Shirley." He nodded to a short fat lady behind the bar.

We sat at a table. There were only a few other people. All men. They watched me from behind their drinks. There were lights with metal hoods clipped to gas and water pipes that ran up through the ceiling. It was still just a basement, I saw, as my eyes got more and more accustomed. The walls weren't even paneled. They were just cinder blocks, painted black. They really soaked up the light. At the end of the room was a little raised square of plywood with a fence around it and green outdoor carpeting, the kind that's supposed to look like grass, tacked to the bottom. More bulbs were clipped along the fence and up the sides, all pointing to the wooden floor.

"Beer?" Herbert confirmed, bringing two bottles back to the table.

It was a stage.

"What happens there?" I asked.

"Where?" He deliberately sat to block my view, even though nothing was happening. Or maybe it was to protect me. "There? People dance."

"People? Like you?"

"I don't dance."

"Well, then who?"

"It's a strip joint. On Fridays. They get some girls in from Cedar Rapids. Drink that slow."

At first, my throat closed up, it was so parched. I fought the urge to cough. My eyes were smarting.

"That is sick," I got out, thinking of Gordon with his magazines. "Really repulsive. Is that all you guys ever think about?"

"Well, it is and it isn't. A man has needs, you know. Even if he doesn't like these needs, he still has them."

"So you started coming here after your wife died?"

"No. Before."

I nodded. It was a beautiful thing, the bottle. It had a long neck. I ran my hand down its side. It was already empty, somehow. A spreading glow, warm and cold, rippled out from my heart.

"Whoa," Herbert noticed. "You really have a taste for that stuff, don't you?"

"I was thirsty." I started to take off my hard hat, but he put his hand on top to keep it there. "What's the matter?"

"Colony girls . . ." he began, then stopped. "You know, Eve, people are intrigued by you."

"Intrigued?"

"You've got to be careful."

"Who, me?"

"All of you. That's why I think it would be better if you weren't so recognizable here."

"What's wrong with being from the Colony?" I demanded with dumb pride. I mean, it was exactly what I had been running away from for the past month. If anyone knew what was wrong with being from the Colony, it was me. But let someone else attack it and I immediately got all defensive.

"Nothing's wrong with it. Hell, I admire you out there. You're really trying to address the problem of how to live. It's just that certain guys get ideas."

"Ideas? In Arhat, Iowa? I don't think so. Can I have another?"

He hadn't even taken a sip of his. Rather than go to the bar again, he just pushed it across to me. I grabbed it as if it was the only solid object left in the world.

"So you come here Friday nights?"

"Sometimes," Herbert admitted.

"How come your son hates you so much?"

He winced. "You been talking to Joey? He doesn't hate me."

"Well, he doesn't like you."

"I'm his dad, for Christ's sake. He's not supposed to like me. Not now. Maybe later," he added sadly, moving the ashtray around.

"You think he's stupid?"

"He told you that? Jesus! No, I don't think he's stupid. I think it's stupid for him to work as a car mechanic, though. I don't want him to piss his life away, that's all."

I couldn't tell if he meant . . . like Joey was doing now, working at some broken-down garage, or piss his life away like his father was doing.

"Now you, for instance." He smiled. "You're not going to make a mess of your opportunities. I can tell. You're very direct. Very focused. The way you got that job on the road crew. That showed initiative."

Suddenly all my courage disappeared. Nothing he thought about me was true. I was a fool, a faker, in my jeans and T-shirt and jersey. With this dumb hat I wasn't allowed to take off. I longed to be dressed properly, a God-fearing Christian girl, in the clothes I had known since girlhood. I wanted to be swaddled in yards and yards of plain cotton. Christ's kid sister.

"What do you do, anyway?" I asked, trying to change the subject.

"Me? I work out at the playground factory, remember?"

"Doing what?"

"I'm a safety engineer. I determine what the chances are of a boy hurting himself, relative to the degree of difficulty necessary to maintain interest and to facilitate muscular and cognitive development."

"A boy?"

"Or a girl."

"Can I have another?"

"No, you may not. You've got to learn to pace yourself."

His mouth was a beautiful thing. His whole face. It was so marked up. I loved his look of concern. I laid Joey's features, his lips and nose and eyes, on top of Herbert's, trying to see back in time, and forward, too, to create this perfect combination. I felt a quiet *settling* going on throughout my body. Magic dust was being sprinkled on me from above. I looked up, the sensation was so real. Maybe it was asbestos from the flaky ceiling tiles.

I don't know how Herbert got me out of the Number that day. I don't have a clear memory of it. We talked a while longer. I remember laughing, laughing too much. Then the next thing I knew, we were back in his little yellow car. He had put the seat up. My knees were pushed into my face.

"Why do you drive this thing?" I complained, looking around at the cramped interior.

"You sound like Joey. Because it's well built, that's why. It's not going to break down on you in the middle of nowhere. And it gets good mileage. You should see what *he* drives."

I looked away, realizing there was a wall between these two, Joey and Herbert, and that nothing got through. Except maybe me. But it wasn't the kind of car where you could lounge around and look sideways out the window. Instead, my eyes were drawn back to the road.

"The reason I got so mad back there, when you pretended to faint," Herbert began, bringing up a question I hadn't even thought to ask, "is because you made me think of Mary Alice."

"Who?"

"Mary Alice. My wife. She was so sick, for so long. I cared for her. She died at home. And seeing you there, lying on the ground, brought that all back. Not that you look like her or anything. Just the feeling. And then, when I realized you had really been OK the whole time—"

"I'm sorry, I'm sorry," I muttered. "I just wanted to be with you, that's all. I mean, you only talked to me for two minutes, and then you were about to go away again. And you never come around to see me."

"You're fourteen, Eve. And you live in a religious community."

"Fifteen," I corrected. "Almost sixteen. And it's not like there's no dating in the Bible, you know."

I was watching his hands on the wheel, the way they made it seem so small and manageable. I wondered if he was the man who crawled into my bed each morning and crushed me with his weight, whose strong fingers spread out to cover my breasts. I squirmed in my seat. Was it love? Or did I have to pee?

But he wasn't sensing any of that. His mind was far away.

"She loved it here." He nodded at the outskirts of town. "She was a local girl. I met her at school. University of Iowa. I'm from Des Moines, myself. We moved back here after college, right around the time she got sick."

"And now she's dead," I said dully. "So, are you going to leave Arhat?"

"Hell, Eve!" He slapped the steering wheel. I thought he was mad again, but he wasn't. It was like I had won some prize. "That is exactly what amazes me about you. One minute you're this screwed-up little teenage girl, and then suddenly you know me better than anyone in the whole world. Yes, I would like to leave Arhat. Tomorrow. And start anew, damnit!"

"You're a soul separated from God," I said. "Moving around isn't going to get you any closer to Him."

"No. But it'll get me a hell of a lot farther away from Them."

"Who's them?"

"Them!" He fluttered his hand back behind us, meaning everyone, all of Town. "My neighbors, my colleagues, my *friends*, such as they are."

"So where are you going to go?"

"I got some feelers out. Got an interview next week, actually. Going to fly to San Diego. That's where I wanted to go, originally. A lot of people from around here do. You know what we call California? The west coast of Iowa."

"I'm from California," I said. "Originally."

"Now, why doesn't that surprise me?"

"What about Joey?"

"Joey could use the change, too. Even if he doesn't know it."

He didn't offer to drop me at the Colony. He let me out right where I would have emerged from the cornfields if I had walked home. The sun was slanting in the sky. The stalks stood absolutely still. They didn't look attached to the ground anymore.

"Thanks for the ride," I called.

Then he said something, and I laughed. I didn't know what else to do. It was not a situation I had ever imagined being in. It was unexpected, so I laughed, like a complete idiot, and ruined what would have been a perfect moment. Instead, he got a puzzled look and drove off.

I waited, then ran into the field and peed. It was already chilly, out of the light. I felt the tension of the encounter hiss down and away. My knees were shaking. I steadied myself by clinging to two thick green stalks. The thought occurred to me that I could hide in here forever, just eat raw corn and lick the dew off leaves. I climbed out and the sunset was beginning. It was going to be the kind where the sun is a red-hot ball being lowered steadily into a pail of cold water. You could almost hear the explosion. I looked behind and saw my shadow, stretching ten miles down the road. The farther I walked, the farther it went in the other direction.

"Do you know how beautiful you look?" he had said. "Do you know how beautiful you look, standing there in the light?"

4

What did I want? Well, love, of
course. But what kind of love? There were so many. Part of me
wanted to be utterly passive, to lie flat on my back and become one
with the curve of the earth. Men would pass over me like clouds,
silently, weightlessly, painlessly, until I was nothing, just a field,
trampled into topsoil by the force of their lust. It didn't matter who
they were, their names, their faces, because I was staring past them.
They weren't love. They were the *agents* of love. Something else
was powering them. Some divine force they were oblivious to. If I
looked up, beyond a hundred men's shoulders, straight into the sky,
what would I see? That was one kind of love. But there were more.
There was the love that would cure me of my great loneliness, the
love for one man who would provide my life with shape and meaning. And even if those limits turned out to be terrible, at least that
was something I could try to escape from, something I could push
against. Each night he would torture me. And I would struggle. He
would cleanse me of my sin with pain. That was another kind of
love I fantasized about, longed for, even. And then there was the
feeling my mystery man gave when he crawled into my bed, into my

waking dreams. I wanted that, too. A warm snuggly comfort that was one kiss away from passion, one caress away from fusing every thought and sensation I had ever known, a lightning bolt that would blow out every nerve ending, erase every doubt and guilt, leaving the old Me gone forever and a new Me in its place. I wanted that overpowering, transforming love, too. I wanted every kind of love there was, all rolled up into one.

The Meeting Hall was a big leaky building set off to the side of the lake. It had been a basketball court once. My shoes echoed on that special kind of floor. It was dark, but there was nothing to crash into. The Colony didn't believe in statues or paintings or even crosses. There were folding chairs leaning against the wall in neat rows, and Bibles, with mushy pages and cracked bindings, stacked on a table. That was all. I walked past the site of so many sermons, where I had learned exactly how to get into Heaven, and kept going. What was past Heaven? The kitchen. Two lanterns were set on the floor. Their glow spread out and out. Mother was alone, sprinkling flour over polished marble. It glittered in the air, it was so white.

"Come to help?" she asked, without turning.

She had tied on an apron that showed her figure. Her hair was up and you could see the muscles in her neck work as she rolled out the crust. There was a look of unnatural concentration in her eyes. Her hands never stopped moving.

She had made Gordon get the marble. It was the one nice thing. Everything else he had picked up at a fire sale or bankruptcy auction: a dirty, grease-stained restaurant oven, a refrigerator that made sounds, the kind of freezer that opened on top, where you had to reach down into a chest. But Mother had insisted on him getting the block of gray-veined marble. She was making cherry pies. It was the night before the Fourth of July. I watched over her shoulder the ball of dough become a perfect circle. It was light and soft and empty. The kind of place where Jesus' face would appear.

"That looks good on you," she said when I finally came around.

"Is it one of yours?"

"It was."

I had found the dress hanging in my closet, freshly washed, still stiff and sweet-smelling from having dried outside in the sun. It fit much better than my old one. I had grown, all this time away. It felt funny to be wearing real clothes again. I was self-conscious, even though there was no one else around. My heels sounded incredibly loud.

"There's another apron."

"How did you know I was coming?"

She pressed the dough into the bottom of the pie plate, poured in the filling—pitted cherries so red they were black—and set it aside. She did the tops later, in that crisscross design that looked so simple but was really a pattern, with the strips going over and under, woven against the fruit. Then she would bake them, four at a time, all night long.

"I'm going to be terrible at this," I warned. "You know I can't cook."

It was true. Cooking set off alarm bells in me. As if learning how to boil water was the first step down some slippery slope to servitude, kids, and facial hair.

She weighed out salt in the palm of her hand. She never measured anything. She cut lard into a big bowl of flour. Since the lanterns were on the floor, shadows flew up into our faces. She began adding water.

"Touch it," she ordered.

I brushed it with the back of one knuckle.

She took my hand and pushed it in up to the wrist. The stuff closed over me. I tried to knead while she sprinkled in more water, a few drops at a time. A shiver traveled back up my arm.

"Where have you been?" she asked. "The last few days?"

"I told you. I've been working. On the road crew, remember?"

"I mean after. You get off at four."

I looked at her, surprised she knew that.

"Just walking in the fields," I mumbled.

"Alone?"

"Of course alone. Who would I be with?"

"When I was your age," Mother said, staring with me deep into the bowl, talking while she watched, like it was part of the recipe, How to Make a Pie, "I had a friend. Myrna. She'd sleep over sometimes. She lived next door. One night this boy we both knew came in the window. He'd been drinking. I'm not even sure he was clear where he was. Except he was, of course. But he didn't know there were two of us there. He was very drunk. He got into my sister's old bed and started bothering my friend." She reached for the pitcher of water and poured in more than before. A whole dollop. I felt the dough change. It came magically away from the sides of the bowl. "She had been asleep. When she woke up, he was already on top of her. I had been awake the whole time. But I didn't do anything. I was too embarrassed. Or scared. I don't know which. I just froze. I remember pretending to be asleep. Pretending it was a dream, everything that was happening. Even though she was . . . almost screaming. A kind of living dream. Make it into a ball, now. That's right. Don't work it too hard or it loses something. Good. Then, when he had left, and my friend was lying there trying not to cry, trying not to wake me, I realized, this was my home and my bedroom, and that the whole time it had been happening, he had thought it was me. I had really been seeing what should have happened to me. It was like being outside yourself and seeing . . . your fate."

"That is one gross story," I said. "What do I do now?"

She took the ball over to the marble square and floured it lightly. I began destroying it with the rolling pin

"Gently." She slowed me down. "Work out from the center. I just never want anything like that to happen to you, that's all."

"What? You don't want me to get raped because I'm friends with a pretty girl?"

Her hands closed over mine. They were always so cool. Or maybe mine were always hot and sweaty. Together, we smoothed it out.

"What happened to Myrna was terrible. But I meant what happened to me. Just listening and watching, just lying there feeling . . . the feeling . . . go *out* of you. And then never having it come back. That's what it was like for me. And I would hate to have you be the same way. Do you know what I mean, Eve?"

I was trying to look anyplace but her eyes. I hated it when adults confessed to me. But lately it seemed like that was all they ever did, like I brought it out in them. All this unwanted emotion. And now even my mother was getting in on the act. When are we going to address my problems, I wanted to ask.

"Look!" she said brightly.

We had made a pie, or a crust, rather. My edges were more raggedy than hers. She showed me how to trim them off and patch the little tears.

"So you have a sister?" I confirmed. "That means I have an aunt, right?"

"All the women in the Colony are your aunts," she said, carrying the pie off to sit with the others.

"Yeah, right." While I had her on the run I figured I'd get as much out of her as I could. "That picture you keep. The one of you. Dad took that, didn't he?"

"What picture?"

"The snapshot of you. The one in your dresser drawer."

"What have you been doing in my dresser drawer?"

"Looking for heroin."

"It's not a picture of me. It's a picture of you," she said, going back to the bowl, mixing up another batch of dough. She did them one at a time. She said they were better that way. That's why it took her so long.

"No, the one of you," I insisted. "In that gown, with those rocks all around you, or whatever they are. Those mounds."

"It's a picture of you." She worked much faster without me, the flour, the salt, the shortening. She was freed. The pastry cutter clinked against the bottom of the bowl. "That was taken when we first found out I was pregnant. You're inside that picture. If you look close enough. That's why I kept it."

I tried understanding. That I was somehow contained in that moment. So it was a mirror. A time mirror. I thought of Gordon's mirror that showed your "true" reflection.

"So he really is my father."

She stopped.

"Who?"

"Dad, I mean. Even though you don't talk about him."

"Well, what did you think?"

"I don't know. I thought maybe my father was someone else. Gordon or someone. And that's why it's not important that I know about Dad. Like who he was, even."

I felt for the back of the apron, where the string was. I hated cooking. She had gotten me interested again, but only for a few minutes. Now I wanted to get out. I hated the Meeting Hall. It smelled. Even under the odor of baking pies it smelled. I'd had a revelation here once: If you wanted to get to Heaven, you never would, because just wanting to get there was so selfish. A sin in itself. So the only way to Grace was Not to Give a Rat's Ass. That was the title of a sermon I worked on in my head for a while. But it never really came together.

"Gordon? Your father?" She was smiling blankly. It was like I had hit her with a door. "You were four when we met Gordon."

"I know. But I thought that was maybe just from when I remember him. That really you'd known him earlier. It would explain a lot of things, that's all. But I guess—"

"Explain a lot of things like what?"

I finally gave up trying to find the stupid apron string and pulled the whole thing over my head.

"Explain what?"

"Nothing," I said. "Really. I don't know why I even said it. I never even thought it before. I have to go."

She was right on top of me. Her face was two inches from mine. She had touched her hair and cheek, and there was flour smeared on them. I had never seen her look so twisted. Her eyes were wild. Like she was jealous or something.

"It's just that he's so nice to me," I finally got out. "I thought there must be a reason."

"He's not nice to you."

"Yes, he is."

"He's not nicer to you than to anyone else. You're all his children here."

It's what Joey had asked, I traced the thought back to its source. He was the one who had wondered if Gordon was my father. I hadn't considered it since, not consciously. It was weird to hear the idea coming straight out of my mouth, when it hadn't even formed in my brain. Suddenly I wished Joey was here to protect me. How would Mother react to his wide, perfect shoulders? She would respect something like that. If I wasn't beautiful, at least I could bring something beautiful home.

"Oh, come on, Mom. Of course Gordon treats me different. He lets me do things no other kid is allowed to do. He lets me work outside the Colony. He lets me hang out at his house. And it's all because of you."

"You think I'm a whore!" she hissed, grabbing me by the shoulders.

"No!"

She was going to beat the crap out of me, but then her eyes dulled over. She got that way she did. All transcendental. She mastered herself, mastered her anger, and then took a deep breath.

"I *know* you don't sleep with him anymore," I said, even though I didn't.

"I'm not the way I used to be. Gordon saved me from that life. You see that, don't you? I'm so much better than I was before."

She was pleading.

It was true. The other women at the Colony were actually much more corrupt. They all wanted Gordon. You could tell. Even if they thought they were dreaming about Jesus and called the whole thing a Religious Experience. But Mother had extinguished her flame. Now, instead of sleeping with everyone, she slept with no one. That was her great accomplishment. Gordon's one certifiable miracle.

She noticed something, licked her thumb, and gently worked away the spots on the sleeve of my new dress, where she had grabbed me.

"Your father runs a pre-owned-car dealership in Tucson, Arizona." She wet her thumb again and did the other sleeve. Carefully.

Concentrating. I stayed perfectly still. "At least that's what he was doing the last I heard. When you're older, you can go visit him, if you want. I wouldn't expect too much, though. He drinks. Or he used to. It's been a long time." She wiped her hands on her apron and tried a new way of doing my hair, combing it forward as if I was a doll. But there wasn't enough of it. "He never had a great deal of interest in you, Eve. Not after we split up. Not before, either. I'm sorry. I'm telling you this so you won't be disappointed. So you won't build him up in your heart as some answer to all your problems. It's Gordon whose love is true. His love is pure. It's not because you're his daughter. It's because he wants to save your soul for Christ. Is that so hard to believe?"

"Gordon loves you," I said.

"Yes."

"No, he *loves* you, Mom."

She pushed my hair back the way it was, then stepped away, as if to admire her creation from a distance. But I was just the same as before.

"Maybe," she allowed. "Once."

"He still does."

She went back to her block of marble.

"You got him to buy you that," I pointed out.

She rolled out more dough.

"So what's Dad like?"

She started ladling in the cherries. Our little chat was over.

"Could you get Gordon to do something for me?"

"What?"

"Do you know about Serena? That she's going to get married?"

She paused for a moment. "Serena? But she's so young."

"She's five months older than I am."

"Who is she getting married to?"

"Ethan, maybe. Or Gerald. Gordon has to decide."

"Good," Mother said, almost to herself. "I'm tired of their looks."

"Whose? Those guys?"

She held up a strip of dough and pinched it off like it was their throats.

"Serena wants to be good," I said. "She's not going to say no to Gordon and her mother. But I don't see why she should be punished."

"Marriage isn't punishment, Eve."

"I know! It shouldn't be. It should be beautiful. That's why I want you to stop it. Before it's too late. To get Gordon to stop it, I mean. Can you?"

She laughed. Then she saw I was serious and stopped.

"Marriage will be good for Serena. And for her husband. You'll see."

"How can you say that? Those guys are pigs."

"All men are pigs." She busied herself weaving the lattice top. Her fingers were so fast. She was pretending to concentrate, so she wouldn't have to look at me. "I can't do anything, Eve. Maybe I could save *you*. If I begged him. Maybe. But Serena . . ."

She shook her head, imagining how hopeless it would be.

"So you're going to let them do the same thing to Serena that happened to your friend."

"What friend?"

"The one who got raped instead of you."

"It's not the same thing at all! If Gordon thinks Serena is ready to get married, then she is. It's His will."

"It'll be worse than what happened to your friend. Because everyone's going to be watching, not just you. And it's going to be in the daytime, not at night. And Gordon's going to be there reading from his stupid Bible. You won't be able to pretend you're asleep."

"The trick," she said, "is not to work the shortening too much. Or else it won't be flaky. It's very sensitive."

I watched a minute more.

"So was Dad different?" I asked. "Or was he like all the others? Did you love him?"

But her thought was with her pies now. They never let her down. One after the other they came out, always perfect, her true children.

The Fourth of July was a huge event at the Colony. Gordon said it was his favorite holiday, growing up. The men built a fire and roasted tons of meat. The women put out potato salad, coleslaw, deviled eggs, succotash, stuff like that. But it was more than just a cookout. It was a carnival. Kids ran wild. There were games and races and contests. It was our day off from the Rules. I used to love it. I remembered running down to the lake, hours early, to watch them light the barbecue and set up the tables. It was all for me, that's what I used to pretend. The whole party. Nobody else knew, but secretly it was a celebration of my own personal existence on earth, of this brief time I walked among them, an ordinary mortal like themselves. It wasn't really the Fourth of July, it was Eve, like Christmas Eve or New Year's Eve, but just Eve. My day. The day before I would reveal my true nature.

And now I wandered through the empty cabin, hiding, trying to get up the courage to go outside. What had happened? I looked down and ran a hand over the smooth, unfamiliar fabric of my new dress. Was this really me? There had been something else in my closet, a white paper bag with HAPPY BIRTHDAY, AMERICA written on it. Inside was a pint of Everclear alcohol, small enough to nestle at the bottom of my dress's deep pocket. It gave me the creeps, to think of Gordon in my room. He would have had to step over my bed. I could see his legs straddling my mattress. His shadow on my pillow. I unscrewed the bottle and the plastic cap crackled.

Outside, it was a perfect day. The sun made me blink. A bunch of nursing mothers were sitting apart from the crowd.

"Well now, who is that?" they screeched, watching me come down the hill. "Is that little Eve? All grown up?"

I didn't answer. I pretended not to hear. I looked up once, long enough to see their babies, these live goiters, munching away at their flesh, and kept my head down, like I was picking my way through some really complicated obstacle course.

"Now you be careful down there, Eve," one mother cooed, mocking me, but jealous, too.

I straightened my shoulders once I was past them. My eyes finally reached some agreement with the intense light and everything came back into focus: the men in their overalls and hats; the women in their long dresses and scarves. The children like their parents in miniature, except they had something else, a freshness that made you smile and feel sad at the same time.

"Eve!"

Angela was in the tug-of-war. She was flushed and excited. Her hair had slipped out of her bun and was halfway down. She waved at me. She was on the losing side. You could tell already. They were getting dragged, step by step, toward the mud pit.

"Eve!" she shouted again, way too animated. "Look at me!"

She was the only girl, sandwiched between a bunch of men. It didn't look as if she was helping that much. I don't think she understood the object of the game. She was just slamming herself into the guy in front of her and then the guy behind. She probably would have liked being the rope, all those sweaty hands trying to tear her to pieces.

"Have you seen Serena?" I called.

"What?"

The music started up, snare drums and a million crashing trombones. It had been going since early morning. Gordon had turned his speakers around and was blasting John Philip Sousa marches. Just one John Philip Sousa march, actually. He had left the sound system on Repeat so it played "Stars and Stripes Forever" . . . forever. It was amazing how different it sounded the twentieth time, like a musical expression of insanity.

"Serena! Have you seen Serena?"

But she couldn't hear.

At the food table Gordon was helping people load their plates. He was dressed up as Uncle Sam. He had a real costume, blue pants and coat, a red vest, a red-white-and-blue top hat. He even had that little wispy beard glued to his chin. He still wore his dark glasses, though, so the effect was kind of sinister, to me at least. But everyone was grateful. You could tell. It had been so long since he had come down from his house. It made the day even more special. When I came up, he took me by the shoulders and hugged me. His costume was stiff, like cardboard.

"Don't you look beautiful," he murmured under the marching music.

"It's great you're here," I said. I couldn't tell if I was drunk, from one swallow of the Everclear, or if he was being weirder than usual. "People didn't know if you were coming or not."

"Neither did I. Not until this morning."

"What made you decide?"

"Fasting and prayer, fasting and prayer, my dear. And this." He let me peek in his vest pocket, where there was a prescription bottle of pills.

"What's that?"

"A little thing I discovered called Demerol. Really helps me out in social situations. You know how shy I get. Can't operate heavy machinery with it, though. That's what the label says. That's why I don't go up and change the music."

"Pills?"

"Well, they're not pills, per se. I prefer to think of them as an apocalyptic version of the Host." He went back to serving up food. "You don't eat meat, do you, sugar?"

"Gordon!"

He squinted at me from behind his glasses.

"Why, it's Eve!" he exclaimed, as if there was someone else next to him, watching us both. "Well, I'll be goddamned! Figuratively."

"Who'd you think it was?"

"No one." He touched his forehead and let out a deep breath. I could see his brain feeling for its skull, trying to get its bearings. "Now, that is a new dress, is it not?"

"I want to talk to you about Serena."

"Eve!" He was still getting it straight. "You find that present I left you? In your closet?"

"What? Oh, yeah." The bottle of Everclear clunked against me. "Thanks."

"I sensed you had a taste for it, that night up at my house. The pure, undiluted essence of things. That's the American version of *eau de vie*, you know. The water of life. Every country has one. Aquavit. Schnapps. And that's ours. Grain alcohol from the heartland. Everclear."

"Thanks again, Gordon."

"You said you were looking for Serena? She and Jewell were just here. I don't know where they went, though."

"This is Mom's dress."

"Your mother's still in the Meeting Hall, making the pies, I believe. She likes the last ones to come out right around dessert time. She's a perfectionist, your mom."

"That Demerol stuff. Is it in the Bible?"

"Well, I'll let you in on a little secret." He leaned close, not actually touching me but whispering into my ear. The fake beard flicked against my neck. It set off this unwanted shiver. "Ain't no *Bible* . . . in the Bible. Ponder that."

"It's Mom's dress," I repeated. "You thought I was her."

"You are her. Half her. And half your daddy. That's your dark side. But I have faith in you, Eve. The goodness in you will win out. You were raised right. Grace is the product of struggle. Happy Independence Day."

He held out my plate. I turned around. A line had formed.

"Look what Serena got."

Jewell was sucking on one of those tubes of colored ice, the kind kids ate. You squeezed it through a plastic sleeve into your mouth. I crouched just inside the willow branches, still holding on to my plate. Theirs were sitting off to one side, already empty.

"From the SuperAmerica." Jewell's tongue was purple. It was on her fingers and lips, too.

"You've been stealing again."

Serena ignored my accusation. Hers was red. There was a ring of it around her mouth. It made her look like the victim of a crime. I stuck my plate next to theirs. She reached into a paper bag and handed me my pop. It was light blue.

"Yours is grape?" I asked. "And cherry?"

They nodded.

"What's mine supposed to be?"

"Sky blue," Serena said, finally swallowing.

"But what's sky blue supposed to taste like?"

"Find out." She went back to nibbling at hers. Apparently it demanded a great deal of attention.

"How come they're still cold? SuperAmerica's miles from here."

"I didn't get them today, silly. I got them last week. I've been keeping them in the bottom of the big freezer."

She was eating incredibly carefully. She examined one side, then the other, touching it with her tongue but not really licking, pressing out the road of frozen sugar.

"The freezer in the Meeting Hall? So you saw my mother?"

"She was baking."

"Did she say anything to you?"

I was afraid she had said Congratulations, or something else that would give away that I had told her about the marriage.

"She told me I looked pretty."

"Nice dress," Jewell said. "Is it new?"

"It's hers. Or used to be." I was suddenly aware that I shouldn't be getting stuff on it. Although it was a little late for that, since I was sitting on dirt, with artificially colored syrup running down my wrists.

"That's her best one," Serena nodded. "I recognized it right away. It looks really good on you, Eve."

"I look like a whore."

"Have you ever actually seen a whore?"

Jewell squeezed off an inch of ice and bit it. Her body temperature must have been thirty-two degrees. Meanwhile, I was trying to lick back a chunk that was somehow melting off the tip of my nose.

"So how come you guys aren't out there?"

"We just decided."

"*She* just decided," Jewell said.

Serena's blood-red fingertips squooshed her pop out a little farther.

I knew what Jewell meant. When Serena decided on something, she got very powerful and determined. And since we were basically a bunch of directionless girls, we usually went along. I licked at my ice. It did have a taste, but I couldn't figure out what. Not a fruit. The sky? The sky didn't have a taste, did it? The ocean? Which I had seen but couldn't remember. What else in nature was light blue? I looked in the bag and saw one waiting for Angela. It was brown. Root beer.

"I shouldn't have eaten all this," Serena said.

"Why?" I asked. "Is there going to be a dress you have to fit into?"

"I don't know." She frowned. "They haven't told me yet."

"Have they told you who it's going to be?"

"They haven't told me anything, Eve."

"It could be romantic," Jewell offered.

"What's that?" Serena poked at the outline of the bottle through my pocket.

"Oh." I dug out the Everclear. "It was a present."

"From who?"

"A secret admirer."

I got the top open and took a sip, pretending they weren't watching me.

"Well, it's the Fourth of July," I argued. "At least I didn't steal it."

They shrugged at the logic. I passed it around. Jewell took a swig with the same guarded stare she had for everything else. She just gave a little genteel cough at the end like a lady at a tea party. Serena giggled.

"What *is* it?" she asked, before she had some.

"It's our country's water of life," I recited.

" 'Danger. Flammable.' "

"That, too."

She drank a quarter of the bottle. I've never seen anything like it. I opened my mouth to say something, but just watched. Her throat opened and closed. Time slowed down. She was so red-streaked and self-contained. Like a sacrifice. I remembered how I was going to save her. Save all of us, somehow. But from what? And how?

"Secret admirer." Jewell sounded a million miles away. "Is it that boy from school? Joey?"

I shrugged. I didn't want her to think yes, but I didn't want her to think no. I set the bottle down in the middle. It was this fire for us to warm ourselves by.

"Do you remember much from before?" I asked, staring into its depths, the line where the clear of the liquor became the clear of the air.

"Mom says we came here when I was six," Jewell answered promptly. She knew what I was up to. After all, it was her idea. "She never says much about before. You don't remember a lot, do you, Eve? Where you come from? If you have relatives?"

I shook my head. We waited, the two of us. I didn't dare look up.

But Serena answered a different question.

"It's not really stealing," she said. "I mean, I didn't go in there to steal. I just went in there. I don't know why."

"SuperAmerica? You went in there without money? What for? The air conditioning?"

"They had things that belonged to me."

"Nothing belongs to you."

"That's not true." Serena reached out and took the bottle again. She tried to explain. "There are these things that glow. Like they were mine once. Things that I lost or forgot about, and now I've found them. That's how it feels. So I just pick them up. I just take them. I take them *back*."

"But it's a sin."

"No, it's not. I'm not stealing. I told you: they glow, the things. They're waiting for me. So it's more like I'm righting a wrong. An ancient wrong." She put the bottle back, exactly where it had been. She didn't seem drunk at all. "Besides, I'm going to be married in less than two months. So until then I can do whatever I want. I'll be a white bride. That's all anyone here cares about."

"Less than two months?" I asked.

"At the end of the summer." She lay down on the ground, curling up, making her fingers into a little prayer pillow and resting her head. Her big brown eyes looked past us, into the willow. "That's what they told me."

"I thought they didn't tell you anything."

"Well, they told me that."

"And what did you say?"

"They didn't ask me, they told me." She was a little ball now, trying to get even smaller. "So I don't have to go back to school, at least."

"Where are you from?" I asked desperately. "Do you remember?"

"From here, of course. What do you mean?"

"Before. Do you remember where you lived before?"

"Mars," Jewell breathed, shooting me a look.

"I'm hoping *he* has it," Serena went on.

"Who?"

"My husband, silly. I'm hoping he has that glow, like the things I take. So when I see him, I'll know. I'll know that it was meant to be."

"It's sick," I complained. "And everyone's just going to let it happen. Me included."

Joey's car was impossible to turn. I watched his hands cross over and over each other on the steering wheel, lining it up with the empty driveway.

"And then Angela came in, covered with mud, because she'd been playing tug-of-war with all these men, and she was babbling about how strong they all said she was, which is a total lie, because her arms are like spaghetti, which actually is what the rest of her body looks like, too. And then—"

"We're here," he said.

"I know we're here. I've been here before, remember? Your party."

It was a white wooden house with red brick over parts of it, but you could tell the brick didn't hold anything up. It was just for decoration. There was the same bad-looking lawn as in back, and a cement pathway leading up to the front door. A big picture window downstairs and bedroom windows upstairs. Even though I'd said I'd been here before, I wouldn't have recognized it.

"Your awful party," I remembered.

Bushes hid the bottom, as if the foundation was something shameful you weren't supposed to see. A chimney stuck up through the shingles. The whole thing looked fake, propped up, like in a play. I could probably push it over with my little finger, this house where I was about to become a Woman.

Say something, I begged silently. He had said about ten words since we'd gotten into the car.

"I liked your mom."

"I noticed."

They had really hit it off. It was a conspiracy. I had come home and Joey was sitting there talking to her. He had changed out of his work clothes. He didn't look nearly as sexy as in his jumpsuit. There was no zipper to pull down. He had showered, too. His hair was still damp. I, of course, was like a piece of roadkill. I had even been thinking, as I opened the door, how particularly ugly I felt. And there they were. They both turned and looked at me.

"She'd sleep with you if you wanted. She used to do it professionally."

"Why do you say things like that?"

"Just trying to be funny."

We were both staring at the house, not moving. From now on, everything I did or didn't do, I could tell already, was going to mean something. If I got out of the car first it would look like I was wanting it more than him. But if I stayed still, it would look like I was nervous and scared. All of which was true, but that wasn't the point. My hands were sweating. I pressed them against my dress. Mother had made me change.

"I'll talk to Joseph," she had said, walking me down to my room, standing right alongside me as if I might bolt. Then she added, in this urgent whisper: "The new dress."

It was cleaned again, miraculously, as if she had been expecting this to happen. The stains I had gotten from the Fourth of July were gone.

"He's very nice," she went on, standing in the doorway, making sure I was really going to wear it. "He's been waiting almost an hour. Where were you?"

"I don't believe this," I'd said. "You mean you're actually encouraging me to go out with him?"

"Why not?"

"What about all those things you said before? About saving myself for Jesus?"

"Jesus was a man," she pointed out, "and clearly you need practice in talking to men. Besides, this isn't about sex, it's about going on a date."

"I still don't get it."

"Remember when you asked me about Serena? And I told you I couldn't help her? Well, I can't. But I can help you. Now, if you don't want to end up like that, then you'll have to start having experiences of your own. Simple, ordinary experiences, like a regular girl would have. I've talked to Joseph. He seems like a very nice boy. And nothing's going to *happen*."

"It's a trick, isn't it?"

She opened her mouth to say something, but then changed her mind. I think she had been expecting me to thank her.

"Can't I wear my jeans?"

"No."

She went back out. I listened to them talking. She didn't ask him about school or anything like that. They were discussing cars, which was pretty amazing. I'd never even seen my mother in a car since we came to Iowa. But she was asking could he fix foreign models? And was it true they had computers in them now? She treated him like an adult. She got him talking. He talked more to her in those five minutes than he had ever talked to me in all the times we'd been together. I wasn't surprised. She was doing what she used to be so good at. Pleasing a man. Acting interested. Making him feel big. It excited her. I could hear it in her responses, these little oohs and ahs of appreciation and pretend amazement. It would be pathetic if she was trying to live through me, I thought, pulling the dress over my head. That would leave her twice-removed from any kind of life. Meanwhile, I was transformed from road-crew girl back to my little Christian Academy self. I sat on the mattress, on the floor, with the big furniture looming up all around me, feeling about six years old. I didn't want to go back out there.

"Aren't you afraid we're going to do something?" I asked, when she finally came to get me.

"You look nice," she said. "Stand up."

I did. She corrected my posture. She tried fixing my hair.

"He wants to take you out for a hamburger. That place where the kids go. On the highway. If you don't want to go, just tell me. I'll say you changed your mind. I thought you would want to. I thought it would make you happy. That's why I'm saying yes."

"It's against the rules."

This look came over her face. "I make the rules. Not Gordon. He's a nice boy. I can tell."

"How can you tell?"

"I just can. Don't worry. Nothing's going to happen."

"Stop saying that."

"He'll be a perfect gentleman." She smiled nervously. "Now answer me: do you like him? Do you want to go out with him? Yes or no?"

"I guess."

She gave me a hug. There was a catch in her throat. She was all emotional. She stood back and straightened my dress, tugged it really hard, like she was trying to yank me onto some path.

"Nothing's going to happen," she assured me again, as we went back out together. She couldn't stop saying it.

"So what's going to happen?" I asked as soon as we were alone in his car. "Are we going to do it?"

"Do what?"

"Sex."

He swerved. For a minute we were on the shoulder. These bumps went through us. Like we were entering a new universe. A rocky ride. Then he straightened us out again. We were heading exactly where he'd said, to this fast-food place off the Interstate. It was basically a parking lot. That's where all the activity took place. The town kids, in their parents' cars or their third-hand pickup trucks, would spend hours eating gross food and making out in the back seat. I sometimes wondered if, with their eyes closed, they could tell the difference between a hot kiss and a really greasy bite of hamburger.

"I thought you'd want to go," he said. "So people could see."

"See what?"

"Us."

"See that you took the freak out on a date?"

"Yeah, I want to embarrass you. In public."

"Maybe I'm embarrassed by *you*. Did you ever think of that? Maybe I'm deeply ashamed to be seen with you."

He shook his head and kept on driving.

"You know, we're not some Stone Age tribe out there," I went on. "I mean, it's not like you're doing me some great favor by taking me to eat beef fat and breathe in other people's car exhaust. I mean, I'm not going to fall down in amazement at an order of french fries. I hope you won't be too disappointed."

We were coming up to the place. Its sign was the biggest thing for miles, so people could see it as they crossed the country, this enormous pagan altar of a grinning black slave boy. It was evening and the light was teetering. The summer air was the same temperature as our skin. He didn't even slow down. The idol zipped by, still grinning. I discovered I was gripping big handfuls of my dress, exposing my knobby knees. I tried smoothing everything out, my heartbeat included.

"What took you so long?" I asked. "I thought you were never coming back."

"I didn't think you wanted me to."

You idiot, I told myself. We could be parked under that hideous statue right now, kissing in its shadow, and you blew it, all because you didn't want to eat a hamburger. Or worse, because you really did want to eat a hamburger and have all those town kids see you with Joey. But you didn't want him to *see* that you wanted that. Or maybe this was the real reason: You were acting like a jerk because you hate this dress your mother made you wear. Because it makes you look like someone you're not. But really you hate it because it makes you look exactly like the person you truly are, a hunched-over Bible bitch. And all because of a stupid dress, which is, in fact, a nice dress, you've ruined your one chance in life for happiness. Or maybe—

"My dad's not home," he said. "He went to California this morning."

"Oh." The road was hollowing out my stomach. I felt light-headed. Things weren't following, one after the other, which I kind of enjoyed, even though it was scary. "So . . . you're all alone?"

He nodded, and I nodded, like, What an interesting totally irrelevant fact. I stared at him across the wide bench of the seat. He was so clean-looking. Not just that he had taken a shower, but the whole freshness of his face, the angle at which it met the world, chin up, confident and happy. My exact opposite. This wave rose, and crested, and broke, all inside me. I think I might have blushed, just from looking at him, praying he wouldn't notice, which he didn't, because the road was taking up all his attention. I mouthed the words *I love you,* and he turned, but he couldn't possibly have heard. I had barely formed them with my lips. Just trying them out. I didn't really mean them. He smiled. Which was like having a javelin buried dead center in my chest.

"Mom says you're not going to do anything," I told him. "She says you're going to be a perfect gentleman. Nothing's going to happen. Apparently she can tell."

"She knows a lot about cars, your mom."

He reached over. I took his hand. His fingertips were hard and squared-off from work. Not rough, though. Not torn up. They were pink. He must have scrubbed them. I turned his palm over to read it, pretending it contained the key to my future.

And now we sat, parked in his driveway, not about to move, either one of us. As if someone had cast a spell.

"You have ovens?" he finally asked, going over what I'd just told him.

"At the Colony? Of course we have ovens."

"But ovens aren't in the Bible."

"How do you think they baked bread?"

"Well, what about freezers, then? They don't have freezers in the Bible."

"Gordon decides."

"Oh."

My stomach was being wrung out like a wet washcloth. We got out of the car at the same time and went into the house. He gave me a little tour and I pretended to be interested. We climbed the stairs. In his parents' room there was this bed the size of the ocean. We fell in, rolling around and around on top of each other, with our shoes still on.

After a few minutes of his trying to figure out my dress, I laughed. "You are never going to get this off."

I sat up and struggled out of it myself. It was like crawling out of a tent. When I could see again, he had taken off his shirt. His chest was smooth and white, a landscape of muscles, quiet and strong and mostly hidden, just these suggestions, making the skin ripple, but so completely *there* that it was unbelievable. I stuck my hand out, straight up and down, like a shield, half-touching, half-protecting me. Then he pressed against it and I just crumbled. He kissed my ears, my breasts, the hollow above each hip. My body arched like an electric current was passing through it. He got on top of me and his weight alone set off these streamers of pleasure. I was drowning. I struggled against him just for the thrill of feeling how strong he was. I tried as hard as I could to move and felt the energy flow back into me as he pinned my arms high above my head and slowly drove them back so our bodies lined up perfectly, and he kissed me so simply, so gently, on the mouth, perfect talking, talking without words, talking with just his tongue on mine and nothing in between, nothing to be misunderstood. Our eyes were open. A slow rhythm already had us in its power. His pants were still on, rubbing against my underwear. Our shoes knocked. That made us smile. I reached behind him. His shoulders were wide, but his back tapered beautifully. I traced its outlines. I couldn't see, so I pretended I was blind and explored every inch of it with my hands. I would hit certain spots and he would quiver, not make any sound, but jump, like I'd flicked a switch. Now our legs weren't pressed up against each other. They were frantically twining, like tendrils on two climbing plants.

"Eve," he said, raising himself on his hands, doing a push-up, really, over me, and then holding it, hovering there. "Eve."

He said it like it was a complete thought. And for once, maybe it was.

I touched his chest. My sky. His face was far away, looking down at me. I kissed him and licked him, felt his muscles quiver and his bones shake. I lay back, completely under him. By now I was so sensitized, even breathing was a sensual act. I breathed him in, everything about him, his essence, and almost fainted. I wanted him to come crashing down on me. I wanted him to grind me into powder. I had this overwhelming urge to be destroyed, reduced to nothing. It shocked me, that it was there inside me, this desire for oblivion, and that it was so intensely sexy. It *was* sex, the urge, for one moment, not to be. To give yourself up. To give yourself away. To be extinguished.

But all that time he was smiling down at me, full of love, or lust, or whatever it was boys felt. Something healthy. He was probably just seeing how long he could hold himself up there, like he was in gym class or something. It was all a game to him. Which is how it should have been for me, too. He didn't have any mentally ill longings. I tried to chase mine away, rolling my head between his arms, knocking against them as if they were marble columns, wanting and not wanting them to become the prison bars of my life, forever and ever.

"You sure you want to do this?" he asked.

"You're worse than my mother."

He pushed on one hand and rolled over, so he was lying next to me. We stared into each other.

"That's her side," he said.

"Whose?"

"My mom's."

I felt around. I had forgotten where we were. On a fringed white bedspread with a raised, nubbly pattern, folded over carefully so it entombed at least four pillows, plus there were a few smaller ones on top. There was also an extra blanket at the bottom, even though it was summer.

"He doesn't sleep here anymore," Joey explained. "He sleeps on the couch downstairs."

We hadn't even messed it up. I'd thought we'd been thrashing around in this tropical sea of passion, but from the blankets and pillows you couldn't tell a thing. It was all glued down. Preserved. I had never talked to anyone half-naked before. My eyes kept following his. Until I realized what he was staring at. I wanted to cover my breasts. But I was afraid he would see I was scared. I ransacked my brain for something to say. Something very cool and sophisticated.

"Are you circumcised?"

It took him a minute to answer, as if he was thinking about it, but I mean he must have known.

"Why?"

"It's OK if you are. But really you shouldn't be. It's mutilation. Which is pagan. Or Jewish. Because they were halfway on their way to Christianity. But they denied Jesus. Because really they didn't want to stop worshipping idols, even if their idol was the Law. But if you follow the Law without self-examination, it's just like sacrificing to the Golden Calf. Jesus told them to look within themselves, but they couldn't, or wouldn't, because they were too busy cutting off their—"

"When you get nervous," he said, "you talk about religion. Did you know that?"

"It's not when I'm nervous. It's when I'm serious. And it's not religion. It's life. What you call religion, I call life. What you push into one little corner of your world—God and the Devil, Heaven and Hell, Grace and Sin—that's what I see everything through. That's the world I live in. And mine's more practical, because, in the end, we're all going to die."

"No shit."

"I'm sorry." I had forgotten about his mother. "I don't even really believe in half that stuff anyway. But even not believing in it is real. More real than . . . what's on TV, or eating burgers in a parking lot, or whatever it is you think about. Town kids, I mean. Not you. I don't know what you think about personally. You don't talk enough, Joey. That's your problem."

"Well, it isn't yours." He frowned. "Anyway, I'm not."

"Not what?"

"Not circumcised."

"Can I see?"

He ran his hand over my whole body, from top to bottom. Especially bottom. It took several centuries. But I had time.

"I thought you freaks all wore some special kind of underwear."

I hit him. We wrestled. I think he was surprised at how strong I was. Then he got up. Suddenly I was alone on this strange bed. Where his mother died, I remembered now.

"Here." He held out my dress. He'd never picked one up before. That was obvious. He didn't know how it worked, this shapeless ball of blue cloth. But he held it out with a kind of reverence, as if he liked me. Even though, if he really liked me, I reasoned, why didn't he take off his pants, come back here, and make me his sex slave for life?

"Not here," he said, reading my mind. "It's too weird. Let's go out back."

"Outside?" I asked. It was getting dark now. I remembered what a bad lawn it was. How many twigs and pebbles had loped in and out of my view as Herbert carried me to safety.

"There's a little house. Just before the woods begin. My dad uses it. We'll bring the blanket."

Evening was just slipping into night. I looked for the tree that—it seemed so long ago now—I had been holding on to when Herbert rescued me. The most likely candidate was this scrawny little sapling. But how could that be? Had I grown six sizes since the start of the summer? Joey took my hand. My feet didn't touch the ground. They churned through the low light. The sun, with its last gasp, pushed back the open halves of his shirt and turned his chest into solid gold. He was talking, telling me things I already knew, about the toolshed, about Herbert and how he made antique furniture. I think he was talking mostly because I had just said he didn't talk enough, and I was moved, again, like when he had held out the dress, to see that he cared about me, what I wore, what I said to him. Other people cared about me, too, but not this way. Mother and Gordon had to care about me. It was expected of them. It was part of their job. But Joey chose to love me. My legs missed a beat and I almost fell. He caught my arm.

"Are you OK?"

I held on to him. Just conceiving of the idea that Joey might love me—which had never even crossed my mind before, because before I had only been concerned with my feelings for him—made me swoon.

"You want me to carry you?" he asked.

"No, no, no." I was down on my knees. I nuzzled against his chest. The sun had warmed it. I tried burying myself there, hiding my tears.

"What?" he asked. I could hear he was worried. I shook my head, rubbing into him, trying to reassure him. But then I started sobbing.

"I'm fine," I called, choking it all back in. Just the thought that anyone, but him especially, might love me . . . I looked up. He had the blanket over his other arm. "Maybe we should just do it here."

"Here? Outside?"

I could see, reflected in his eyes, all kinds of puzzlement and panic. Don't blow this, a voice inside me warned.

"Never mind," I said, getting up, brushing off dirt, wiping away tears. "Come on, show me the toolshed."

"How'd you know it was called that?"

"What?"

"How'd you know we call it the toolshed?" he asked.

"You just told me."

"I did? When?"

I slid my hand under his belt, reached down, and found his penis. He stopped. He stopped everything. A total shutdown. Then he kissed me. A long, quiet, serious kiss. He took me in his arms and picked me up. I made myself light for him.

There are two of me. At least two of me, I decided, wrapping myself around his neck. Two Eves. And when we both want the same thing, we are unstoppable.

The toolshed was changed. There was sawdust in the air and chisels left out on the bench. Herbert had been working. A half-finished piece of furniture stood in the corner covered in thick plastic. On the floor, there were curls of wood.

"My dad," he said, as if this was him, Herbert, and he was introducing us. I had to keep reminding myself that Joey didn't know we'd ever met. I looked for the tank of oxygen but couldn't find it. Maybe I had imagined that whole visit. The room felt so different, so much more normal, just another suburban dad's hobby-shop hideaway. Joey kicked at the mess. He put me down and I helped him clear a spot.

"What does he do?"

"He's an engineer."

"No, I mean here."

"I just told you. He makes furniture. Weren't you listening?"

It annoyed him even to talk about Herbert. He laid the blanket out and folded it over once, so there was a little bit of cushioning. We both stared.

"I'm a virgin," I said. "I just want to make that clear right from the start. I mean, so you're not freaked out. I'm probably going to bleed a ton. All over the place. Like . . . a hemorrhage or something. It's going to be disgusting."

He nodded.

"Are you surprised?"

He shook his head.

"What's so funny?"

He was grinning again. I was his own private joke. I sighed and started to take off my dress, but he stopped me. He reached down, all the way down, to the hem. He gathered it up slowly, with both hands, and in one pull, like a magic trick, had it off me.

"Do that thing you did before," he asked shyly.

"What thing?"

"You know. Just now."

I tried to unbuckle his belt and almost crippled him. It was funny how hard it was to do familiar things backward. I pulled on the leather and cinched it way too tight. He gave a little scream. Then I finally got it loose and eased down his pants.

"It's wrong," he mumbled. "The way they keep you all up there. By the lake." I'd never heard him sound so nervous. It was the first sign I'd ever had that he might be human. "Don't you think it's wrong, Eve? That place you live in?"

I didn't answer. It was so much fun to hear him be scared. Not in a mean way, but it's just that I had spent so much of my time with him in absolute terror of saying and doing the wrong thing. While he always seemed so secure and in control. And now I could tell he had no idea what to say or do next. Then it came to me: he was a virgin, too. It was obvious.

"There's too much room back there." He tried to speak more clearly, but his voice cracked. "I mean, even before Mom there was. But now especially. The house just seems so big."

I took his penis in my mouth. He came down to me, collapsing slowly like a dynamited building. I didn't know what I was doing, but it was not exactly rocket science. Plus I had a pretty good idea, from his reactions, of what he liked. In fact, the only danger was that I might go deaf. When he came—I don't know what I had been expecting exactly, but it was not like the back of my head got blown off—I was amazed by how much he could feel. And how much his feeling affected me. All the grossness I had been afraid of was nothing, not in comparison to how real this was. This was my life. What had been happening before was nothing compared to this moment, the two of us lying there, struggling, helping each other out of ourselves, safe in our own little church. He was so grateful. There was only one window, facing the woods, but that light, and the light leaking in through the roof and cracks in the walls, soon even that was gone. We had to get closer, just to see each other. We took off the rest of our clothes. He found a flashlight and set it with the bulb straight down so it gave off a tight white glow. Our moon.

"Look." He showed me his bare arm.

I kissed it. The muscle. Worshipped it. The swelling rise under the skin.

"No, *look*." He pointed to a patch that was maybe one tiny degree darker than the rest. "That's where you grabbed me in the car. Remember? When I was driving too fast? When I was taking you home that night?" He reached up. "I got these bruises about two days after. Four fingers and a thumb. I didn't know what they were. Not at first. Then I figured out they must be from you. I could barely lift my arm."

"I'm sorry," I whispered back.

"You don't understand." He settled on top of me. So easily. Not heavy but not light. There was just this feeling of rightness about his body. "I didn't think you liked me. I wasn't going to try and see you anymore. I was going to forget all about you. But I couldn't, because it *hurt* so much every time I moved. Every time I tried to do something."

He flexed his elbow, remembering.

"I'm sorry," I said again, holding him. "Does it still hurt?"

"No."

"I wish it did. Then I could make it feel better."

It was time. I knew it was time. But the floor was like rock. We were under the piece of draped furniture. I got the bright idea of reaching up and grabbing the sheet of plastic. I thought I could wad it up and put it under my head like a pillow. There was nothing holding it down. I gave a tug and it slid right off.

"Just a minute." I tried to cram it all under me without breaking the mood. I knew I looked awkward, but I didn't want to get my brain bashed in by the cement.

Joey was poised, crouched. He was on me, but his weight was hovering. I could feel him coiled inside himself. He looked up, past me. I waited.

"It's OK," I said. I thought maybe he was expecting some final permission, though I would have had to be a maniac to say no now.

But he just kept looking. Not at me. Past me, and up.

"What is it?" I asked.

He stood up. He got off me and walked away.

"Joey?"

I was already, in my mind, not a virgin. It's like when you're about to cross a road and in your plans you're already on the other side. So I just lay there for an extra minute, waiting for the future to catch up.

But it never did. Instead, it went off in some other direction.

I turned around, still on the floor. Then I saw it: Herbert hadn't been making fake antique furniture after all. At least it didn't look like anything you could sit in or eat off. It was just a shapeless hunk of wood, an open lipstick tube or a miniature totem pole. But Joey was staring at it, hypnotized. I looked at his penis again. It beat with his pulse, moving up, and then going down, and then up again, but a little less each time. There was still some sticky stuff on the end.

"I'm sorry," I said. I was back to apologizing for everything. "Should I put the plastic back on?"

I got up to cover it again. Standing, I could see more what it was: a statue or a sculpture. He had been carving. That's what all the tools and curls of wood shavings on the floor had been. It rose out of rough wood, this woman, naked, grossly misshapen of course, your typical man's fantasy. That part ridged and grainy. You could still see the tree. But the face was smooth and doll-like. Her lips were half-parted and her eyes were empty. She was like a little girl. I liked her shoulders better, the halfway point between the clumsy body and the blank face. They were delicate and had just been lightly sanded. They almost looked real, except they didn't have any arms, which made her look helpless and incomplete.

"Is it your mom?" I asked, coming up alongside Joey.

I tried to hold his hand, but he wouldn't let me. I looked over and he had this expression of *hatred*. I stepped back, as if he had hit me.

"It's you!" he said, flailing at the wood carving instead. "Can't you see? It's you!"

"No way." I was turning dark red. It wasn't me. It wasn't anything like me. For one thing, I was surprised it wasn't tipping over, her boobs were so big. I looked at the face again. Then I remembered Herbert's stare when he had taken me home that time after work, how he had seemed to be taking an inventory of my eyes and nose and mouth. "I don't look like that. You're crazy."

"You know him," he said quietly. "I thought I saw you in his car one time, but I couldn't believe it. I was even going to ask you, but . . ."

"Joey, it is *not* me."

"I can't believe it," he said to himself. "You and my dad. That is so sick."

I stared, trying not to let her change into me before my eyes. It might be me, I began to admit. One of many. It might have been the lost girl he saw that night, on the floor here, so long ago, so sad and drunk and confused. Herbert's Eve.

. . . but not yours, I wanted to tell Joey. I'm yours. In every sense of the word. I am yours. All you have to do is make it so.

He had been watching me out of the corner of his eye. Watching me look at the statue, or bust, or totem pole, whatever it was. He saw my face soften. And I think that's finally what ruined it. That we could have still made love up until then. Maybe he was even excited, because he could have gotten back at his dad, won a battle in some stupid secret war they were fighting. But when he saw that I liked the statue, or had sympathy for it at least, maybe that I was even a little flattered by it, that killed him. He turned away. I went over to the corner and found my dress. After I got my shoes on, I looked down and saw my panties were still on the floor. I stuffed them in my pocket.

"Hey," I called softly from across the room. It seemed impossible that we weren't still going to be the two greatest lovers of all time.

He was sitting there, back in his clothes, looking at the sculpture, rocking a little as he hugged his knees, trying not to see me. He was trying to tune me out, wishing me away. I wanted to tell him everything, what there was to tell. Which was really nothing, now that I thought about it. I mean, we hadn't even kissed, Herbert and me. He'd just given me oxygen that night. And then a ride later. He had said I looked beautiful. But was there anything so bad about that? It wasn't even true! I should have said something. Explained. But I knew that to Joey it wouldn't matter. I had, in some way, betrayed him.

I walked to the door and turned. He was still staring at the hunk of wood. His back was so beautiful, straining through his shirt. I don't know why I loved that about him in particular, but I always had. From the moment I first saw him. From when before I even knew who he was. He had been walking down the hallway in school, away from me. And something about his back, the way the shoulders swelled and then the sides narrowed, made me doubt everything I had ever believed in, from the floor being solid to the immortality of my own soul. I had watched him until he disappeared. Maybe that's why I keep screwing up, I thought sadly. Because I'm in love with this vision of him leaving me, of him walking away.

5

"So your mom was right," Angela said.

"No, she wasn't. What do you mean?"

"Nothing happened."

"A lot happened!"

We were in Angela's bedroom, which was nicer than mine, even though she and her dad had a much worse cabin, one of the farthest from the lake. It was so tilted the walls and ceiling didn't line up. There was this sinister black wedge of space in every corner. You could feel the tilt walking down the hall, too, as if you were being pulled sideways. But Richard had put a lot of work into the rooms. He was incredibly organized and handy. When he opened the door he was holding a measuring tape.

"Angela's sick," he said.

"I know. That's why I brought this tea. From my mother."

"Your mother?"

He made it sound as if it might have been poisoned if it came from her. Richard was this bloodless man with no eyelashes. He was so pale, his hair and lips were almost white. He looked at me with a suspicious, doubting expression. Basically, people came to the Colony for two reasons: either they were afraid of something, some part of the outside world that tempted them, that turned them into craving, godless animals, and so they came here for shelter, or they came because they had such a need for order that they couldn't take seeing anybody else have a good time. That was Richard. He wasn't happy unless he was following a rule. Or stopping other people from breaking one.

"Ginger tea," I added, because there was a prohibition against caffeine. "Can I just bring it to her? I'll only stay a minute."

"I was pleased to see you at Service," he said soberly.

"Oh yeah. Me too. I mean, you were good."

He stepped aside, as if that was the only reason he was letting me in, as a reward for having sat through his yawner of a sermon.

"Angela!" he called, in a voice that made my blood run cold. Nobody ever asked about Angela's mother. People said she had left Richard for another guy. Personally I wouldn't have been surprised to hear he'd cut her up into small pieces. Each the same size. "You have a visitor!" He looked down at the tape measure. "I'm resquaring our window frames."

I nodded.

Angela's room had homemade dolls with fairy-tale dresses, a dollhouse, too, and a chest of drawers with a white doily spread on top, the oil lamp perfectly centered. The carpet was salvage, a little stained, but it had a nice pattern, and at least there wasn't just a bare splintery floor like in our cabin. Against one wall stood a school desk, the kind with the chair and tabletop attached. It was bolted in place. It looked like some instrument of torture.

She was blowing her nose, shivering in an old-fashioned bed with four posts. That's the only thing I was jealous of. Her bed. She had a flannel nightgown buttoned up to her chin.

"So you kissed and rolled around a lot." She shrugged. "So what?"

"Well, it's a lot to me," I said cautiously.

I realized she hadn't gotten it, that despite acting so cool she had trouble imagining me even getting naked with Joey, much less the rest. She sneezed. She had been sneezing since I came in. Her nose was red, which made it look even more pointy, a carrot. Still, I felt bad for her, even if she was dismissing what I had thought was my Nobel Prize for Sex Fantasy. Of course I hadn't told her about later, the toolshed and the statue of the naked woman. I had said that we stopped, by mutual consent, two clean-minded teens. I figured that was so corny-sounding she might actually believe it. The real dirty stuff, about Herbert and his obsession and the possibility that I would now marry him and become his full-time artist's model, was something I thought better to keep to myself. But making out with Joey was news from the front. Our lives, otherwise, were so dull. I had interested her when I was whispering the story on her bed, but now she was trying to act very casual and unimpressed.

"I met a guy, too," she said, pulling the blankets up higher.

I looked at her. I couldn't tell if that was supposed to be good or bad, by the way she said it.

"You should drink that while it's hot."

She had put her mug of tea on this cute round table next to the bed. It was going to another world, visiting Angela's house. Everything was clean and thought-out. When you wanted to put something down, there was a little table for it. When your eye traveled, there were things to see. I wondered if that was why Richard hit her sometimes, because there was some flaw in her he wanted to correct, the same as when you "resquare" a window frame (whatever that meant). But no, it was that way in everyone's house, I admitted. Everyone else's. They were all summer cabins, just a few rooms and a bathroom, but only ours felt so run-down and temporary, with the furniture and everything, ourselves included, floating on this sea of bareness. That was Mom's style, to act like we weren't going to be here for that long, though in fact we'd been here longer than anybody. But to get comfortable was to doubt the transience of the everyday world, to blaspheme your belief in the Second Coming.

"I'm not really sick," Angela whispered.

"Oh."

I looked down at my own cup. Then why was I drinking this stupid stuff? Maybe it would stop me from getting whatever it was she had, which was beginning to look like a particularly bad case of craziness. She leaned closer, pulling the covers with her.

"He has a motorcycle," she mouthed.

"Who?"

"He gave me a ride."

I could barely hear her.

"And that's why you're pretending to be sick?"

She nodded and sat back. I don't care what she said, she looked feverish. Her eyes were intense. She was searching my face for . . . I don't know what. Disapproval, maybe. Or appreciation. Envy?

"A motorcycle," I repeated, hoping that would get her going again.

"Shhh! A Harley-Davidson. A Hog," she recited.

"Is that big?"

She closed her eyes and shook her head from side to side in superior knowledge. "You have no idea, Eve. I could barely get my legs around it."

"Wow. Who is he?"

"Him?" She sounded much less impressed by the guy. "Oh, he's just some guy."

"What's his name?"

"He didn't say. I didn't say my name either."

"You went on a guy's motorcycle and you didn't even know his name?"

She sneezed again, the whole time she was talking, a string of sneezes, like she was trying to get something out.

"I was on my way to town and he passed me once . . . Then, when I was on my way home, he came back, from the other direction, but much slower. And I guess I looked up. Because he did have this shiny bike and it was pretty loud. But I mean, I wasn't staring or anything. I was just walking. It would have been more noticeable if . . . if I hadn't looked. So then he passed me again and did this turn, so he was right alongside me, riding next to me. We tried to talk, but even when they're going really slow, those motorcycles make so much noise. So he asked if I wanted a ride . . . and I said yes."

"I think you're allergic to something."

"I'm in love." She grabbed me, she was so excited. "It was incredible, Eve. The seat isn't really a seat, you know. It's just this long piece of leather. That's how it feels. You slide down and hold on to the bike really tight with your legs. And when he revs it up you become part of the engine. This power just goes right through you. He doesn't believe in helmets, so I was looking over his shoulder, clutching him like my life depended on it, which it did, when you think about it, and everything just *flew* by. I mean, we reached eighty miles an hour. I read it on that sign where the Interstate goes over. He said we could be in Nebraska in two hours."

"Nebraska. Gee, that's great."

"Well, anywhere. Nebraska was just an example."

She gave up trying to hold it in and sneezed some more. Sweat was beading on her forehead. It was a rainy Sunday afternoon. She hadn't been at Service. She was the only one missing. That's how I knew she was sick. Everyone else had been there because of the rumor that Gordon was coming. He did, but it was a disappointment. He didn't preach. He watched. He watched Richard lead, but he also watched all of us. He sat in the front row, half-turned in his seat, with his dark glasses on, even though we were inside. It disturbed people, his not giving a sermon. They thought he was back, after the Fourth. Back among us. Instead, he just gave us this stare, as if he knew what we were thinking.

"We went to Sharon," she said slowly, reliving it, savoring the ride, mile by mile, bump by bump.

"Sharon?" That was the next town over. It had a grain elevator. It was even smaller than Arhat. It didn't have the railroad. "What did you do in Sharon?"

"Nothing. We didn't stop the whole time. That's what made it so great. We went right through Sharon. Then we turned off on these dirt roads. We barely said a word, Eve. The whole time. We just rode. That's what made it so . . ."

". . . sick," I supplied.

"Romantic." She closed her eyes again. "It was the happiest day of my life." Then she opened them, worried and panicky all of a sudden. "But something terrible happened. Right at the end."

"He threw you off the bike and raped you."

"God! Why do you always say these horrible things?"

"I'm sorry."

"I told you, it wasn't like that. It was about riding around. It was about freedom."

I pretended to vomit. I couldn't believe how disapproving I felt. From start to finish. Suddenly I was every mother in the Colony. I wanted to go to Richard and tell him to lock up his daughter. I was shocked to see how prudish I was when it was someone else, and how nauseated I was at the thought of her having a good time with a guy, at just the picture of her riding around on a motorcycle. And when you considered what *I* had done . . .

"Someone saw us," she said. "In Sharon. Someone saw *me*. I don't know what he was doing there. I mean, I don't think he recognized me, but I was wearing my dress, so he knew I was from the Colony. I could see him watching us in the bike's little mirror. He was surprised, I could tell."

"Who? One of us?"

"No. That man who comes here to see Gordon sometimes. The Town Supervisor."

"Olney."

She nodded.

"Well, so what?" I shrugged. "He saw a Colony girl on a motorcycle. Big deal."

"Don't you see?" She took my teacup and put it with hers. It was like I was the little girl now, the one who had to have things spelled out. "That's why they're making Serena get married."

"Huh?"

I tried relistening to everything I had just heard.

"It happened a month ago," she explained. "Just before they told Serena that she was . . . betrothed."

"I don't see what one has to do with the other."

"It was me!" I could feel her trembling. The bed was actually shaking. "Don't you see? That man told Gordon. I know, because Gordon came here and talked to my dad."

"He came and talked to my mom, too. It doesn't mean that—"

"Don't you see, Eve? That's why he's making her get married. Because Gordon thinks it was Serena. I mean, on a motorcycle, going away from him, to that guy, Serena and I probably look pretty much alike."

In your dreams, I thought.

"So he describes her that way to Gordon, and then Gordon decides to get Serena all settled and pregnant with some Colony guy before she does anything more with Murt."

"With who?"

"Murt. My boyfriend."

"Your boyfriend?"

"Well, kind of."

"I thought you didn't know his name."

"Well, I do now," she said. "I mean, we've gone for rides a few more times since then. He picks me up right outside the Colony."

"Murt? What kind of name is that?"

"It's just a name," she answered impatiently. "That's not the point. You're not getting anything, Eve."

"Well, I'm trying," I said. "So that time at the Luncheonette, when Gordon was saying how your dad was worried about you . . ."

"That's when he still thought it might be me, but then he must have decided it wasn't." She stuck out her lower lip. "Because Serena's so pretty, I guess. Probably he thinks no one would ever be interested in wanting me on the back of their motorcycle. But Murt does. I can tell."

"It must be short for Merton."

She ignored me. "But every time I see Gordon he looks at me and my knees knock. I mean, they actually hit each other and I have to hold on to something. I'm still afraid he'll see. See into my soul."

"See what?" I asked harshly. "You're not doing anything, right? You're just going for rides on a motorcycle. What's so bad about that?"

"I'm scared he'll see it's my fault that Serena's getting married," she whimpered, looking right and left, even though we were alone. She lowered her voice even more. I could barely hear. "I keep thinking he really knows and he's just torturing me. He's letting Serena get closer and closer to getting married, and he's waiting for me to confess. It's like he's testing me and I'm *failing*." She had worked herself up into a hysterical fit. She threw her arms around me and hugged me, sobbing, as if I could save her. But all I wanted to do was wriggle free.

"So that's why you didn't go to Service today? Because you knew he'd be there?"

She nodded, weeping into my sleeve.

"But you've got to tell him," I said. "You have to confess, Angela."

Her head jerked up and almost hit me. That was the thing about Angela and me. We weren't compatible. As soon as we got close, we bounced away. She sneezed again. But the thing was, we always *were* getting close. We kept trying. We couldn't help it. We kept bumping into each other. We were going down the same path.

"What do you mean confess?" She stuck out her jaw. "I haven't done anything. Why should I confess?"

"To save Serena." It seemed so obvious to me. "If you tell Gordon it was you on the motorcycle, then he'll call off her marriage."

"But it wasn't me," she said.

I looked at her.

"It wasn't me," she said. "I made it all up. Just now. Just to fool you, because you were telling me about all the sick things you did with that boy."

"Joey," I said slowly.

"That's what I'll say. If you tell. I'll tell him what you've been doing."

"I'm not going to tell. *You* have to," I argued. "You have to, Angela. Look at you. You're not the kind of person who can keep a secret. And you can't play sick for the rest of your life either."

"I think I really am sick now. Maybe you should go." She squirmed away from me and lay down under the covers. "Thank your mother for the tea. I know *you* didn't make it."

But I didn't go. I stared at her weepy, reddened face. She was still trying to be a little girl, to crawl back into that world.

"You think God could have a daughter?" I asked.

"What?" Angela sneezed.

"A daughter." I stared out her window. "He had a son. Why not a daughter?"

"And what would happen to Her?" She snuggled down deeper into the mattress. "Would She be crucified?"

"I don't know." I frowned. "I haven't thought that far ahead."

Richard knocked on the door. Angela jumped, wondering if he'd been listening. He didn't say anything, though. His footsteps faded down the hall. He had just been doing his prison guard act. Visiting hours were over.

I had to be alone. You'd think in such a big empty place as Iowa that wouldn't be a problem. But there was nowhere to go. It was raining and everyone was busy inside. Idle hands were the Devil's playthings, so after Service we worked, polishing, scrubbing, tinkering, hammering, cooking. The lake was beautiful, receiving tears from the gray sky. I tried staring straight up and a single drop hit my eyeball. I staggered. But it wasn't the Lord coming to take me. I was just some idiot teenage girl who didn't have enough sense to come in out of the rain. Where could I go? There was the willow. Maybe the tight-knit branches would keep out the water. But somehow I knew that our sacred spot was contaminated now. Our childhood friendships were wrecked by lies, by jealousy, by envy. I was envious of Angela. I couldn't believe it, but I was. I envied her love affair with a big quivering motorbike. That's how crazy I was. I envied them all. Serena with her white wedding. Even Jewell, for being so self-contained and self-sufficient. At least she was in control. Me, I was just getting carried this way and that, bashing into things, making these sudden spurts that felt like action but only seemed to carry me further and further away from everything I wanted. Which was because I didn't have the faintest idea what it was I wanted. I wanted whatever was worst for me at the time. Or whatever I couldn't get. I couldn't, no matter how hard I concentrated, really think of a goal. All I had were wants. This kind of restless, free-floating hunger.

I looked up at Gordon's satellite dish. It was the closest thing to a cross, not because of its shape, but because it stood so high and looked so alien from nature. And because of the way it pointed to Heaven. It began to move, responding to some command. He was adjusting it. It made a grinding, creaking sound, shifted its long narrow finger a few feet, and then settled back down. The raindrops, getting heavier and heavier, *pinged* off its surface.

I had wanted so desperately to be alone, and here I was, alone, standing with my shoes full of rain, but somehow it wasn't what I wanted after all. Surprise! I wanted to be alone among strangers. That's what it was. I wanted to be with people who didn't know me. I was nostalgic for school, of all places, where I'd been so miserable. All those deeply dumb town kids who'd gawked at me. Where were they now when I needed them? I wanted Joey to show up in his magic carpet of a car and take me to the hamburger place. And we would make out in his back seat with the rain shielding us like a curtain. It would drum on the roof, and the damp from our clothes would bring out all those funny forgotten smells. I could even imagine the soft, lukewarm french fries, with ketchup on top, lying half-eaten in a waxy cardboard container. Red and yellow. I was crying at the thought that none of this would ever happen. Even though it seemed so possible, it would never come to be. And I was hoping the whole time that someone would come out and get me. That they would see me and take pity on me and put their arm around me and invite me in. But no one did. I took a step. My feet squished. It was a funny sound. I made it again. I was some creature emerging from a swamp. I stuck my tongue out and drank the rain. I made the squishing sound again and again, up the hill, away from the lake and its cabins, which were beginning to glow now, one by one, as the afternoon got dark with clouds and people lit their lamps. I wasn't walking, I was just making noise. I was just proving to myself that I existed. I looked down and saw I was soaked. Why do they like these, I wondered, feeling each breast. I found if I tipped my body forward, so my center of gravity actually lay in front of me, my feet would quicken to follow, and I could take step after step, over-coming whatever had been making me feel I was neck-deep in mud. I leaned into this imaginary wind and found myself in a kind of con-trolled fall, up the rest of the hill, onto the muddy, disintegrating Colony road. It was more like a streambed when it rained. But I kept falling through it, over obstacles, gaining confidence with each step. Confidence in what, I couldn't exactly say, just that my center of gravity, the essence of the new Eve that I was becoming, was always in front of me and I had to catch up. It was a game, like try-ing to catch your shadow, but it got me places. Pretty soon I was on the highway, where trucks plowed through ruts of water, igniting these spectacular sheets that lashed me with asphalt-scented spray. I yelled, wordless yells at the invisible sky. I was so happy all of a sud-den. Happy sad crazy alive.

Since you couldn't get lost in Arhat I decided to discover the mid-dle of town itself. I remembered reading somewhere that to solve a maze you were supposed to take every left-hand turn. Once I got to the nine-block "business district," I tried that. It was pouring now. A wind would adjust the rain, tilt it this way and that. Sometimes, as a joke, it would twist around so, even though you were bent over, it would find a way to smack you right in the face. I grinned, dripping. I was soaked to the skin already. My dress wasn't even a dress anymore. It was this dark see-through body stocking. Gordon would have been peeved if he had known he was making us wear such a slinky outfit. I am technically not in violation of the Dress Code, I defended myself. I watched my legs and admired how strong they were. I was definitely developing muscles this summer, if nothing else. And anyway, no one could really see me. There were people around, but they didn't count. They were all enclosed in elaborate raingear, these little houses they had constructed, portable tents from which they peered. Some actually stopped. One guy raised his visor and kept his hand there, as if he was saluting, as I passed.

"Praise God," I shouted, thinking of the Flood.

It was what they expected. It kept them at a distance. I didn't want them to think I needed help. If they wanted a crazy girl, I would give them a crazy girl. I took a left-hand turn where I had never even noticed a road before. It wasn't, really. It was a pathway, but paved, so I guess that counted, running narrowly between the drugstore and an insurance office. But if this was the Flood, I suddenly thought, where was I going to get two of everything? Two lovers, that would be the hardest. A daytime lover and a nighttime lover. And another one, too. A secret lover. A stowaway in my Ark of passion. Would Herbert marry me? Would we sleep in his wife's bed, where she had died? How would Joey feel about that?

The alley was a disappointment. It just let me out on the next block over. I moved to turn left and almost walked into a wall. I was spun around. The traffic signals seemed to be facing the wrong direction. They swung heavily, like an elephant's red, green, and yellow earrings, on chains, far out over one of Arhat's precious intersections, telling the driving sheets of summer rain to Slow and then Stop. I was backwards, that's all, I assured myself. I squinted and saw an old man trying to light a cigarette under a fringe of awning. Even though he was out of the rain he was having trouble because of the wet wind. He couldn't get the match lit. Or, when he did, it went out. Once, he finally got the flame to the cigarette, but it wouldn't burn. I stared at him for a full minute before I realized it was Gillie.

"Can I help?" I asked, standing there, shivering.

"Damned matches," he said, not looking up, striking one over and over again.

"It's Eve," I said. "From work. From the road crew. Remember?"

"Uh-huh." This time he did look up, but only briefly. He didn't seem at all shocked by my appearance. Or even interested. I guess he had seen it before, a soaked, practically naked girl. Apparently it wasn't as important to him as a good smoke. "Damned safety matches. Used to be you could scratch a match on anything. Your teeth, even. Now . . ."

He threw the damp book down, then took the cigarette out of his mouth and carefully worked it back into his breast pocket, sheltering it from the rain and wind, as if he was feeding a pet mouse. He wasn't wearing a slicker either. But he was dry, the way old people are. Bone dry.

"What are you doing out here?" I asked.

"Bingo," he said, and I noticed now we were standing in front of the building that had the Veterans of Foreign Wars upstairs.

"They play bingo here?"

"Every Sunday."

He watched me huddle and step on one foot, then the other. I was trying to squeeze the water out of my socks. There was hair in front of my eyes, but my arms were plastered to my sides. I had adopted this pose of waterlogged modesty. I fought a horrible hallucination that I was mutating into Herbert Biswanger's statue of me. I tried to keep my eyes from looking down in case my chest had swollen like a pair of huge sponges.

"No smoking in there." He nodded contemptuously over his shoulder, then seemed to take it all in: me, the street, and the rain. "Wet?"

"A little."

"Better come inside."

We climbed wide stairs to the second floor. It was a big room. There was a stage with flags on it, the American one and then a bunch of others. There were long tables arranged in rows and gray folding chairs on both sides. The same chairs we had at the Colony, I noticed. There must have been about seventy-five people, old and young, men and women, all hunched over cards. Some had four, some had eight or sixteen. I guess you had to buy four at a time. Their heads kept traveling all over them as a number was called, so they were in constant motion, bobbing and squinting, as if they were trying to see through a haze. On stage, two men revolved a little hamster cage of cubes. One cube would finally get caught in a metal cradle and they would fish it out, examine it, and call "O 73!" Electricity passed through the crowd. Heads made wide, swooping circles over the grids of numbers and letters. They all had green magic markers, poised. There was one woman off to the side, sitting behind a table with an urn of coffee and a plate of sweets you could buy. People hadn't taken much. They were too busy. Everyone had his head down. They didn't notice Gillie and me standing in back.

"What's the prize?" I asked.

"Money."

It was a two-story building. You could hear rain on the roof. The woman came over and asked if I wanted some towels. She went out and found a few thin white ones. I dried my hair and face. It was hot. The floorboards creaked.

"I 16!"

"What does bingo mean, anyway?"

"Bingo?" Gillie looked at me. "It means you win."

"I know, but—"

"It's the name of the game." His eyes, now that I wasn't shivering, seemed to travel over me with more interest. "How old are you?"

"Sixteen. Almost."

"Sixteen! Then how did you get work as a flagman? That's what everyone wants to know."

"Gordon. The man who founded the Colony. He asked the town supervisor, Mr. Olney."

"Olney!" Gillie's hand reached for his breast pocket. Then he remembered he couldn't smoke. "Well, that explains it."

"You know him? Mr. Olney?"

"I guess."

"What's he like?"

"Not worth the gunpowder it would take to blow him to Hell." He looked out over the room as he said it. "You should see it when somebody here wins. He jumps up and down. Acts like he's having a fit. Everyone pounds him on the back, smiles like they want to kill him. Then it starts all over again."

"So why do you come?"

"To watch. I know everyone in this room. From birth, practically. I know who's sleeping with whose wife. I know who's about to go broke. I know who's pregnant. And I know who's dying."

I tried following that, as if it was a story. But of course it wasn't. He was just talking. I always felt Gillie was trying to tell me something and that I was never getting it.

"Used to be you could smoke," he grumbled.

I looked with him. Here they were, the kids from school, just five or twenty or fifty years later. The men with the bingo machine were like priests, speaking in tongues.

"B 3!"

"O 64!"

Or maybe they were citing Scripture from a book nobody knew anymore. Just giving chapter and verse, but not the words.

"B 13!"

It was the sad end of something. The end of Town. Or worse, after the end, when people still performed their rituals but had forgotten why.

"What do you do out there, anyway?" Gillie asked.

"Pray," I said, trying to consider exactly what it was we really did. "Read the Bible. Do chores. Sing."

"Sing!"

"Well, we don't have TV," I explained. "It's mostly what we don't do that's important."

Some lady got bingo, and it was exactly as he'd described. The Holy Spirit descended on her. Suddenly all my contempt drained away and I realized these people were going through the same spiritual exercises we did, only it wasn't getting them anywhere. Instead of the Bible they studied a gibberish of numbers and letters. Instead of Grace and peace they got money. But they kept coming, they still sensed they needed something. Even Gillie, who was too smart to play, he still came for the feeling of togetherness. Of community. They all wanted salvation. And it was just so terribly sad that they weren't getting it, that they were being given this pathetic little consolation prize of fifty dollars instead. Gordon was right. I had a calling, or an urge, at least. I looked out over the crowd and thought, These are my people. Then I stared down at my dress. It was crinkly like crepe paper. Right. Get up in front of my people and be arrested for indecent exposure. But still I had this overwhelming desire to make my way to the stage, knock over the dinky metal cage like Christ scourging the Temple, and preach to them all, tell them about their immortal souls and what they could do to start *cleansing* themselves, before it was too late.

The walk home was harder. My feet were soaked. Instead of straining forward, I had to heave my body up and then let it come crashing down with each step. But that was all right. I was glad to pay. There's nothing wrong with suffering. Sometimes it's a sign that you're thinking things through. That's what I had done, the whole trek along the highway. I had considered my predicament and decided on a course of action.

It stopped raining. The dirt road was mud, so I stuck to the forest, feeling my way through trees, letting leaves tip their load of water over my eyes and down my back. When I got to the Colony, all the cabins were dark. The Perpetual Flame was still going, though. Gordon's big-screen TV. There was this distorted amplified laughter coming from the house. I walked right by our cabin, circled the lake, and went up the hill. Usually I came down to Gordon's house from behind, from farther up the hill. That way no one could see. But since it was late and everyone was asleep, I climbed up the path. It was steeper than I remembered. And more forbidding. The house loomed the closer you got to it. The dish and the black wraparound porch were like warning signs telling you to go back. I waited for the television picture to get bright enough to show me the small enameled knob on the porch's screen door.

"Look," Gordon said excitedly, as if I had just come back from getting a Diet Coke in the kitchen, not appeared, uninvited, hopelessly muddy and wet at . . . 1:30 a.m. I now saw. I had never been up so late. "Look, it's *I Love Lucy*!"

"Great," I answered tonelessly. He was in his BarcaLounger, but it wasn't launched yet. The leg rest hadn't flipped up and the back wasn't tilted. It was still just a thick chair.

"You don't understand." He was on the edge of the seat, peering through his dark glasses at the washed-out black-and-white picture. Between the shade and the brightness I don't understand how he saw anything. "It's *I Love Lucy*. It's this episode's first transmission. I was just pointing my dish at random. Sweeping the heavens. It's the original signal. This is the way it really looked."

"Oh."

The place was cleaned up. All the gadgets and packing peanuts and boxes had been pushed into one corner. As if he'd had to clear a few spots for company at the last minute. But who would he have for company up here besides me? I looked around for the packing crate bar. It was still there. The one fixed point.

"You don't understand the significance of this," he muttered. He was following the movements of the actors—they were talking some kind of English, but it sounded foreign, screaming and whispering, full of feelings that didn't match their faces—with a kind of quaking excitement. "I have stumbled on the original television transmission. This is not a rerun. These signals never die. They just bounce through space. Now, I checked my guide. There is no satellite where my dish is pointing. I am just probing the Void. This is absolutely like contact with an alien culture."

"An alien culture?"

"Well"—he shrugged—"the Golden Age of Television. Call it what you will."

The bottle of Everclear was almost empty. I filled a glass and sat down on the couch.

"Did Jesus drink?" I asked.

"Did Jesus drink?" Gordon considered, using about one-tenth of his brain while he stared at the picture. "Did Jesus drink? Well, He would have if He had to deal with the kind of bonehead questions that come my way."

"He turned water to wine," I pointed out. "The Bible doesn't say what He did after that, but I can't imagine Him just sitting there while everyone else got pie-eyed. Then there's the whole question of His blood. 'This is my blood.' If it turned into wine, when it was still inside Him, then technically He'd be drunk. Like in those tests they give for drunk driving. His blood alcohol level would have been 100 percent."

Gordon pointed the super-deluxe remote control at me and pushed a button. For a minute I thought he might actually have managed to mute me, which was what I knew he was trying to do. I took a sip of the Everclear and tried my voice again. It still worked.

"Sorry," I said.

"What's on your mind, Eve?" It was as if he had just recognized who I was and realized that it was odd, my being here.

"Nothing." I took a big swallow. "Can I just sit here with you and watch?"

"Sure. But you don't want to watch this." He'd lost his enthusiasm for *I Love Lucy*. He reached down and picked up another control box, the one that adjusted the dish. There was a grinding sound as it repositioned itself. The house shook slightly.

"Looks like you've been on a hegira," Gordon said, while we waited for it to lock into a new position.

"A hegira? What's that?"

"A hegira's a pilgrimage or time in the wilderness. It's the period from when Muhammad was driven from Mecca to when he returned in triumph. It marks the start of the Muslim calendar."

"How come you never want to talk about the Bible anymore?"

"Bible's like sex," Gordon said. "More you talk about it, the less you do it."

"I haven't been on a pilgrimage," I said. "I went to town."

"Arhat on a Sunday night. That sounds like a contradiction right there."

"I went to bingo."

"Ah." He started calling up channel after channel. I watched with him. I wasn't sure if I was supposed to say stop when there was something I wanted to see or if he was searching for a particular show. "It's fixed, you know."

"What?"

"The game at the VFW."

"The bingo game is fixed?"

He nodded and kept flipping.

"Certain tiles are weighted, so they get chosen more than others. It's an old scam."

He wasn't trying to find something to watch. He was just flipping, knitting together his own show from these quick pictures.

"Got to keep up a rhythm," he said.

After a while I gave up trying to watch and just looked at him. Gordon. He was so delicately constructed, almost frail. His head seemed too big for his body. And when he wore those dark glasses, it was as if he was deliberately depriving himself of his power to see.

Like it was getting too painful for him to look into everyone's heart. His gift had become a curse.

"How come you don't have any hair on your chest?" I asked.

"What?"

He turned. The TV happened to be showing this enormous map. A man was in front of it, explaining what the weather was going to be in Texas.

"Your chest," I said. "You have hair on your arms and legs. And you shave. But your chest is bare."

He looked down, as if I was the one with X-ray vision.

"I remember," I explained, "from a long time ago. You and Mom took me swimming once."

"You remember that?"

I nodded.

"Why, that was back in San Francisco," he said wonderingly. "You were afraid of the ocean. You'd have a fit when the waves just touched your little toes. So I took you in my arms and we walked in, step by step. You couldn't have been more than four. Finally I got you all the way in. You were so trusting. You never cried once. I can't believe you remember that."

"I just remember your chest. I don't remember the rest."

"Funny," Gordon sighed.

I drank my drink. It was time. I opened my mouth to say what I had rehearsed on the walk home. My confession.

"Surgery," he said.

"What?"

"I had surgery when I was a young man. They cracked open my chest. Shaved it first. For some reason the hair never grew back."

"You had surgery . . . on your chest?"

"On my heart. I had heart surgery."

"How old were you?"

"Sixteen. About as old as you are now, come to think of it. I died. Briefly. On the table. Then they brought me back. It's from then I date my ministry. That moment."

"You died?"

"For seventy-three seconds."

"What did you see?"

"What did I see?" He took off his glasses and rubbed his eyes. "Something remarkably similar to that, actually."

On the TV there was a big swirling circle. A tornado. These choppy pictures of it. Photos taken a few minutes apart. Pictures from above the sky.

"I saw everything from the top corner of the room," he said. "Like those mirrors in stores that are supposed to stop you from stealing? Everything was kind of fish-eyed and unreal. But in fact, it was super-real. I could see that we were living on a curved planet and that actually the curve is incredibly sharp, like a marble. Everyone was tipping slightly, sliding off to one side or another. Some people were sliding toward each other, and others were sliding away. But they acted as though they were standing on level ground, which was one of their many problems. They didn't accept how precarious things were, that they were constantly falling. And I realized that if I embraced this world—which I could, because it was round and really very small, and I was big all of a sudden, huge, with long ape-like arms that could hug the universe—if I embraced this world, then I could save it. I could rescue it from chaos and destruction. These doctors were going crazy trying to start my heart again. So I took pity on them and came back. It wasn't really that I was spared. It was more that the world was spared, by me. By my deciding to return and hold on to it. For the time being."

"Wow," I said slowly.

"Look at that damage." He whistled. They were showing pictures of a demolished farmhouse. Gas tanks with no gas station. "But the force of that vision has faded over the years. It's like all you remembering of that day at the beach being my bare chest. When I look back, all I can feel is the certitude of the destruction. And that I couldn't accept it. That we were all going to die. So I willed it not to be. Not for that day. But what I can't feel anymore is the sureness of salvation. I can't find the hope that used to fuel me."

"It was me," I said. "I was the girl on the motorcycle."

He looked at me blankly. I drank from my glass even though it was empty. I was sick. I could feel the Everclear sloshing up against the walls of my stomach.

"It was me," I confessed again. "It was me Mr. Olney saw in Sharon. On the back of that motorcycle."

"What are you talking about, sugar?"

"I've sinned!" I screamed. "How many times do you want me to say it? I was . . . with this guy. We did things." I wanted to throw up Joey's sperm. They were still in my belly, wriggling around, these minnows with monkey faces, appalled that they had ended up in the wrong place. It was so unnatural. It was an abomination. I wanted to purge myself.

"You did things? Sexual things?"

I nodded.

"With who?"

"None of your business."

"Well, excuse me, but I think it is my business. It'll certainly be his business when I find the boy in question and break his kneecaps with my ball peen hammer."

"It's not his fault. It's mine. He didn't force me. Like you said, guys'll stick it anywhere. Not that he . . ." I was torn between trying to tell the truth, even though it was in the form of a lie, and wanting to lie well, so I could save Serena, even though that would mean exaggerating what I had done. But does a confession work if you make your sin out to be worse than it is? That's what I couldn't decide. "I mean, we didn't actually do *everything*. But we did enough."

I hung my head.

"Enough to make you feel . . ."

"Filthy."

"Good," Gordon said. "That's why you've been out in the rain. Trying to wash away your sin."

"Maybe." I hadn't thought about that. I hadn't really thought about my night with Joey, what it meant, how it made me feel. I was too concerned with the event itself. It was gossip. Or news. Or a secret, something *not* to tell. I hadn't looked inside myself to see if I was different. If it had changed me.

"But you can't wash away the stain from the outside. You can't wash it away with plain old rainwater. You have to wash away the stain from the inside. With the Blood of the Lamb. Is that what you want me to say?"

"Well, it's true, isn't it?"

"It is if you want it to be, Eve. I'm not going to do your dirty work for you, though." He sat back and shook his head. "I let you go on the road crew just to avoid this kind of shenanigans. I thought manual labor would drain off some of that promiscuous energy you get from your mother. Plus, I figured that hideous outfit they make you wear might scare guys off for a while. But I guess my fashion sense is stuck back in 1968."

"What energy of Mom's? What are you talking about?"

"Well, your mom, she was like a . . . queen bee or something. You must remember a little bit from that time. She just drew men out of the woodwork. It's this talent she had. Not that she asked for it. In the end it almost destroyed her. It's what she's spent her lifetime dealing with."

"I'm not her."

"No," he said, staring at me. "You got a little bit of the used-car dealer in you, too. I keep forgetting. Where'd you meet this boy, anyway?"

"He's not a boy," I answered feebly. "He's a man. He's got a motor-cycle."

"Sure he does. What color?"

"That's not important. What's important is that I'm the one Mr. Olney saw in Sharon. So if anyone should be punished, it should be me."

"Punished?"

"Well, married. Whatever."

Gordon smiled. I hated it when his teeth showed. They ended so abruptly. They were all crowded to the front, like passengers trying to jump off a sinking ship, and there were no molars. That's why his cheeks were so caved-in.

"About when was this? What time of day?"

"I don't remember." I got up. Which was a mistake. The floor had risen several inches since last time.

"The Weather Channel," I heard him say. "Now, isn't that the ultimate tool of the Devil? All you have to do is step outside to see what's happening in God's Heaven. But no. Satan wants to keep you chained to this little box, so he can paint this grotesque picture of Creation. His Creation. And make the whole world appear like a parody. A cartoon. His aim is not to drag you kicking and screaming to Hell. That's a common misconception. That's what he wants you to think. His aim is to bring Hell to your everyday life. So damna-tion is a seamless thing, and death merely seals a bargain which has already been struck. That's what most people don't realize. You can't repent at the last minute and be saved. Well, you can, of course, because Jesus is infinitely merciful. But you won't. After a lifetime of sinning, most people *want* Hell. They crave it. Just like they hurry home to watch TV at night. They don't sell their soul. They give it away. They beg Beelzebub to take it. They make a swan dive into the fiery lake. Their last words are 'Wait for me!'"

"Is that what I'm doing?" I asked. The glass neck and the rim of the cup were chattering against each other. All his talk about damnation made me shake. What was left of the Everclear leaped out and slopped over the side.

"I don't know, Eve. What are you doing? You tell me."

"Well, I thought I was confessing."

"Confessing to something you didn't do. Which doesn't make you a sinner as much as a typical sixteen-year-old."

"Fifteen." I sat back down on the couch. I was still holding the bottle. I put it on the floor. It wobbled crazily, but finally stayed up. "And I did *so* do all that. Why would I lie?"

"Olney saw that girl in the afternoon, while you were busy stopping traffic out on the highway. I checked. Besides, whoever she was, she was wearing a dress. That's how he knew she was a Colony girl. Whereas you were probably still trying out for the All-State Lesbian Team, in terms of attire."

I opened my mouth to answer, but didn't say anything.

He rubbed his eyes as if he was tired of seeing.

"But it wasn't her," I insisted. "It wasn't Serena."

"Whoever it was"—he yawned—"is going to learn something about my anger. I give you quite a long leash, but there's still a choke collar at the end of it. I got to hand it to you, Eve. You really had me going. I give you credit for that."

"But if you don't think it was Serena, then why are you making her get married?"

"I'm not making her get married. That's a choice Serena made of her own volition."

"Even if it's against the law?"

"It's not, technically, against the law. There's a case to be made that because she's a member of a religious community, the age at which she chooses to marry is covered by her right to worship. See, in the Bible, girls married very young."

"She'll do whatever you say, Gordon. We all will."

"Speak for yourself! You, actually, are the most obedient of my children. Even if you think you're going off on your own unique lamebrained adventures. Angela, for example, is totally out of control, from what I can tell. As for Serena, she's quite a headstrong girl. She'll only do something if she really wants to. And she wants to do this."

"She doesn't want to marry Ethan. Or Gerald. She's sixteen!"

"Ethan or Gerald? You mean *our* Ethan and Gerald?" He laughed. "She's not marrying Ethan or Gerald. Who told you that?"

"Well, whoever you pick."

"I haven't picked anyone. I don't know what you're talking about."

"Well, she's getting married, isn't she?"

"I am taking Serena," Gordon said. "Hell, Eve, didn't you know?"

"Know what?"

"I thought she would have told you by now," he went on more gently. "Serena is my betrothed, Eve. She's going to be my wife."

There was a map of the United States on the big screen. I saw a smudge over Iowa. The rain. But it was tiny. Almost gone. Mostly there was a big emptiness. "A Bermuda high," the man in the suit was saying, sat over the entire middle of the country. An H appeared, with rings around it. An onion. A Bermuda onion. The whole thing wavered, as if it was being seen through flames. The heartland was going to "bake for several weeks."

Gordon had gotten out of his chair. He took the glass from my hand. I thought he was going to touch me, put his hands on my shoulders, but he didn't. The gesture got canceled somehow. Instead, he stood in front of me. Not that tall, even though I was sitting. But he seemed far away.

"I'm tired," he tried explaining. "It's like I got tired blood or something. I look out over all of you, and I love you. I do. But it's not like my love can move mountains anymore. That's how I used to feel. Hell, that's how it used to *be*. I made this place. By sheer will. I carved it out of nothing. You'll never know how hard it was. Not fixing up the houses or buying the land or dealing with all my enemies. That was exhilarating. But making you all come together. Thinking of your happiness and spiritual well-being twenty-four hours a day, seven days a week. It's . . . I got a taste, just a taste, of what it would be like to be God. With a million, billion little particulars of other people's lives running through your head all at the same time, so that you lose any sense of yourself, except in relation to your worshippers. Lately, though, I ran into a wall."

"You're marrying Serena?"

"She has a certain quiet center that I admire. She'll be a pool in which I can refresh myself. I'm talking to you like I talk to no one else, Eve. I'm hoping she'll revive me, enable me to go forward. And she's young. I need that. I crave that."

"I'm young," I whispered.

"You're too much like me." He smiled. "We're two peas in a pod, you and me."

"Don't say that."

"It's true. Serena will be more like a transfusion. That's what I'm hoping. She'll be fresh blood."

"Will she move in here?"

"Of course. She'll take her rightful place as my wife. Things will be different. The Colony's established now. It's like a business. Self-supporting and all. It's time to change gears. We have to find new methods for perfecting ourselves. This will signal the end of my time away. I intend to move among you again. I don't want to be this . . . mystery man on the hilltop anymore. I've been lonely up here. I've felt so isolated."

"What about Mom?" I asked dully.

"Your mother will understand."

"I don't understand."

"I want children," he said simply.

I had to throw up. I lurched off the couch and looked for the door. Gordon watched, then turned away. He knew he couldn't help. I looked back once. He was entranced by the big screen. There was a woman on it now. With padded shoulders. Selling something. He still talked to me, but I could tell his attention was with her. I remembered what he had said about how, late at night, the people on TV became real to him. Life-size.

"I hope you'll still come up and see me," he was saying. "I don't want this to interfere with what we've got. I value our special relationship, Eve. And I've still got a lot to teach you. Not just by example, either."

I blundered past the corner where he had pushed all his things, the catalogue-bought toys and gadgets. Where he had cleared the couch for her. Maybe for her mother, too. He had probably asked for her daughter's hand, thinking he was being very old-fashioned and proper. As if she was going to say no! Hate. The other side of love. I felt this mud slide of hate obliterating every spark of devotion I had ever felt for Serena. It rose up in me, and I pushed frantically through the kitchen, past its tower of Diet Coke cans. The moon was out now. I stopped at a bush and felt it all come out, wave after wave. I was on all fours, crying and vomiting and trembling. I was sick. Of course I was sick. I had sat with Angela, who had a fever, and walked around for hours without a coat in the pouring rain, and then gotten drunk. I had to be sick, I told myself. After a few minutes there was nothing left, but my body kept on heaving. My fingers dug deep down into the Iowa earth, so soft and black. Snot ran from my nose, mixing with the puke and tears.

I began to laugh.

6

"Breaking Up Is Hard to Do!"

was another kind of article they always had in those teen magazines. Some of the suggestions were jokes: "Sit Down with Your Mom and *Really* Talk About It," which might work if she hadn't been *really* jilted by the same guy. Or, "Go Somewhere with Your Best Friend," which, again, didn't take into account the possibility that your best friend might be marrying the jerk in question. I finally settled for "Buy a New Outfit," went to the Salvation Army, and got another pair of jeans. I made shorts. Or tried to. I cut each leg off just above the knee. But I didn't cut them very evenly and kept trimming each one to catch up with the other. I finally stopped at the pockets. At least they'd be cool. After the rain, a heat wave had come and all the crops were turning brown. I also got a T-shirt, without any writing on it, just bright white. My choice in shoes was still either work boots or heels, so I went barefoot, squeezing my toes over the hot ground. It felt so good, the sun on my thighs, my back burning, that delicious shiver going through my shoulders. I had the sense of freedom you get when you know you're supposed to be somewhere else. Because it was Sunday morning again, and this time I was missing Gordon's big

Return Sermon. At the highway I walked on the thin strip of grass between the shoulder and the drainage ditch. Cars blew clouds of exhaust. It smelled like the breath of some huge animal. The grass tickled. I tried to think of walking as touching. The soles of my feet were palms. My toes were fingers, exploring. But if walking was touching, then was touching walking? Were your hands really feet? When you ran them over a surface, concentrating on what you felt, did you travel to a different place?

Both their cars were parked on the gravel outside the cemetery. Joey's big black monster and Herbert's little yellow subcompact.

"Hi!" I called, waving.

They had brought clippers, a spray bottle of cleanser, and a rag. Both looked as if they had come from church. Herbert had a jacket slung over his shoulder. Joey wore a shirt with a collar. I had never seen them together before.

"Look," I said. "Shorts!"

I turned around, modeling them. Colony rules, except for our school uniforms, were very simple: no skin showing above the wrists, above the ankles, or below the neck. ("I guess that covers every-thing," Gordon used to say.) I felt I extended infinitely in every direction. Like the rays of a star.

"I made them myself. I mean, I didn't sew them, but I cut them off."

"You sure did," Herbert said.

Joey didn't say anything. He just stared.

"I should have hemmed them." I looked down. "These threads keep unraveling."

"No, no. The threads are nice. They're decoration."

I came closer. It was a new plot, near the edge. The stone was shiny, only rough where they had cut in the letters. You could see the sky reflected. I did the math. She had been forty-seven.

"Mary Alice Berry Biswanger," I read.

"That's how I knew she loved me," Herbert sighed. "When she took my name. Her own was so much nicer."

"It wasn't hers," I said. "It was just her father's. That's why we don't have them. Last names, I mean."

"I can't imagine being just Herbert."

"But that's all you are. The rest is ancestor worship. It's pagan. Someday you won't even be Herbert. Your soul will just be this shiny soap bubble, and when it pops you'll rejoin God. That's what happened to her. Mary Alice Berry Biswanger."

"You think?"

"Of course."

"How did you know we'd be here?" Joey asked. I could tell he didn't like me talking about his mother. Which of course made me want to do it more. I had this uncontrollable urge to bug him.

"You told me you come out on Sundays. Remember?"

"I told you that?"

Well, one of you did, I thought. It didn't really matter which. They were just two aspects of the same thing. The same *phenomenon*, Gordon would say. It was just a question of which one I would end up with.

I sat cross-legged in the shadow of someone else's stone. Cemeteries didn't creep me out. Dying was the first thing I'd been taught about. Dying and the certainty of Redemption. Herbert's eyes focused past me, on the highway. I turned to look with him, but there was nothing. Just cars and the early sun, already beating down. You could see heat ripples rising from the pavement. Joey was still mad at me. Of course he had plenty of reasons to be, finding out that I knew his father when I had said I didn't, and now the way I was interrupting their private moment, but I think what really bothered him was my shorts. He kept looking away from me, then looking back, as if I might have changed in the intervening microsecond.

"What was she like?"

"Quiet," Herbert said. "Very intense. It's hard to put into words. A great mother."

"She didn't eat," Joey said.

"She did eat. Just not very much. Lord knows I tried to get her to eat. And then, toward the end, it was the cancer, not . . ." Herbert shook his head. "We've been having a little discussion. About the future."

"Oh. Did you find a job in California?"

"Well, now how did you know that?" He looked over, trying to figure how much Joey knew. About us. About how much we talked. "I might have, actually, now that you mention it. In San Diego, doing some civil engineering for the Parks Department. Still waiting for word."

"That's great."

"Well . . ."

"You don't want to move?" I asked Joey.

He stared away from my legs and shook his head.

"You are a mind reader, Eve." Herbert was still lost in admiration that I could see the most obvious things in the world. When it came to other people, at least.

"Why not?" I asked Joey.

"I have family here," he said.

"We're family," Herbert snorted. "You and me."

"They let you walk around like that?" Joey asked.

"Like what?"

"Like . . ."

He didn't have to say any more. It was another one of his one-word sentences. I was beginning to think he wasn't so stupid, which would be bad, because then I would have *nothing* over him. He made me feel I was in one of those dreams where you're walking around naked. And I had thought I looked so nice. I looked at my legs again, trying to see if they were suddenly fat or ugly.

"Son!" Herbert said sharply.

"It's ninety-eight degrees," I said. "Can't I wear shorts?"

Joey got up.

"Joseph Biswanger!" Herbert boomed. "You come back here right now!"

I hugged my legs to my body, but my arms were bare, too. There was no way to cover up my nakedness. I was a creature out of its shell. Herbert, meanwhile, was bright red.

"Well, *fuck* him, pardon my Italian. Don't you listen to a word that boy says, Eve. He's just upset about moving." He looked down briefly to confirm something. "You have beautiful legs, for what it's worth. They're so white."

I heard the big black car starting up, trying to drown us out with its roar. I imagined how its engine would feel if it was right under me, sending a purr up my spine.

"They're white because they've never been out in the sun," I said moodily.

"Well, you should be careful, then. Maybe we should get you inside."

I stared up at him.

"See, you don't understand the first principles of carving."

"Which are what?"

"Which are that you can't go backwards." He cupped his hand over my breast. One of the wooden breasts. He hadn't done any more work on the statue since I saw it last with Joey. Apparently he knew we'd been here, in the toolshed. He had come back from California and found the plastic sheet still off. And Joey had barely spoken to him. It was weird to see it there, his wedding ring resting on this knot that was supposed to be my nipple. "The boy blames me for Mary Alice's death."

"Why?"

"I have no idea. We did everything she wanted. We moved back to her hometown. She went into Des Moines once a week to see a therapist. We had a child. We tried to have more. She was sick. She'd get better for a time, but then . . . The doctor gave us a book. You know the story of Persephone? It's a Greek myth. This girl got kidnapped and taken to Hell and ate a pomegranate. And because a pomegranate has six seeds, she had to go back there every year for six months. Which is why we have winter," he finished lamely.

"What's a pomegranate?"

"It's a kind of fruit. I've never actually seen one."

"What are you talking about, Herbert?"

"It's like she was a balloon, bobbing on a string," he tried again. "And anything she ate weighed her down, stopped her from getting to this place where she had to go." He shrugged his shoulders. "She had an appointment. A date. Someplace else. With someone else. She couldn't stop starving herself."

That was where we lay down, I thought, looking at the floor. Where his shiny church shoes stood now. That was where Joey stopped loving me. The statue, in daylight, didn't look quite as grotesque.

"So when the cancer came—" He sighed. "I don't know. Maybe part of me felt relief. Not that I wanted her to die, of course. But at least it was a real illness. With treatments and maybe a cure. It couldn't be my fault anymore. It was Hell, but it wasn't a Hell of my making, in some way. Which was like a weight had been lifted. And the boy saw that in me. Her being sick, I mean really sick, gave me this part to play. I didn't have to pretend things were all hunky-dory at home anymore. I didn't have to hide my feelings. So maybe I overreacted. Maybe I reveled in that a bit too much. Accepting sympathy. Being the grieving husband. The dad. I think Joey saw that. That I was playing a part. And it pissed him off."

He wasn't facing me. He was talking to the statue. I came up next to him and took his hand off my breast.

"They're too big," I said.

"Well, of course they're big, Eve. I told you: it's carving. You can't undo mistakes. So you've got to proceed carefully. Now your face I've seen. I know that part of you. The rest was guesswork and I was just roughing it in. I can't believe it upset you so much. It's just a little project of mine."

"Me?" I asked. "I'm just a little project of yours?"

"Christ!" He walked away from me.

The difference was: when Joey walked away, it was to leave me, but with Herbert it was to put some distance between us, so he wouldn't be tempted.

"Now you're angry, too," I complained. "What is it about me? I'm always getting people angry."

"You say things."

"Like what?"

"You ask questions."

"What's wrong with asking questions?"

"It's the kind of question you ask."

"Could you still have sex with your wife? When she was starving herself?"

He coughed. I couldn't tell if it was a laugh or a sob.

"Good question," he said dryly. "Not often. I think she regarded me as the ultimate pomegranate."

"What's that supposed to mean?"

"Nothing, Eve. Stay there, will you?"

He looked at us, my statue and me. Light filtered in from the window, but because it faced the woods there was still this feeling of privacy. It was our own little place. Our sanctuary. The wood made it a living, breathing space, not just a man-made box. It was where I wanted our wedding to be held and our life to be lived. Joey could have the house. Herbert and I would live back here. Or the other way around. It didn't really matter. We would meet in the kitchen, the three of us, for meals. I would have to learn to cook.

"So you haven't had sex in a long time," I reminded him.

"Just don't move, all right?" He picked up a chisel. "No small talk in the Bible either, I suppose."

"I don't see why people don't want to have real conversations," I complained. "I mean, I don't know anything. I'm fifteen. I want to learn about things. I want information. It's like everyone knows this big secret but won't tell."

"There's no secret, Eve."

"There is," I insisted. "You just forget it's a secret because you already know it. But I don't. So I have to ask questions."

"I have not had sexual relations in a long time," Herbert stated numbly, like it was a sentence in a foreign language. "OK? Now, I would like to continue work on my statue, if that's all right with you."

"Why?"

"It calms me," he said. "Working with my hands. It clears my head."

"So you want me to pose?"

"I just want you to be yourself, Eve. Will you stand over there, please?"

"Sure." I shrugged.

I went over to the window and stood. He cleared his throat a few times. I stared out at the trees. They were so pathetic. They were wilting in the sun like weeds.

"It would help," he said, "if you took off the rest of your clothes."

"What do you mean the *rest* of my clothes?" He was making me feel bad about my shorts again.

"Slip of the tongue." He was standing there with the chisel at his side. "Just take off your top."

"No way," I said. "That's disgusting."

"But . . . I mean, don't take offense or anything, but I know what happened between you and Joey."

"He told you?"

"It's pretty obvious, isn't it?"

"We didn't do anything." I crossed my arms over my chest.

"I don't know exactly what you did," he said carefully. "And I don't particularly want to know. But since I found your brassiere in my dead wife's bedroom, I assumed that—"

"I won't get naked so you can make a statue of me."

"You make it sound like voodoo or something."

"Well, that's what it is, isn't it? I mean, you're trying to practice magic. Which is dangerous and stupid and won't work. I'm here. You can touch *me* if you want. Not that . . . thing."

I wasn't sure if I wanted to. I wasn't attracted to Herbert. I didn't long for him. But that in itself was very appealing. That I could handle it somehow. While with Joey I was at the edge of this crumbling cliff. Herbert was safe.

"Where's the oxygen?" I asked, looking at the bigger tools pushed up against the walls so the sculpture had its own little circle of holiness.

"I sent it back to the medical supply house after that night."

"You said it was for you. That you got dizzy sometimes."

He smiled. "I didn't know you then. No, it was hers. From her sickroom. Toward the end, that's all I could do for her. Help her breathe. For some reason I didn't want to let it go. It was some kind of painful reminder. But then, after you used it . . ."

His hands hung at his sides. They looked so useless. I came over, took the chisel out of his hand, and put it away.

"Just pretend I'm her."

I thought it was a good idea. Practical.

"I can't," he said. "I thought I could, at first. I mean, that was the general idea. To talk to you like I talked to her. Nothing more than that. It's the talking I miss more than anything. But you turned out to be a genuine person in your own right."

"Sorry."

He smiled and shook his head.

I'm not a person, I wanted to tell him. Everyone keeps wanting me to be, but I'm not. I don't want to be a person. Not yet. And if you take me in your arms right now, I can put off that moment a little longer.

He was strong. Or maybe I was getting better at being picked up. When he'd lifted me high enough, I wrapped my legs around his waist, squeezing him tight. If walking was touching, and touching was walking, then what were my bare thighs doing to Herbert Biswanger?

"Christ," he groaned.

"Please?" I said.

"It'll hurt."

"I want it to hurt. It's supposed to hurt, isn't it?"

"Let go, Eve."

"It's OK," I whispered into his ear. "It's even legal, I think. If that's what you're worried about. Because of my religious beliefs. See, in the Bible, girls married at an early age. So that—"

"Let go."

"I can't."

"Eve."

"I can't," I panicked. "It's a cramp or something."

My legs were locked around his waist. This pain was shooting up each calf. It was so bad I began to cry.

"Put me down!" I screamed.

"I'm trying!"

He lowered us both to the cement. My whole pelvis was in agony. I thought maybe I was having a baby. Could it happen this fast? Herbert felt around behind him, to my ankles, blindly, as if there was some knot he could untie. I screamed again.

"Shut up!" he snapped.

"I'm paralyzed. I can't feel anything."

"You're not paralyzed. Just hold on a minute. Here." He very gently took my legs and lifted them just enough so he could move back. "There."

I gazed at them, these cold, fatty-looking tubes lying lifeless on the floor. I had squeezed so hard they must have fallen asleep. Now they had that burn in them as the blood started to come back. It was excruciating.

"Jesus Christ," he said.

He was standing away from me now. As if I was dangerous. When I couldn't even move! All I could do was lean my head back against the base of that stupid statue. He looked away and wiped his forehead with a handkerchief. Then he took a deep breath.

"It would be wrong. You're going to have to trust me on this. I am just . . . so full of sadness. I'm brimming with it. And I don't want that to be your first experience, what you remember. Some fat, middle-aged man's tears. You deserve better."

He reached down into his pants. I could see him trying to push his penis back into his shorts. It was such a pathetic human gesture. One I'd never seen before. I filed it away. Like it was a clue. But what was the mystery? All I knew was that it was more real than the words coming out of his mouth.

"That's what would make it so right," I said. "You being sad. That's what would make it more."

"More than what?"

"More than just sex. Because you really need me."

"Don't be so melodramatic."

"It's true," I told him. "Don't you see? You're lost without me."

Herbert drove me home. I was disappointed, of course. But also not. I had seen how tortured he was, how hard he fought his desire. It made me feel weirdly proud that I was important enough to make him suffer. Of course I wanted more. I wanted him to say those things, to act all noble and troubled and concerned for my well-being, and *then* help me out of my clothes, show me exactly what to do, make it clear I had no more choice in the matter, and very deliberately and thoroughly make me a woman, with the concrete floor butting against my shoulder blades, the oiled tools watching me from the walls, the smell of wood dust in the air, and even that hideous half-finished statue looming overhead. I pictured it so clearly. I still couldn't believe it hadn't actually happened. Sleep with His Father! I had been all ready to headline my letter in the

Reader's Suggestion Box, commenting on last month's article, "When He Says He 'Just Wants to Be Friends.'"

"You and Joseph," Herbert asked. "What exactly have you two got going on?"

"Joey? He hates me."

"I doubt that."

He pulled off the highway where the Colony's dirt road began and killed the engine.

It was still light. Only early afternoon. I had snuck away while everyone was at Service. I didn't know how I was going to get back to our cabin now, in tiny shorts and a T-shirt.

"He's screwing up, Joey. I don't know how to help the boy. And this latest bit about not wanting to go to San Diego . . ."

"Are you really going to move?"

"I'd like to. If I get the job. I don't know what to do, though. Joey's got a real bug up his ass about leaving."

"Want me to talk to him?"

"If you think it'll help."

I smiled as I got out of the car. It felt good to be taken seriously. Like an adult. As if I could actually influence events. In my mind I saw that gesture Herbert had made, trying to push his penis back, and I decided that this morning had been a good thing. Not sleeping with me had been good for his character. It was this refusal he had to make, so he could pride himself on having made it. Once.

He leaned out his window. "So you'll talk to Joey?"

"Sure," I called back. I was tightrope-walking on a ridge of rocks, part of an old stone wall that must have marked the edge of something once. I didn't turn around. I knew he was watching.

From the woods I ran downhill to the stunted tree that grew outside my bedroom window. No one saw me. I waited a minute, squeezed past its branches, and pushed up the glass. When there was enough space I hoisted myself, fell headfirst onto my mattress, and just lay there, breathing. There were people in the cabin. I could hear talking, women's voices, coming from the other room. I changed my clothes, stuffed my shorts and T-shirt back behind the bottom drawer along with my wine-stained black party dress from long ago, and was about to go in there when I realized how dumb that would be, appearing from the bedroom when I'd been out all day. I gathered my Colony dress around my waist and climbed back out my window. Then I circled around to the front door and came in, smiling.

Mother had her sewing box out. Serena and her mother were there. Serena's mom sat in a chair. Serena stood on the wooden stool. It had been moved to the center of the room. She was draped in white fabric. It was a fitting.

"Wow," I said, planting myself on the floor so I could look up at her.

It was already part done, the dress. Mother must have been working on it for at least a week. Probably longer. She'd hidden it from me. It looked very traditional, floor-length of course, cotton, with lace trim and a high collar. Serena was uncomfortable, balancing on the three-legged stool, staring off into nowhere.

"Isn't it gorgeous?" her mother sighed.

She was this very nice woman who acted as if she had been struck by lightning. Her hair stuck out in all directions and was white at the ends. Her eyes were a watery green. She believed everything you told her and jumped at the sound of a sneeze or a cough. Her name was Eulalia.

"You must be very proud," I said to her.

"Praise God," she answered, gazing up with me at Serena.

Mom was on her knees, with pins in her mouth, going along the hem.

"Where have you been?" she managed to ask.

"Walking," I said. "How did it go, the announcement?"

Nobody answered. Eulalia pretended to lose herself in the trailing folds of the gown. Mother shuffled around to the back, pinching the fabric up so you could just glimpse new heels, very high and white.

"Cool shoes."

"I don't think they liked it," Serena said.

"Don't be silly, dear," her mother objected. "They were just surprised, that's all. They were expecting Gordon to preach, and instead—"

"Instead, he just announced our engagement and sat back down," Serena explained.

"Lord knows *I* was surprised," Eulalia confided in me. "When we were summoned, I mean. It was out of the blue. It was like . . ." She stopped, totally at a loss for words.

I nodded sympathetically.

"I thought Serena might be in *trouble*." She laughed. "Imagine that!"

"Imagine that."

"But Angela's father didn't sing," Serena pointed out.

"Richard never sings, dear."

"But usually he pretends to. He moves his lips. This time he just stared."

"It doesn't matter what they think," I said.

She looked down at me from the silly height of the stool. We hadn't seen each other since I found out. I had made sure of that. I was afraid I would punch her in the nose or go to the lake and hold her head underwater for an hour. But now, seeing her crushed by this dress, trying not to fall out of her teetery two-inch heels, I found anger wasn't what I felt.

"Gordon can do what he wants," I went on. "It's his job to lead. It's our job to follow. To learn from his example."

"You're such a good girl, Eve." Eulalia began to cry.

"Mother," Serena sighed.

"Besides, Richard's a jerk."

"He's an Elder," Mother corrected. "And Serena's right. Richard didn't like the announcement. He feels threatened."

"Threatened?" Eulalia frowned. "Why, whatever for? It's not like my little girl won't make Gordon a loving wife."

"Can I come down now?"

"He doesn't like Serena's betrothal because it puts someone between himself and Gordon," Mother said. "It dilutes his power."

"I'm sure an Elder doesn't think that way," Eulalia murmured.

Mother stood up and stretched. I watched while she lost herself picturing how the finished dress would look on Serena. In that unguarded moment, she didn't feel my gaze. Something had changed. Just in the last few days. She was still exactly the same. She still had a young woman's body. But now it looked the way a cigarette did when it was left burning. She was this perfect replica of her former self, in ash.

"If Richard has problems with Serena's betrothal, then he'll raise them," Mother said, staring. "He's not a humble man. And there are others who listen to him."

"You think Gordon knows that?" I asked.

"Of course Gordon knows. But he has to follow his heart." She turned and smiled at the dress. "What do you think?"

Serena's mother started to cry again.

"Can I come down?"

I got up and held out my hand. Serena poked with her heel, feeling blindly for the floor.

"Don't step on the material," Mother warned.

I held Serena by the waist. It was funny. Her dress was so billowy, it was big enough for both of us, like a parachute. We giggled. When she changed, I tried to imagine her through Gordon's eyes. What did he see when he looked at her? Beauty? Or did he even think of her that way? What kind of marriage would it be?

We talked a while longer, the four of us, about the wedding, what kind of food there was going to be, the flowers. Gordon was going to preside, which struck none of us as weird at the time. Who else would lead? I couldn't imagine him kneeling down before Richard or any other of the Elders to receive their blessing. It all seemed perfectly reasonable. It was even pleasant, talking about something so conventional and normal for a change. A wedding. A marriage. Eulalia was all moist-eyed. Mother was practical, concentrating on the planning. Serena was quiet, the way a bride should be, and I was the Friend, supplying the enthusiasm she was too modest to show. When the dress was put away, Mother made lemonade and brought out cookies. Serena and I stayed a little while longer, then we left them there, the two women, and went outside.

The heat had broken for the day, but everything looked limp. Grass blades were bent over. The air felt chewed. We walked up the hill and looked at the willow, but didn't go in. It was quiet. Only a cloud of bugs was making noise, buzzing and whining. They were lit up by the sun, racing around inside this invisible ball. Their universe. And the whole ball was drifting.

"When did you know?" I asked.

"Right from the start," she said.

"So you lied to me."

"I was afraid."

"Of course you were afraid. That's why you should have told me as soon as he asked you. So I could help."

"I lied because I knew you'd try to stop me."

"Don't you want me to?"

She sighed and parted this imaginary curtain from in front of her face, then ran her hands back through her hair.

"I've always known I was going to marry him," she said. "I've always known that I was going to live there."

She nodded down to his house. You could barely see the antenna that stuck up out of the dish, the leaves on the trees were so thick. It was high summer. Everything was getting more of what it wanted than it could handle. Things grew like crazy in Iowa. That's why you had to be careful what you planted.

"You can't even say his name."

"Gordon." She turned to me. "I knew you would try to talk me out of marrying Gordon. That's why I lied."

"But you hate him!"

She didn't deny it. She looked around once, with this careful stare, to see if anyone could possibly be listening to us. She was like a politician's wife, considering all the consequences before allowing herself to feel. That's how she'll be with him, I thought, surprised to see this side of her. I never realized her quietness might have to do with being shrewd. I thought she was innocent.

"I'm scared of him a little," she said. "But he'll love me and be good to me. And I can help him with his work."

"Help him? How? By doing what he says?"

"There's nothing wrong with obedience. If you're obeying someone you believe in."

We walked past the willow. There wasn't much farther to go. On the other side of the hill, the back field of someone's far-off farm began. An old fence tilted. Its wires were still strong, but the posts were dried out and cracked. The field didn't need a fence anyway. It was a wall of oats. The evening made it a solid block.

"I don't *want* to love him," Serena said. "I don't want to love anybody. I'm not like you. Love scares me. I just want to do the right thing."

She took my hand. We were both little girls again, dwarfed by the big sun going down and the endless crop. She kissed my palm, pressed it flat against her breastbone, and held it there.

"You have to come visit," she said. "I can't talk to him. Nobody can. He says you're the only person he can relax with. He says it used to be your mother, and now it's only you."

"We don't talk. He just watches TV."

"He says he feels comfortable with you. You have to come, Eve. I don't want to be alone with him."

"You talk about me?"

"You're almost all we do talk about."

"I'm going to be so jealous."

"Jealous! I'm the one who's jealous of you, silly."

I could feel her heart beat. She held my hand there a moment longer, making some point, then gave it back to me. She turned and stared down the hillside. She looked so womanly. It had happened, what I always knew would. She had turned beautiful. But it wasn't the change I had expected. I had thought Serena would be this really attractive young woman one day. I'd thought she would show us all the way. Instead, she had gone right from being a child to being a wife.

"Let's run," she said.

This time I ran with her. We held hands. We ran faster and faster until our feet left the ground. We held out our arms, and the air puffed our sleeves and ballooned our dresses. I felt my cheeks flatten and the evening air roar in my ears. We were in perfect harmony. Our pounding was one rhythm. We made this single cry, this shriek, and took off from the top of the hill.

"I'm going to buy you a bus ticket," I panted, when we got to the lakeside. I was light-headed. "I'm going to buy you a bus ticket to wherever it is you came from, and I'm going to give you money. I've got money from my job now. And you're going to *go*. You *are*, Serena. You can find some relatives and stay with them. I'm not going to let you spend your life trapped up there in that haunted house."

She smiled.

"Would you come with me?" she asked.

I stopped gasping and looked down at my shoes. All dirty again, as usual. While hers, right opposite me, were spotless. Even though we'd been through the exact same things.

"If you want me to."

"What would happen to your mom?"

"She'd . . . go crazy," I admitted.

She put her hand under my jaw and made me look up again. I got hit with this incredible power coming from her eyes. I don't know how else to describe it. Like a weapon she'd never used before. It was the way Gordon could look at you.

"I'll do whatever you want," I said.

"Then stay. Stay here. And help me. Because I need your help."

Singing began coming from the Meeting Hall. They were having Evening Service inside, despite the heat, maybe because it was such a special occasion, Gordon being back and announcing his engagement and all.

"I have to go there," Serena said.

I nodded. She was someone now. She had standing in the Colony. She had returned, not just by herself, but as the person who had brought Gordon back. Mother was right, she had put herself between the Elders and Gordon. She took her hand away and walked toward the hymns.

. . .

"That's not just beer, is it?" Jewell asked.

"It's a Scottie. It's beer and lime juice."

"And tequila," Walt burped. "Don't forget the tequila."

"It's what we drink after work," I explained.

It was a few weeks later. There were three pitchers in the middle of the table. Six of us were there, everyone but Victor, our boss, and Gillie, who never came. Walt and Big John and a few of the other guys. I had started working harder. I flagged cars very authoritatively. I stepped right in front of them, playing chicken, daring them to hit me. I watched their bumpers slow and then come to a stop an inch away from my knees. The whole point was not to move, not to flinch, even. Then I would wave for the tar spreader or dump truck to come in, walking backwards, facing their huge grilles, leading them across the highway. If I looked up, Walt, or whoever was driving, would mouth "Get out of the way, you stupid bitch!" and I would nod, pretending they had communicated some very serious technical information to me, then hustle around to the waiting traffic and shoo the cars on their way, or scold them for lingering. I liked being in charge, controlling things. I wanted to apply these talents to my personal life. I wanted to flag people in and out, make them stop, while the necessary repairs were made to my happiness, then have them go and leave me alone. That was important, leaving me alone. But not ignoring me. There was a difference.

And as I got more comfortable with the crew, they started inviting me to come along to the Number. Well, maybe I just came. I don't know if they actually invited me. But I could tell at a certain point it was all right. Except maybe with Victor. He was still worried I would do something that would get him in trouble with

Olney. And Gillie, I could tell he didn't like it. He would stare after us when we left from the Road Commission parking lot. But he never said anything. I liked the feeling of togetherness after a really hard day. And I liked the drinking. It was scary how much I liked drinking.

"Do you want water?" I asked Jewell. "Or anything?"

She didn't answer. She was still taking in the Number, its shag carpet, black cinder-block interior. There were more people than when I'd come here with Herbert. It was after work. She didn't stand out too much in her dress. A few guys might have stared. But she didn't seem to mind.

"I would never have found this place," she said.

"Me neither. Not by myself."

"So what do you do at the Senior Center?" Walt asked.

He had immediately acted interested in her, even though when I introduced them I saw her give this pretty obvious look of distaste. But men are totally blind, I had come to realize. Or maybe a guy like Walt thought her not smiling at him was some kind of challenge.

"I just try and make their lives a little more comfortable," Jewell said. "Wheel them places. Help them go to the bathroom. Change their clothes. Talk to them. Or listen."

"What do they say?" I asked.

"The same as you and me." She shrugged. "They're not really so different. They're just old. They give me advice sometimes."

"You got to have something," Walt pleaded.

"They have Coke?"

He jumped to his feet and went to the bar.

"Is he the one?" she murmured, staring after him.

"I thought so," I said. "Don't you think?"

"I guess. You know him. I don't."

"Well, all he has to do is buy us a bus ticket. We're not asking him to rob a bank or anything."

"He has to keep his mouth shut about it, after."

"He likes you," I teased.

She nodded solemnly.

"Jewell," one of the guys asked. "Is that your real name?"

"It's what they call me," she answered.

The guys liked her laid-back, sleepy look. They tried to shock her, but they couldn't. In fact, they were much more relaxed with Jewell than they were with me. Maybe because she was dressed as a Colony girl. There wasn't any of the awkwardness I sometimes felt when I accidentally brushed against one of them, or when I had stumbled and Big John reached over to hold me up as if his arm was an extension of the road grader he operated. We had both mumbled and looked away. They treated Jewell more like their kid sister. She sat there, sipping her Coke, giving as good as she got, smiling back at them, answering their dumb questions and returning their even dumber jokes, making them laugh.

"What happens over there?" she asked, nodding to the little raised plywood stage.

The guys giggled.

"That's where Walt takes his naps," one said.

"With a fifty-dollar bill rolled up in his mouth!"

"Shut up! Fifty-dollar bill," Walt muttered. "I've never even *seen* one of those."

"They have dancing?" She stared at the spot.

"Friday nights," I said.

They all looked at me.

"Well, it's true."

I drank my beer and felt it replace the blood in my veins. I liked the idea of having greenish-yellow fizzy blood, of being an alien.

You could drink out of your own mug if you brought one in. They would keep it for you behind the bar. All the rest of the guys had one, some with their name etched in the glass. One was in the shape of a curved Viking horn. Walt's, of course, was a woman's torso. We stayed later than the rest of the crew, and we kept him with us. It wasn't hard. He was talking almost exclusively to Jewell. I was surprised, not that he was all over her, but that she didn't seem repulsed by him. By the time we left it was dark.

"Jewell," Walt kept saying. "That's just the prettiest name."

He looked over her dress in this perverted way, as if it must be *revealing* something, because its purpose was so obviously to hide.

"You have kids?" she asked.

"Two girls. Lisa and Cheryl."

"Lisa and Cheryl. So you must know women."

"Well, I guess I do."

She was doing all the work for him. She even took his arm, after he stumbled once. His elbow brushed up against her side.

"Because I have a favor to ask."

"A favor? Sure. For a pretty girl like you."

"Hey, what about me?" I called. I was on the other side of them and they were veering off.

"Eve!" Walt called across. "Where are we going, Eve?"

"The Park Hotel," Jewell said.

"The Park Hotel?"

He tried to stop. But Jewell just kept walking and overrode his hesitation. Walt's face was red. His light brown mustache had more expression than anything else. His eyes were glassy and his mouth made a pursed little O, like the opening of a balloon. But his mustache was twitchy and puzzled. It was all that was left of his brain and it was asking, What am I doing here?

"It's just to buy a bus ticket." Jewell smiled. "Remember?"

"Bus ticket?"

"Didn't Eve tell you?" She shot me a look, but I just shrugged. She hadn't said anything about telling him first. "You're buying us a bus ticket for a friend."

They were still arm-in-arm. His legs were working, but his neck was all rubbery. He kept looking down at her breasts and then back up at her face. Like one of those springy figurines people have bobbing on their dashboards. If Jewell hadn't been steering him he would have walked right into a wall.

"They sell them at the desk," she went on soothingly. "The hotel is the ticket agent. The bus stops in front. We need a one-way ticket to . . . Durham, North Carolina?"

I nodded. I had asked Mother. Not directly. Not: Where did Serena's family come from? But she knew, by my asking, that I was planning something. Something bad. She hadn't answered right away, but she made sure it came up again, naturally, a little while later, and then let slip that Eulalia had a sister in Durham. "Tobacco country," she had said, as if that was the point, a little picturesque note in idle conversation, not the kind of information I'd been begging for all my life and that, until now, she would have died rather than reveal. She even knew the sister's last name.

"Here."

Jewell held out her hand. I dug into my own pocket for the money and gave it to her.

"That's OK," Walt said automatically. "I got it."

He must have thought we were still in the bar. I didn't realize how drunk he was. Or maybe it was just this gravity that Jewell had him in. She was like a planet with a moon in her orbit. She was so determined.

"Take it," she said.

He wiped his mustache with the back of his hand. "Well, why can't you just buy this ticket yourself?"

"Because everyone in this town talks," she explained. "If a Colony girl buys a ticket, it'll get back to our parents and our friend will be in trouble. But if you buy it, then it won't seem so peculiar."

"A bus ticket? To . . . ?"

"Durham," I said.

"You know," he said soulfully, "sometimes my pecker feels just like a dog's nose. Does that ever happen to you?"

"Make sure it's one-way." Jewell put the bills in his hand and closed his fingers over them.

I watched, fascinated. How come everyone else knew how to get people to do things for them? Walt toddled off. We saw him straighten his shoulders. He was drunk enough to know he had to think before climbing the steps to the dilapidated hotel's tilting porch. Then he disappeared inside.

"You think it'll work?" I asked.

Jewell nodded.

"How did you do that?"

"I just pretended he was one of the guys at the home." She shrugged. "People really don't have a clue. All you have to do is keep going where you want. And hold on to them. They're just looking for someone to take them places."

She rubbed the side of her dress he'd been pressing up against, as if she was brushing away whatever he'd left there. "You heard about the meeting?"

"No," I said. "What meeting?"

She shook her head. We both sat on the curb. The woman who ran the Park Hotel was this crazy lady who kept her money in a cigar box instead of a cash register. Walt would be in there awhile. I noticed, for the first time, that it was actually "The Hotel Park."

"I can't believe you, Eve. Don't you talk to your mother? She knows everything."

"Not about the Colony," I said. "I'm sick of it."

"Because Serena's marrying Gordon?"

"She's not marrying Gordon. That's why we're here. Remember?"

Jewell banged against me. That friendly shove which was her own personal way of communicating. She was trying to cheer me up.

"All you can do is give her the ticket," she reminded me. "You can't make her use it."

"So then why are you helping me get it?"

"So we'll feel we did everything. Everything we could."

"What meeting?" I didn't want to think about how I was going to convince Serena to go, because, frankly, I had no idea. She had her eyes fixed on this prize and what did I have to offer her instead? Some nutty flight to nowhere.

"Richard," Jewell stated, and just let that hang there in the warm Iowa night. "He called a meeting of the Elder Council. For tonight. They're concerned about Gordon's betrothal."

"Well, they better be. Because Serena is going to totally destroy them. Do you realize that, if she goes through with it, this sixteen-year-old girl is going to have more say than all those old farts put together?"

"It's serious." Jewell stared at the front of the hotel. "A lot of them think Gordon's losing control."

"Of his church or of his mind?"

"Both."

"Well, that's crazy," I said. "We're his creatures. It's not for us to judge. He's *forming* us. His actions give our lives meaning. Judging

Gordon! It's like trying to judge God. I mean, how can a part understand the whole? You can reject Gordon or you can accept Gordon, but you can't judge him. Anyway, I'd rather sin Gordon's way than lead a life of ordinary virtue. I mean, there's no way I'm going to do what *Richard* says. He doesn't have a single spark of the Divine in him. Besides, he hits Angela."

"No one's even seen Angela," Jewell sighed. "She's been in bed for a week."

"Is she sick again?"

"Or something. Do you realize you were just preaching there, a minute ago?"

"No, I wasn't."

"Yes, you were. You were preaching."

The moon was full. I watched a cloud pass over it. The near and far of things didn't make sense. I felt I could reach out and touch that cloud. But Joey was so far away.

"So what's going to happen?"

"If they're all united, they may stand up to Gordon at Service. In front of the Colony. Ask him to explain himself."

"Good luck." I smiled.

"It's serious, Eve." She turned to me. Her eyes were intense, for Jewell. "It's serious for your mom. And for you, too. That's why I'm telling you. It's still a secret."

"You underestimate his power."

Jewell searched my face for something. "I can never figure out whose side you're on," she finally said.

The screen door to the hotel whined and Walt came out. He was very happy with himself. He skipped a step coming down off the porch and almost ran across the street.

"Got it," he waved.

Jewell examined it. I looked over her shoulder. This little slip of paper with four pages. Each said Arhat, IA, and Durham, NC, but in a different color. Like the four Gospels. Jewell smiled.

I let her walk him home. Now that she'd told me her method, I could see it, how she treated Walt like some senile eighty-five-year-old, letting him say whatever he wanted, even letting him get away with gross stuff, like staggering up against her more than he really had to, while she guided him firmly along.

I don't know why I was sad. We had gotten the ticket. It had gone far better than we could have possibly expected. I walked through the empty town, feeling exhausted from work and the Number. I looked up at the moon again. Why had I missed Joey just now? I tried to remember. It was when Jewell was telling me all about the Elders conspiring against Gordon and how it could be bad for Mother and me. Just then I had the most soul-emptying, devastating need for Joey, for his chest, that wall of bone and muscle and perfect skin. I stopped and almost lost my balance, it was such a strong hallucination. He's just a detour, I reminded myself. That's what I had decided. Herbert was actually my future. My hope. And Joey was just this detour, this sometimes fun, sometimes scary car ride that always brought me back to his father. But maybe it was really the other way around. I couldn't remember, anymore, who led to whom. They all became this big circular mess. My love life. Which had no love in it and wasn't a life. Instead of heading toward the highway, I crossed the railroad tracks and found Duffy's Automotive. It looked different in the dark. There was a second floor, which I hadn't noticed before, with a light on, one rounded yellow window facing the street. From below, looking up, I could only see the ceiling. A black car blocked both garage doors. I ran my hand over the curve of the headlight's big blind eye. It was dusty.

"Hello?" I called, pretending it was a magic bottle and if I rubbed it right a genie would come out. "Hello?"

It was his car, I was pretty sure. I tried to see if there was an armrest or anything else recognizable inside, but it was too dark.

"Joey?" I called cautiously.

I looked at the window again. What was Joey's car doing here? And did that mean he was up there? Maybe with another girl. Whose eyes I could imagine ripping out with my nails. I would have to grow them longer so I could really claw them out. I looked down at my grimy hands. If I tried it now I would just smudge her makeup. She would definitely have lots of makeup, applied just right. Like those girl models in the magazine. "Super Blush in Just Sixty Seconds." And how long would that take, to grow the kind of really long nails he probably likes? Cheerleader nails. And to learn how to dress so he wouldn't look at me as if I was a whore, when all I had wanted to do was to wear shorts for the first time in my life? By the time I made myself over the way he liked, he would have already married this other girl and had children. It was all too complicated. I found a big rock on the ground and heaved it at the glass. Luckily, I missed. It just clunked off the side of the building. The place was so old that for a minute I thought it might all come tumbling down. Nothing happened, so I picked up the same rock, which had come rolling back to stop almost right at my feet, and heaved it again. This time it landed closer. A cloud of brick dust flew up and a whitish spot appeared on the wall. Then a face came to the window.

"Is that you?" I asked. With the light behind him I couldn't tell. I just wanted it to be him so bad. The shoulders definitely were right. But somehow the rest of him might not be. Whoever it was, he wasn't wearing a shirt.

"Is that *you?*" he asked back.

"I think so." I looked down. It *was* me. Amazingly. Only he could make me . . . me. Oh God, I thought, feeling this gush of cheap love. I'm just Walt Connerly with breasts. I gave my whole body a little shake and swore that this time I wouldn't act goofy.

"Are you naked?" I heard myself shout.

Even though it must have been past ten o'clock and we were in this deserted patch of blacktop near the railroad tracks, I could see him wince and look to either side.

"What are you doing here, Eve?"

"Just walking." Then I got bold. "What are *you* doing here? Why aren't you home?"

"Oh, my dad and me . . ." His voice trailed off. "You know."

He grinned. I was doing this unintentional dance for him, making a big circle with one toe, hopping a little to music that had come on in my head. I was free-falling down an abyss of desire. Plus I had to pee. I always had to pee at crucial moments in my life. But it was all pointless, I realized, because he had this girl behind him, pouting on some mattress, probably a female version of himself, which meant instead of being strong she would be pretty, but in that same intimidating way. She'd be rolling her eyes, waiting for him to get rid of me, with this really dumb expression, the kind guys like because it's this absolutely blank screen they can project whatever cheap fantasy they want onto. I couldn't actually think of any girl in school, but I had the strong suspicion her name was Jill. Or Tracy. Or Cindy. One of those cutesy-poo names where if you scramble the letters around they spell out VOMIT. And the irony was that my being here, humiliating myself in front of him this way, was just making him seem even more cool to her. More desirable. So my very presence was doing me harm. But there was nothing new about that.

"Duffy lets me stay here," he said.

"Duffy. You keep talking about this Duffy. But I don't think he exists. I think he's like your God."

He nodded, as if I might be right.

"So who is she?" I asked.

"Who's who?"

He looked down at me, puzzled.

"I have to pee," I said.

"Come on up."

Around the corner, a staircase clung to the side of the building. It didn't look like there was any other way in. If it fell off, we'd be marooned up there, on the second floor. All alone, just the two of us. For years, probably. I would have to give birth to our child with no help. I held on to the wooden banister and kept going up, up, up, until Joey opened a door. He was wearing pants. And he had put his shirt back on, which made my heart plunge a little bit, but it was also touching, his modesty. He led me down a little hall and showed me the room, which was so white. You could see it had been the attic. The roof came down on either side of the window. But it was freshly painted and cozy, not at all what you'd expect over a garage. There was this brightly striped rug that didn't quite cover the old wooden floor, a chair, a pile of Joey's clothes folded in one corner, and an unzipped sleeping bag laid out on a mattress. But no girl. I looked around. A lamp, with its cord trailing across the room and out into the hall, where the only electrical outlet must have been, was by the one pillow.

"What were you doing?" I asked.

"Studying."

"Studying!"

I looked. It was our math book from last year.

"I flunked," he said. "I have to take it over again. Unless I can pass a test."

I sat on the sleeping bag. I was trying to be graceful, but it was lower than I expected and I kind of fell the last few inches. I was still wearing my boots from work. They felt like some newly invented mixture of lead and mud. I yanked one off and then realized my feet might smell. But it was too late.

"Math is actually one of the few things I'm good at," I said.

He nodded, still standing there.

I looked down at the sleeping bag. "So you're camping out."

"Kind of. My car broke down, too. So I work on it here, late."

"Did you and your dad have a fight?"

"Not out loud."

"Was it about me? Because if it was, I'm really sorry. It's just that it was so hot that day and I never made shorts before. So when I cut the legs off—"

"It wasn't about you."

"Really?" I was disappointed. "Are you sure?"

He was wearing the same kind of shirt I had seen him in that day at the cemetery. It wasn't buttoned. Its two sides hung unevenly, as if there were two halves of him that didn't line up and this crevice of naked flesh in the middle. The chest I had been fantasizing about a moment before, the one I wanted to break over like a wave.

"He got that job in San Diego."

"Oh. Great. So are you going to move?"

"He says you didn't do anything. You and him. That you just talked."

"He said that?"

"It's true, isn't it?"

"Of course it's true."

"So why didn't you tell me?"

Somehow I thought that just talking with Herbert was more like lovemaking, and that what I'd done with Joey, even though it was more like lovemaking, had really been talking. I shook my head and looked down at the problem lying open on the floor.

"Well, this one is easy."

"Maybe for you."

"Oh, that's right. I forgot. You're stupid. Excuse me."

He sat down on the other side of the book.

"Do you flunk things at school just to get back at your dad? Or because you feel guilty about growing up? It must all be about your mom, right?"

"I thought you had to pee."

"Why does it make you so uncomfortable whenever I ask about her?"

"Why do you ask about her so much?"

"Just to bug you," I admitted.

He flopped back on the mattress. His shirt fell apart. I lay down next to him. I was so tired of talking, of saying the wrong thing. And yet it seemed to be my only talent, the only thing I could do spontaneously, unerringly: screw up. I found this spot, between his arm and his side, and nestled there.

"I like your car," I said. "I hope it's going to be OK."

"I liked your shorts."

"Really?"

He nodded.

We smiled. We fit together so perfectly. Our lives that had come before had been this long separation. A separation we only knew about now that it was over. The word "flank" welled up in me. A word I didn't even know I knew. I laid my head against Joey's flank and rubbed my hair against his white skin, an animal preparing its bed for the night.

"Are you going to go with him? To San Diego?" I asked.

"No way."

"What can you do instead?"

"Stay here. In this room. Quit school, which I'm no good at any-way. Work for Duffy."

"Why?"

Tears were leaking out the corner of his eye and down his cheek. Like some mysterious fluid flowing from a car's engine. I licked them from the hollow of his collarbone. But his voice didn't break and his body stayed absolutely still.

"Once," he said, "I came home from school and she was staring out the window, just looking right past everything. She got that way, sometimes. This was when she was sick, but I knew that look from before. From when she was starving herself. And I asked her what was wrong, and she said, Nothing. So I went to my room, and she came upstairs a little bit later and sat on my bed. She put her fingers through my hair." He swallowed, staring up at the ceiling. "She said there was nothing wrong, but that sometimes she just didn't feel that *attached* to this world. That's what she said. It's like if she didn't concentrate she would just break free and float away. I couldn't tell if that was a good thing or a bad thing, in her mind. Anyway, she said that I was one of the only things that made her want to stay. Not Dad. Or anyone else. Just me."

His face wasn't really smooth, it was downy, with these unimag-inably soft hairs. He didn't have to shave yet.

"And now she's gone," he complained. "It's like I couldn't hold her. I didn't interest her enough. I dream sometimes that I'm hold-ing on to her, but then I let go, or maybe she lets go, but anyway she falls. Or I fall. We're both just spinning away from each other. In space. Like astronauts. And I get so mad."

I had finished licking the tears from his collarbone and worked my way up his neck, to his jaw, and then his ear.

"We could go," he said.

"Go where?" I asked. I thought he meant some other place in town, which I didn't want, because this room seemed perfect to me. The perfect place to lose my virginity.

"I mean go in the car. Once I get it fixed. You and me. Go together someplace."

It sounded like a pretty cool idea. It sounded . . . possible.

"How come you'd leave Arhat with me but not with your dad?"

"Because you remind me of her."

Then maybe he got scared, because he changed the subject. "What about *your* dad? You never talk about you. Tell me something about you."

"My Father sent me here," I said, hovering over his face, watching his features relax out of small-town suspicion to reveal their beauty. Yes, beauty. His eyes were so wide. "His only daughter. To save mankind. To save you, in particular."

"Me?"

I nodded.

"I thought your shorts were beautiful," he said again. "I couldn't take my eyes off them."

"Shhh."

"I couldn't take my eyes off *you*. You're beautiful."

"Don't talk anymore," I whispered.

"I think I love you, Eve."

"I have to pee," I said, getting up.

"Just trying to bug you," he yawned, and rolled over to where I'd been. The warm spot. He had this big smile, looking up at me, nuzzling into the empty space. "It's down the stairs. Want me to come?"

"No. I'll be right back."

"I'll be here."

I followed the yellow extension cord down the hall to some rickety stairs. The garage was cooler. It smelled of gasoline and car exhaust. I couldn't find a light and blundered around past tools and parts, but finally found the little toilet. I sat and prayed. Usually I didn't use words in prayer. You're not supposed to spell things out. After all, He's God, that's the whole point. He pretty much knows. But this time I didn't want to leave anything to chance:

"Lord, forgive me if I've blasphemed, but I'm feeling things I never felt before and I can't believe they're just animal lusts. They're Divine. I have a spark of the Divine in me. And if I feel Godlike I must have a Godlike mission, and Gordon always says, Start small. Meaning with myself, of course, but also with those around me, whose lives I can really affect. That's Mother and Serena and Joey and Herbert. And even Gordon. Jewell and Angela, too, I guess. But Jewell doesn't need my help, and Angela wouldn't take it if I rammed it down her throat. Anyway, I'm sorry if I sounded a little full of myself back there, but all I'm really doing is acknowledging the You in me. This night with Joey is going to be like a spiritual marriage, even if it's not sanctified by the ritual of any church. So please don't disapprove. Don't strike us dead with a bolt of lightning or give me my period." I held my breath and checked. "Thank you, Lord. Thank you, Jesus, my Brother and Savior. Amen."

Feeling my way back up the stairs, feeling the walls with both hands, with my arms spread out and my heart beating wildly, I sent a PS:

"A sign would be nice. I know people are always asking. But really, what else do You have to do? I'm in the dark here."

I followed the yellow cord back to the room. The lamp was still on, but Joey was asleep. His mouth was open and this thin trickle of drool was soaking into the soft lining of the sleeping bag.

"Thank you, Lord," I sighed obediently. "Maybe I can do something for You, one day."

I couldn't even get out of my clothes. Because then I'd be naked and he'd be dressed. I crawled in next to him and drew the flap, the top half of the bag, over both of us. I found the zipper and slowly zipped us in, turned off the lamp, and lay back. He sensed me, without waking, and laid his arm across my chest. It was heavy, like the length of wood you fix across one of those old-fashioned barn doors to lock it. I snuggled under its weight, its protection, and ran my hands inside his shirt. He made a sound, some satisfied feeling from wherever he was.

"Sure, I'll go with you," I said.

7

That night I dreamed America

was a steak. I dreamed the bony gristle of each coast, and then the meaty middle I had to chew, chew my way through, with aching jaws. I was waiting to meet this person, holding up my end of the bargain, but so far there was no one, just endless mountains of white coral. My boots made scraping sounds over the harsh surface.

Watch out, I warned myself. This stuff is razor-sharp. It must have all been . . . reef once.

I explored the ancient seabed a few steps at a time. There were no plants. No people. Just me. The scraping sound got louder and louder and—

It was evening in Arhat. The sun was going down. A radio was playing. What was left of the dream slowly drained away. Outside, the air was warm and soft. Even the street gave, as if the asphalt had just been poured. I turned my sloppy smile to the light.

"Good morning."

It was my father. He was middle-aged, with a high, moussed head of hair, fancy shoes, and chewing on something. I looked more closely and saw it was a toothpick. His face was shiny, painted on, as if he had had plastic surgery. He was perched on the fender of a pick-up truck, with one shoe on the chrome, the other on the ground.

"You ever *eat?*" he asked.

Because suddenly I was thin. Overnight I had wasted away. He stuck his hand down my shirt. There was so much room. His fingers investigated all the emptiness, then closed around my body and gave it a squeeze.

I tried to talk, but what came out wasn't even a whisper, just air squeaking in my empty lungs. He held my heart in his hand.

"That hurts, what you're doing," I managed to say.

"I could make it hurt more," he offered, friendly.

"Do you realize your son could be arrested?" a voice asked impatiently. "This girl is below the age of consent."

"I think technically there's a case to be made that, because of her religious beliefs, the Constitution guarantees—"

"Religious beliefs? She's fifteen!"

"Almost sixteen."

"She doesn't have the religious beliefs God gave a common dog."

I kept my eyes closed. I tried to go back into my dream. It was pretty awful, but it had to be better than this. One of them pulled down the zipper. It felt so oiled and mechanical, systematically unlocking our happiness. Morning air broke the warmth of the sleeping bag.

"See?" the second voice said triumphantly. I could hear his relief. "They're still dressed. They didn't do anything. They probably don't even know how. I mean, they're just a couple of kids. I think what we're dealing with here is more a friendship. Nothing sexual."

"What do you call that?" Gordon asked.

"Well, that's biological," Herbert objected. "The boy's asleep. You can't really hold him responsible."

"Eve!" Gordon yanked my shoulder, almost pulling it out of its socket. "Rise and shine, sweetheart. Time to face the music."

"Easy!" Herbert called. "Easy, now."

I yawned, pretending to wake up. I had vaguely heard them calling from outside, then tramping up the stairs, but I didn't think they were real. I still didn't. Joey was real, even though he was asleep. He lay there, warm and loving, guarding me, enfolding me.

"Eve!" Gordon said. "Come on, honey. I got shit to shovel and fish to fry."

Sun was streaming in the small window, spotlighting the mattress, my beery clothes and puffy, grit-choked face. Herbert stood a few feet back, looking uncomfortable, not knowing quite how to act, not sure if he should pretend to know me or not.

Herbert here . . . me looking like garbage, I noted mechanically. But by now it was such a common equation I didn't care. If he ever saw me with clean hair and decent clothes he probably wouldn't know who I was.

I avoided Gordon's eyes.

"What time is it?" I asked.

"Six-thirty a.m.," Herbert supplied. "Mr. . . . Well, Gordon here, he was concerned, naturally, when you didn't come home last night. Your mamma suggested you might be at our place. And I knew this was where Joey had been staying. So."

"We didn't do anything."

Gordon's dark glasses reflected the two of us, shrunken and contorted by the curve of the lenses, caught in our web of sin, Adam and Eve discovering their own nakedness. I moved to cover myself, even though I was still wearing clothes.

"I guess the apple doesn't fall very far from the tree," he sighed. "I cured your mother of this affliction and I can cure you. I just hoped it wouldn't come to this, that's all."

"Who are you?" Joey was awake. He hadn't yawned or stretched. His eyes had just opened, and there he was, sitting next to me, staring back at Gordon and his dad.

"I am, among other things, responsible for this young lady. This girl, I should say."

"What are you, her father or something?"

Gordon looked Joey over. "Son," he said softly, "right now I would take it very easy. Because the only leg you got to stand on is that one making a mockery of your shorts."

"We were studying math." I looked around for the textbook. "Algebra. Then it got late and—"

"I don't care if you were rehearsing the balcony scene from *Romeo and Juliet*." He glanced over his shoulder at Herbert. "I'll leave it up to this boy's dad to decide an appropriate punishment."

"You don't have to go, Eve," Joey said, staring back at him. "You can stay here. If you want."

And do what? I felt like asking. Of course I had to go. It was just a question of on what terms. Of how much trouble I was in.

"Come on, Eve. Your mother's waiting."

"Stay," Joey ordered.

"Oh, will you just be quiet?" I snapped, and then turned to Gordon. "Listen: we didn't do anything."

"Why do you even care what he thinks?" Joey asked. "Who is he, anyway? He's just some blind guy."

"Son," Herbert warned.

"He's not *blind*."

"Yes, he is." Joey was spoiling for a fight. So naturally he picked one with me.

"No!" It shocked me to realize that townies assumed Gordon was *blind*. So then everything he did, finding his way around, or even buying a girlie magazine at the Luncheonette, must have taken on this creepy significance to them. All because he wore dark glasses and was the head of some "cult" on the outside of town. "God, you guys will believe anything." All because they believed in nothing, of course. So this vacuum of True Faith they had was filled by any junk that happened to be floating around. "He's not blind. He has a *condition.*"

Gordon laughed. He opened up his crocodile mouth and showed us the darkness. It was like a third black lens.

"Nevertheless, the boy's absolutely right, Eve. You could have done him in all nine orifices specified by the Tantric doctrine of the Buddha and what business is it of mine? It's your own soul to use or lose. But there is your mother to consider. She's worried sick about you."

"We didn't do anything," I repeated, numb.

"Well, then come home and tell her that yourself."

"Eve," Joey warned.

It was an impossible situation. I got up. My body felt bruised from the sleeping bag. And my jaws were sore, as if I really had chewed my way through America. I saw them all pretending not to look at me: Joey, still in bed, staring straight ahead, angry; Herbert shuffling his feet and examining the floor; Gordon unreadable behind his dark glasses and poker face.

You sure can pick 'em, Eve, I thought.

On my way down the stairs, I tried holding myself straight up and down, like if I tipped over, I would spill something. Wisps of dream still clung to me, along with cigarette smoke from the Number. I remembered my father perched on the pickup truck fender. His grip. Reclaiming me. I could still feel a kind of evil pressure fingering different parts of my body.

"What's this?" I demanded, when we got out front.

"New wheels," Gordon said proudly. "What do you think?"

It was a Camaro, a Z-28. I knew cars now, just out of self-defense, so I wouldn't fall asleep from boredom when Walt and the guys critiqued the various models that came through our road block. No, it was more than that. Cars were also these mystical means of escape. And they were very male. This one was low-slung, with sunken, lizard-eye windows and a throbbing engine. It was fire-engine red.

"Got tired of walking," was Gordon's theological explanation. He went around to his side without opening my door. "Well? You coming?"

I looked up to the second story of the garage. Joey wasn't there. I didn't really expect him to be. He was furious at me. I could still feel it, coming out of the silent building in waves. I tried sending my love, this small weighty thing, a jewel or a grenade wrapped in silk, up high through the already-burning air. It sailed right in the open window, a perfect throw, and landed on the sleeping bag, where it bounced, once, silently, and lay there, glowing. All my love.

Gordon raced the engine.

"Nice car for a blind guy," I said, getting in.

"Well, now they just sense my power but don't know what to attribute it to." Gordon chuckled. It didn't look as if he'd driven in a while, because he took us to sixty miles an hour in about two seconds and had trouble keeping on his side of the road. Luckily it was an early weekend morning. Arhat was deserted. "They're too spiritually retarded to see it's just the Word, giving me strength, making a kind of aura that surrounds my person. You familiar with the concept of the mandorla? The body halo? Sometimes I catch a glimpse of that. In full-length mirrors. Or reflected in the TV screen. Instead of accepting that I might be chosen by Jesus, they get all pseudo-scientific-superstitious. 'He's blind. But when I made that face at him . . . he seemed to *see*!'" He laughed again and shook his head. "They're the ones who are blind, of course. Like lemmings in full flight from salvation."

"We didn't do anything," I said.

"None of them are worth your time, Eve. Not that boy or his sad sack of a father, either."

"What do you mean . . . his father?"

"I picked up on that. Him spouting that same line I laid on you. All about the Constitution and religious beliefs. Now, where do you think he heard that? He's not smart enough to come up with it himself, that's for sure. Why do some women always go for intellectually inferior men? That's what I want to know. You are just thrashing around in a sea of error, child. You want to drive?"

"No."

"Go ahead. Put your hand here. Feel the power. That's a 5.7-liter engine."

He picked up my hand and put it on the bottom of the steering wheel. Then he let go, not just of my hand, but of everything. I was driving.

"Gordon!"

"Let the Holy Ghost inform your every motion," he yelled over the acceleration. We were coming up on the sign that showed your speed.

"Stop!"

I wasn't in the driver's seat, so the road seemed all wrong to me, way off to one side. I wanted to turn, to get us farther over, but I knew that was an illusion, that I had to stay perfectly still, even though it looked as if I was running us right into the oncoming traffic.

"Are you pure?" Gordon asked, flooring the gas.

"Yes!"

"Did you let that boy defile you? Honestly! Be honest, Eve!"

"No!" I shouted.

It was a lie detector test. I swerved slightly. How much I swerved was how much I was lying. Or thought I was lying, because maybe I *was* defiled. How could I tell? What did that mean? I had never considered myself pure to begin with, so it was impossible to say. I was trying to *reach* purity, that's what no one seemed to realize. People at the Colony all saw life as some downward slide you could slow, or maybe even stop for a time. But falling, to them, was inevitable. They counted on it. They were so pessimistic. They even made Heaven seem like some temporary refuge, with Hell lapping at its gates. I wanted to fall . . . up. Was that possible?

I aimed us for the underpass. The sign read 90 MILES PER HOUR. We shot through, with just a brief moment of darkness, a blink. On the other side Gordon eased off the pedal and gently worked my fingers loose from the wheel.

"Really responds, doesn't it?" he said proudly. "You did great, Eve. You're going to be a great driver."

"I am never going to touch the steering wheel of a car again," I vowed.

"Oh, sure you will. You're a regular speed demon. You should have seen your face."

We were coming to the Colony. I wondered what he was going to do. Where he was going to hide the Camaro. But he didn't. He barely slowed down, turning onto the dirt road. Suddenly we were being thrown around, bouncing off the roof and the doors.

"You can't keep this car," I warned. "They'll kill you."

"Kill me or worship me," Gordon said. "Either one of which will be preferable to the miserable state I've been in for the last six months."

"What about those pills?"

"The painkillers? I stopped taking them. See, I was fighting my true nature, trying to tame it to fit into this world I created. But then, one night, I think when I was watching *The Love Boat*, I realized that the only way I was going to survive was to bend things to fit my needs, not the other way around. I had to take you all with me on this ride. Once I accepted my intentions, my desires, if you will, I felt so much better. So free."

The Colony was spread out beneath us. He waited. Maybe for me to thank him. Whatever it was, I sensed he didn't want me to go yet.

"Richard and the others," I said. "They're having meetings. They didn't like it, your announcement, about marrying Serena. They're . . . conspiring against you, I guess."

He ran his palm over the carved-out recesses of the dials, caressing each one. "I always wanted one of these."

"Don't you care?" I asked.

"It's God's will." He shrugged. "If He feels I am no longer qualified to bear His mantle and exercise His authority, then I should be cast out. That's what the Elders are for."

"What would you do then?" I asked. "What if you were . . . cast out?"

He turned to me and grinned. "You ask such good questions, Eve. That's the sign of an intelligent mind. I guess I'd make up for all the lost years, is the answer. Have me a good time."

Kissing Gordon was probably the most unthinkable thing in the world. So why was I suddenly thinking it? Because he had put the idea in my head, of course. He had reached into my brain and put it there. And now he was sitting back and watching it the way you watch a flower bloom.

"Is that why you bought the car? In case you have to go?"

"This? I leased it, actually. It's a much better deal that way."

And sleeping with Gordon, being slowly and impersonally and expertly raped by him in the back seat of his red Camaro, that wasn't even a concept my brain could handle. Someone else had definitely implanted it. Rape, of course, was just what a female Jesus would have to endure. It was true suffering. And yet being raped by Gordon would almost be not losing my virginity at all. Because I knew him. Because I didn't want him, not the way I wanted the others. It would all take place on a different plane, a kind of extension of what had gone before, of childhood. And we could get away, Gordon and Mother and me! We could ride across the country in this supercool car. I don't know how I managed to fit the two fantasies together, but I did. It seemed like the perfect solution. All our problems would be solved at once. Of course, there would be a whole new set of problems, like me, nine months later, giving birth to a two-headed baby, but still . . .

Without taking his hooded eyes off me, he flicked a switch. The lock on my door popped up. So I couldn't have gotten out if I'd wanted to. He still controlled me, from inside and out.

"We're going through a time of upheaval," he said. "Best thing you can do is keep your head down."

"What do you mean?"

"See, a lot of people think I let you kids run wild. They question my methods. So when one of you does something . . . like this Colony girl who was seen on a motorbike with some local kid? It reflects badly on me. It weakens my position. Especially in respect to the Elders."

"I'm sorry," I said.

"Stop apologizing. You didn't do anything wrong, remember? Now listen up: In people's minds, for better or worse, your mamma and you are associated with me. More than anyone else here. Maybe it's because I knew you from before. Maybe it's because your mamma and I were special friends once, or because I sense something in you I once felt in myself. For whatever reason, people *suspect* you, Eve. You and your mom both. Now, if things go badly for me, then they're going to go badly for anyone around me, too. That's how it works. So it might be better if we put a little distance between each other from now on. I told your mom the same thing last night."

"I'll bet she loved that."

"She's tougher than you think. And she's a far more committed Christian than anyone else here. She understands."

"What's going to happen?"

"I don't know," he said honestly, and drummed the top of the dashboard with his long fingers. "I do not know."

I looked with him, out over the Colony, and felt his fear that it might all be slipping away.

I was grounded. Mother didn't even want to hear my explanations. When I tried to talk, she put her hands over her ears and hummed. I had to stay in my room all day Saturday, only coming out to eat and pee. I tried to talk to her each time, but she just stared past me as if I was this smudge on the windowpane of her life.

Sunday was the same. I was going crazy, trapped on my little mattress, although it was also kind of purifying. All my lunatic fantasies got worn out from being played over and over in my mind. By the afternoon I had cleaned everything I could, folded all my clothes, washed my face, said my prayers. I was actually ready for bed at about five o'clock. I felt I hadn't slept well in years. I wanted to have the sleep of a little girl, to close my eyes when it was still light, while there were still the reassuring sounds of voices and footsteps outside—the Grownups—to feel my body get all warm and soft and boneless, like bread dough rising, and dream sweet dreams. I was just about to get undressed when Angela's and Serena's faces appeared in my window.

"Eve!" Angela whispered.

"What happened to your eye?" I asked, and then immediately felt bad, because of course it was obvious what had happened. There was this deep red-black ring underneath it and off to one side.

"What?" she said. Then she pretended to remember. "Oh, this?"

"Eve," Serena said. "Can we come in?"

"I'm grounded. I don't think my mother will let you visit, but you can ask. I was just about to go to bed."

"We know you can't come out," Serena said. "But we have to talk. You haven't heard yet, have you?"

"Heard what?"

"Jewell," Angela whispered, choking on her excitement. She was thrilled and terrified. She was also breaking out, I noticed. She had these nervous pimples on the side of her nose.

"What about Jewell?"

"Jewell's gone," Serena explained quietly. "She left yesterday. Can we come in?"

I helped them climb through the window. We sat on my mattress. Angela let us use makeup on her. We convinced her it wasn't a Satanic tool of vanity if you used it to cover up a black eye, but more like medicine. Besides, her father couldn't really get mad at her for trying to hide what he had done. And it helped calm us. It gave us something to do, the three of us. Serena and I sat side by side, tending to Angela while she tried to act brave. We were all trembling. Because for all our talk of rebelling and escaping, it was unthinkable that any one of us would actually do something like leave the Colony. I kept repeating it to myself, trying to accept the fact. It seemed so simple, but it was also unbelievable. Jewell had gone away.

"What happened?"

"Nobody knows," Serena said. "Yesterday morning, while every-one was at Morning Prayer, she left. She took a few things with her. And she left a note for her parents, telling them not to look for her. Someone saw her outside that hotel in town. Where the buses stop."

"How did she even get the money for a bus ticket?" Angela com-plained. "I mean, what she did at the Senior Center was volunteer work, wasn't it?"

"I don't know," I heard myself say. "I didn't even know she was unhappy."

"Well, of course not," Angela pouted. "You're too busy thinking about yourself to notice anybody else's feelings."

"Me?"

"Shhh," Serena soothed. She was covering up the pimples, too. "What did you do to get your dad so angry?"

"It's not her fault," I said.

"I know it's not her fault. But still, would you like me to have Gordon talk to him?"

"Talk to my dad? Yeah, right," Angela giggled.

"I could help you. Gordon could help you."

"Gordon's the one who's going to need help," Angela bragged. It was her most unappealing side, that anytime you tried to be nice to her she took that as a sign of weakness and turned into Richard. "At least that's what my dad says. He says Gordon's violating the Covenant. Especially now that Jewell left. He says that just goes to show we're given too much freedom. That's what got him mad, actually." I saw her flinch, as if his hand was still moving through the air. "He's so concerned for us. For our well-being. It just tears him up when he sees something like Jewell getting in trouble with some guy."

"Is that what it was?" I asked.

"Well, what else?" She shrugged.

Then I realized that Angela was excited, almost hysterical, because she had been *saved*. Now everyone would think Jewell had been on the back of that motorcycle. And she wouldn't be around to deny it. So Angela was out of trouble.

"And then did you see that car Gordon bought?" she asked excitedly.

"Leased," I said.

They both looked at me.

"It's cheaper that way," I explained. "At least that's what the guys on the road crew say."

Angela rolled her eyes. "If I hear one more thing about those idiots you work with . . ."

"There." Serena smiled. "You look good."

And she did. She looked really good.

"How did you do that?" I asked. "How do you know so much about makeup?"

"Well, don't make it sound like a miracle." But even Angela was pleased, peering into the mirror.

"I've been using makeup for over a year. It's the first thing I ever took. A little compact. From the drugstore. They're so small."

We both turned. If she had been using it, you couldn't even tell. It was part of her. Angela pretended not to be surprised.

"So that's how you got Gordon."

"Right," I said. "Like you'd really want to be marrying him instead."

"No. But it's just not fair, that's all." She began to cry. "I'm sorry. I'm thinking about Jewell."

Serena nodded. We all were. Even though she had gone, we were the ones who felt alone. We could all see her on that bus, with nothing, just a determined look. And every mile taking her farther from God. She wasn't an Outsider. She was one of us. And now she had taken part of the Colony with her, leaving us smaller and more threatened somehow. Vulnerable.

But I was mad, too. She had used me! I was finally figuring it out. She had spotted me as the dumbest of the three and used me right from the start, from when I first said we had to do something for Serena. That night, when she walked Walt home, she hadn't done that out of the Christian goodness of her heart. She had done that so she could go off with the bus ticket. The one I had paid for. She had just sat there, all this time, looking so sleepy and uninterested, and really these wheels in her brain had been spinning.

Angela was scared to stay too long. It was evening, but still light. She was supposed to be at home. Her dad had been meeting with the other Elders all afternoon. Services didn't start until sunset. We helped her out the window. Serena stayed with me. But there was an awkwardness.

"You think that's true?" I finally asked. "What Angela said? That I'm so busy thinking about myself I don't notice when other people are in trouble?"

"Nobody saw Jewell was in trouble," Serena answered. "Not enough for her to want to leave here."

"Angela was with us. When I talked about buying a bus ticket. For you to use. The one Jewell took. You think she'll figure it out?"

"You want me to give you a makeover, too?"

"Probably not," I went on. "Probably she's so scared of Richard finding out about that biker boyfriend of hers she isn't even thinking about telling on anyone."

"I could make you really beautiful, Eve. Not that you aren't already, but . . ."

I watched Serena's face. Now I could see that she wore makeup. It explained how she managed to mask any reaction.

"You know, don't you? Angela told you. About her boyfriend? She can't keep a secret."

Serena got up.

"Don't you want to hear how I got grounded? Or do you already know that, too? Did Gordon already tell you?"

"I haven't spoken to Gordon today."

"You mean he didn't send you here? To find out about us?"

"I should go."

"Why won't you talk to me?"

"I can't." She looked down at herself. She was warning me not to tell her too much, not to put her in a position where she would have to go to Gordon with something I said. Or have to lie to his face when he asked her about it. Because if I didn't actually tell her, then she could keep quiet, even if she knew the real truth in her heart.

"Are you worried Gordon will be cast out?"

"If he is, I'll go with him," she answered.

"Why do you think Jewell left?"

"I don't know. It's not like she told me anything."

"No. Me neither. Her parents must be going crazy."

Serena nodded. She looked at me as if I might have something more to say.

I remembered Jewell, it was the last picture I had of her, when we were waiting across from the hotel, saying, "I can never figure out whose side you're on." I couldn't either. I went back and forth. Was I a Colony girl? If I was, shouldn't I tell Serena what I knew, so they could track Jewell down and bring her back? But of course I would never do that, not in a million years.

After I helped her climb back out the window, I lit my candle. I don't know why. It was still light. The flame looked so inviting, this soft shifting shape of heat, like the blade of a shovel. I held my palm centered right over it and felt the first layer of my skin burn. I could see Jewell sitting on the curb across from the hotel again. Then, before that, in the Luncheonette. And under the willow. Listening. Watching. While all of us talked about things we knew absolutely nothing about. The future. But she knew. She was making her future.

"Eve?" Mother called.

I blew out the candle.

She was still working on the wedding dress. It was almost finished. She was sewing a lace cuff around the sleeve.

"You heard about Jewell?"

"What's that smell?" she answered, not looking up.

"I want to go to Service," I announced.

"Not tonight." She bit off the thread and smiled at me. "I thought we could spend some time together. Talking."

"You're not going?"

She shook her head.

"But you always go to Service. Besides, they may challenge Gordon tonight. You must have heard."

"It's God's will."

"You mean instead of going to help out Gordon you're just going to stay here making that stupid dress?"

She held it up and away from herself a little bit. "This dress could fit any one of you."

"But Gordon wants Serena."

"But Gordon may be cast out," she reasoned, and went back to work.

She straightened out a seam.

"So if Gordon's cast out . . ." I tried following her argument. "Then you think someone else will take his place? And *he'll* want to marry?"

She bent close over the clouds of white muslin.

"Like Richard?"

"I would never make you do anything you didn't want to do."

"Richard?" I repeated. "You've got to be kidding."

"He looks at you. You don't see it, but I do." She went on sewing. "And he could be influenced. Quite easily."

"He beat up Angela again."

"That girl needs a mother."

"I need one, too," I said.

She finished the seam and started to cry. I went and tried to hold her, but there was no way in. I squatted and tried to find her face. Her beautiful face. The tears were biting into it like acid.

"You'd really do that?" I asked. "You'd hope they cast out Gordon just so you could set me up with Richard?"

"He doesn't want us," she said, "so why should we want him? Don't you understand? I gambled everything, our whole life, on one thing. And I lost."

Her shoulders, the dress she was holding, they all crumpled over into this ball of heaving fabric. Then she opened her arms and took me in. How many times I had wished she would do something just like this! But now that it was happening, I was totally unmoved. She hugged me so tight, and cried and cried, and a funny thing began to happen. I felt her coolness passing over into me. Her cold, critical approach to life. I felt my body taking it on. It gave me strength.

I got to Evening Service late. Richard was speaking. It was crowded, a full house, except for Mother, who wouldn't come no matter how hard I tried to convince her. I think it was the first one she had ever missed. Gordon said she needed to go to prayer services the way an alcoholic needed to attend AA meetings. I went down to the lake first. It was a beautiful evening. Every color was pure and elemental. There were no shadows, or it was all shadow, one long, thin shadow that took the glare off things so you could see past their surface down *in*. Into the grass, into the water, into your own skin, even. By the time I ran up to the Meeting Hall, the doors were closed. I had to push one open a crack and squeeze in. Some people turned. I stood in the back and peered over shoulders, looking for Gordon in his usual place up front. But he wasn't there. Neither was Serena. But Angela was. It was her first time back. She was sitting up front. Serena had given her a good makeover. There was no way you could see she had a black eye. Richard was droning on and on. He had gotten some confidence from having led for so long when Gordon was up in his house, but that only made his preaching worse, that he thought he was good at it. You could see him congratulating himself at the end of each sentence. It wasn't even preaching. He was just holding up a Bible in one hand, as if it made everything he said right, and going on and on about the "Word of God." At one point I thought he stopped and looked at me.

When you hold up that Bible, I felt like calling back—heckling, really—you hold up a lightning rod, not a club.

And then I thought, What a weird thing to even *think*.

"The Word of God," he said, "is right here. We don't need Interpretations. We don't need Dispensations. We know Right from Wrong. The Word of God. It's spelled out for us. Satan didn't write the Bible. God did. If it isn't in here, it isn't in God's Plan."

Angela nodded at each phrase. More people were sneaking looks back at me. I couldn't figure out why at first. Then I realized what Richard was talking about.

"Our young flowers. Our most precious treasures. Yes, our . . . jewels." He hung his head. Angela wiped a tear from her eye. I saw how she was careful not to smudge the foundation Serena had laid down. She was there to prove what a good dad Richard was, raising her all by himself, and what a little supportive Miss Priss she had turned into, as opposed to the whores and heathens Gordon had encouraged us to be. I wondered for a moment if Richard was right. I mean, look at Serena. Look at Jewell. Look at me, if you dared. We were all so screwed up.

"No one doubts Brother Gordon's inspiration in founding this Colony, this outpost of virtue in a sinful world, this beacon in America's night of immorality, this lighthouse in a sea of pornography and Godlessness. But sometimes even the seer loses his way. And when one of our own, one whose soul has been entrusted to our care, is lost to us, and to herself, it pains us all deeply. It pains *me*"—he touched his chest—"deeply."

Jewell's parents were there, holding on to each other, pale and weepy. Richard paused in front of them. "And it makes me question certain things. It makes me recall the signs I ignored. Omens, if you will."

You should go, I told myself, feeling more and more stares, quick ones, little darts thrown by people whose eyes were already facing forward again, these flicked poison-tipped stings that were adding up, accumulating in a prickling red that spread over my face as Richard went on to titillate them with suggestions of our "wildness": we wore "unseemly" clothes, skipped Services, had been spotted in "inappropriate places" carrying on "intimate conversations" with Outsiders. Go, Eve, my own inner voice counseled. Leave here now. While you can. Before they reach down into the big freezer, start passing out the T-bone steaks, and club you to death. Mother was smart not to have come. Did she instinctively realize that Richard would try turning the Colony into a Christian lynch mob? Or had Gordon warned her? And why wasn't he here? With his authority, with his gift, with his fearsome power, he could have saved us. Plus, I reminded myself, Gordon is *right*. He is following a calling, wherever it takes him, not relying on his puny "intellect" and "reasoning" to tell him what to do next. How can your brain comprehend God? I wanted to yell. How can a million more rules hope to fence Him in? Once you accepted the fact that Gordon was a glowing coal, breathed red-hot by Jesus, then all his actions made their own sense.

But it was as if Gordon didn't want to save himself, or us, anymore. He had lost interest. I couldn't understand why he was being so self-destructive. First withdrawing, so someone like Richard could even get a toehold in the Colony's consciousness by preaching to them so much, then practically goading them into rebellion by announcing his betrothal to Serena and deliberately breaking all the precepts he had preached. Even if Jewell's leaving wasn't his fault, he had done so much else to set the stage for this disaster, this confrontation, that almost anything would have provided the final spark. And then he didn't even come to defend himself. It was as if he wanted it to happen. That's really what was fueling their anger, I realized. The people in the Colony felt abandoned.

Richard was trying to whip the meeting into some kind of frenzy. You could see they were reluctant to act against Gordon in any kind of concrete way, though. I mean, they owed their souls to him and they knew it. It was a tribute to his teachings and caring that they were so slow to join in, even without him there to defend himself. But that only made Richard angrier. He started railing about everything, shaking his Bible, painting this picture of the Colony the way *he* would run it. Girls shouldn't be allowed to go to school. No kid could go to town without an adult. Services, of course, should be mandatory, for everyone. He kept calling us all White American Christians, whatever that was, and warning how we had to keep ourselves pure. Not just our souls, but our *blood*. People actually responded to that: they nodded and murmured. By the end, he was almost openly proposing himself as an alternative to Gordon. He got them to agree to send a delegation of Elders up "on high," which meant up to Gordon's house, and say it was the will of the Colony that unless changes were made, the kind of changes Richard had been talking about, that Gordon should pray and "consult his conscience" about remaining our leader. I kept expecting the door to roll back and Gordon himself to make some dramatic entrance, with Serena at his side, for him to raise his hand and have a thunderbolt come down to shake their pathetic arrogance off them, so that they would fall trembling to the floor and pray to him and to God for forgiveness. But it didn't happen. And as they decided to send this word to Gordon, all of them giving an uncomfortable, wavering, sheeplike nod (there had never been a vote taken in the Colony before, to me that was the ultimate proof that Richard, for all his arguments, didn't understand anything, that he was turning our time of sacred worship into something as profane as an *election*), almost half of them looked back at me, to see what I would do or, God forbid, say. My face was burning. I felt for strength, groping inside me, wishing the Holy Ghost would descend in flame to transform me into a powerful speaker. Some totally other person. Where was my calling now? But growing up wasn't like that. I was still this stammering, blushing, gawky girl. Their stares slowly pushed me out of the Meeting Hall. When I got outside, I ran. I ran crying down the hill, so mad at myself, wishing the night would swallow me.

8

My mystery man didn't come

the next morning, the lover who would crawl into my bed, into my mind, and make everything all right. After a while I rolled over and got up. Then I realized something else was missing, too: footsteps. It was just turning light. There should have been footsteps outside my window, the whole Colony assembling for Morning Prayer. Without thinking, I got into my dress instead of my road-crew outfit and ran down the hall.

"Mom?" I called softly.

I opened her door a crack.

"Mom," I said. "Prayer."

"I'm not going." She was still in bed, curled away from me, facing the wall. But it was light outside. She should have been up.

"Are you sure?" I asked.

"Go."

I didn't know if she meant, Go to Morning Prayer, or just, Go, let me sleep. I stared a minute longer and left.

Outside, mist made a white scum on the banks of the lake. Birds were screaming. It was that precious half hour in summer when the air is still cool and fresh, before anyone has ever breathed it. I ran down to the shore, feeling my legs pound the baked earth. How many times? A million times. That's how often I had made this short magical journey. To prayer. Through repetition, Gordon taught, through unthinking repetition, you could develop your spiritual muscle, then suddenly one day look around and find Heaven in a blade of grass. That's what happened to me that morning. I wasn't thinking, I wasn't dreading, I was half-asleep and just doing, going to prayer, and even though it was a ridiculously short walk, a hundred feet or so, it turned into the kind of journey a pilgrim makes. My whole life, all that had gone before, suddenly took on the look of a quest. And now here I was at the spot where we gathered, and there was no one! I looked around. Were they at the Meeting Hall? I looked up the hill, but the big doors were shut. I looked all around. The Colony had made a collective, unspoken decision not to show.

"Morning Prayer!" I called. "Morning Prayer!"

My voice sounded flat and empty. The birds were louder.

Well, who needs them? I thought, walking to the front, where I would normally stand. Then I went a little farther and stood on the bare patch of ground where Gordon or, more recently, Richard faced us, leading the congregation. I turned and looked out over all of them, all their absences. This is what it would be like to preach, I thought, feeling the power well up in me. I knelt, even though there was no one, and bowed my head. I didn't pray in words. I didn't have a conversation with God. And I didn't just open myself up and disappear into Him, either. I willed His presence just as strongly as He willed mine, and together we met. I can't explain it any better than that. It was this newfound strength. A quiet that came over me. A stillness. When I opened my eyes, a red-winged blackbird was flying across the sky, leaving scarlet dots that lingered and glowed in the air. It circled a few times, waiting for me, then took off. I watched its trail of pure color disappear up the road and got up off my knees to follow, feeling such gratitude that I forgot to say Amen.

A car was waiting outside the Colony entrance. Herbert's little yellow import. He was asleep inside, his chin on his chest, his arms hanging slack with his palms wide open.

"Hello," I said.

He sat up and looked around. He didn't know where he was.

"I've been drinking," he sighed.

"Got any left?"

He stared.

"Were you waiting for me?" I tried again.

"I guess." His face had melted in the summer's heat and then reset, all sagged and folded. He rubbed his eyes. "I thought you might be in trouble. After Saturday morning. Figured I'd catch you on your way to work."

"Trouble?"

"Well, because of getting caught with Joey. Are you OK, Eve? They do something to you? You look different."

"They didn't do anything to me. What do you think, that we have torture chambers or something?" I did feel different, though. Then I figured out why. "I'm wearing my dress, that's all. You've never seen me in my Colony clothes before. And with my face clean. This is how I really look. It's a total turnoff, right? I can't believe it. You like me all dirty."

"No, no. Not at all. But . . . you can't go to work that way, can you?"

"Why not?"

"I don't know. I guess you can do whatever you want. Need a ride?"

"Sure."

We drove without talking. He was going extra-slow, even for Herbert. I stared out the window, watching my walk, the route I usually took. At the point where I would normally turn off and disappear into the cornfields, I looked over at him.

"I'm sorry," he said. "That's what I was camped out there waiting to say. I'm sorry about the other morning. That I didn't protect you."

"Protect me? From who?"

"Well, from Gordon, I guess."

"It's not your job to protect me from anybody."

He shrugged.

"I still can't believe you guys all thought he was blind."

"Yeah, and he can *drive*, too. It's amazing."

"Gordon is not blind."

"No. I suppose, in a deeper sense of the word, he's not."

I wanted to stomp my foot on top of his and make us go *fast*. Gordon was right, as usual. Driving his stupid car had given me a taste for speed. I wanted the outside world to match what was going on inside me, to mirror this racing, anxious, alert sensation. As if now, finally, something was going to happen. My life. And all because I had prayed one more time, and followed a bird down a road, and finally realized that what you do becomes who you are.

"Why were you drinking?"

"No particular reason."

"You got that job in San Diego, didn't you? And now Joey won't go with you."

"Jesus," he said. "You got a crystal ball or something?"

"Joey wants to stay here."

"I thought you were going to talk to him."

"I did. That's how I know."

"Job starts in two weeks," Herbert grumbled. "I already gave notice at work. Going to put the house on the market today. I want to drive out, get settled, and register the boy for school. They got good schools out there. But he won't budge."

"He wants to be near his mother. Things that remind him of her."

"That's crap. He wants to be near *you*."

I began to think, for the first time. Ever. And this . . . plan started taking shape in my head. A real plan of action, not just a bunch of wishes.

"You're probably right," I said casually. "Joey would probably go to San Diego if I came, too."

Herbert drove into Arhat, Iowa, population 8,000, down the main drag, which was still just the county highway but thick with boxy buildings and revolving signs and diagonal parking. The car bumped as we went over the railroad tracks. Trains hardly ever came through anymore. The town's original purpose for being was gone. So there was this dead spot at the center. He flicked on the windshield wipers once, to push away an early autumn leaf. I watched them settle back down in their little troughs.

"Beg pardon?" he finally asked.

"I mean, we can all come. The three of us. Don't you see? We can take both cars. Yours and Joey's."

It had suddenly occurred to me, why did I have to choose between them? Why not have both?

"To San Diego? You want to come, too?"

The Road Commission garage had a salt spreader they used in the winter, a bunch of plows, mowers, and other vehicles. The doors were left open all day. The guys were already inside, getting ready to climb into the truck. Herbert parked far enough away so they wouldn't see us.

"Face it," I said, "there's no other way you're going to get Joey to come with you. He's stubborn, just like his mom was, right? But if I was coming—"

"If you were coming, that blind preacher of yours would have the State Police on me so fast that—"

"He's not blind." I laughed. "*We've* been blind, until now. At least I have. Listen: if I can fix it so Gordon won't do anything when I leave, so that he *couldn't* do anything, even if he wanted to, then would you take me? Would you take us both, Joey and me?"

"What are you talking about, Eve? Take you and do what?"

"And be happy," I said. "Don't you want to be happy?"

I put a hand on his leg. He stared at me as if he was planning another one of his sad statues, like he was cataloguing me, trying to possess me. But only in his mind. His soft hands were just lying there at his sides. He's scared, I thought. Just like Joey. Everyone is scared. Of what?

"Don't you like me in a dress?" I asked.

He was bigger than I thought. Bigger and stronger. Joey was strong, too, but he was compact. There was more of Herbert, all the years of pain and loneliness, I guess. We kissed and it was as if I had awakened a mountain. I was lifted . . . and then I never came down. I was just kind of deposited on this slope. The world was actually tilted. Everything was at an angle, the ground, the sky.

"Wow," I breathed. It was just like before, when he had given me oxygen. Then I saw we were both all the way over on one side of the car. The shock absorbers and springs were responding to our weight.

"This is a disaster," he said. "You understand that, don't you? That it's a disaster?"

"Absolutely!" I would have agreed with anything. My morning lover had finally arrived, a little late, but in the flesh. "You want to kiss some more?"

"I will talk to Joey," he began very carefully, "and *if* he agrees to come, and if you swear to me that there won't be any problem with you leaving the Colony—that Gordon and your mother give you

their permission or their blessing or whatever you want to call it—
then I will take you as far as San Diego, California."

"And what about once we get there?"

He shifted in the seat, trying to work himself free. But it was such
a cramped car. I saw his hand shoving awkwardly down inside his
pocket again and tried not to smile. It must be so weird, being a
man, not being able to live inside yourself, not being able to keep
any secrets. For example, I knew now that whatever he was about to
say, it would mean the exact opposite of what he felt.

"That's all, Eve. I'll give you a ride. I'll take you away from here.
But once we get to California, you're on your own."

Right, I thought. You're actually going to shake me loose. After a
kiss like that.

"You here to work?" Victor asked, eyeing my dress.

"No," I said. "I mean yes. But not right away. I have to see someone first."

"Who?"

"Olney."

Victor drove me. He was mad. He didn't want to know what I was
doing. All he asked was if anyone on the crew had been bothering
me, and when I said no, I saw how relieved that made him.

"What could he do to you?" I asked. "I mean, if someone *had* been
bothering me?"

"If it was my fault? What could Olney do?" He squinted at the
road, scratched his beard, considering. "Mess with me. Mess with
my head."

They were in business together, Olney and Gordon. I didn't
know exactly how, but I had seen him, more than once, going up
the hill to Gordon's house. He was the only Outsider who came to

the Colony on a regular basis. He always had papers for Gordon to sign or forms to be filled out. Everything to do with the work crews, where they went, how much they got paid, all that went through Olney. He was different from most townspeople. He didn't act awkward, didn't stare at us as if we were animals in a zoo or look away as if we all had this gross, highly contagious birth defect. Olney was actually worse. He'd stop and call "Hello!" across the distance, watch the men and women give these nervous greetings back as they turned and hurried away. Once, I saw him corner a five-year-old and kneel down to talk to him, just to see that trapped look in his eyes. "Hey, sport," he'd said. "What you been doing with yourself?" I know that sounds perfectly harmless, but you had to be there. You could feel it, the urge he had to *tame* whatever was in front of him. I was standing about twenty feet away, out of sight, watching as he tousled the boy's thick blond hair, got up, and went on his way, leaving the poor kid absolutely paralyzed with fear. Then I looked down and saw that I hadn't just been "standing there" after all. Without thinking, I had hidden behind a tree, crouched low to the ground, my hands clutching bark. That was Supervisor Olney.

Which was the very reason he would be tempted to help me, I reminded myself, pushing open the heavy glass door of the Municipal Building. He wouldn't be able to resist the opportunity to mess with my head.

It was early, not even eight o'clock, but Victor said he was always the first person in. I saw him through the open door to his office, frowning over some papers, a full cup of coffee steaming on his desk. He didn't wear a suit. In Arhat, Town Supervisor was a part-time job. He dressed like a workingman, jeans and a T-shirt, but the jeans were new, deep blue, with a crease, and the shirt was so tight you could read what brand of cigarettes was in his breast pocket. He had a lot of black hair, piled high, with just a few threads of gray, and quick blue eyes that smiled at me while his hands automatically put the papers he'd been looking at away, jammed them into a soft leather pouch. They crumpled, because he wasn't looking at what he was doing.

"Eve," he said.

I stopped. I hadn't expected him to remember my name.

"How's it going, Eve?" He was exercising this magical power, just by knowing me. He closed up the pouch and put it on the floor behind his desk. With that out of the way, he could really look at me. Since I'd started going out into the world, I had gotten used to men's stares, how they looked at you like you weren't supposed to notice; how they glared, blaming you for their own fascination or repulsion, or whatever it was they felt; how they gazed with this stupid cowlike expression, expecting you to . . . to do what? But the look Supervisor Olney gave me wasn't about my being a woman. It wasn't even about my being a person.

"Sit," he ordered.

I sat down and smoothed my dress. He smiled as if he'd won some small victory, and waited.

"It wasn't me," I began. "On the motorcycle, I mean. In Sharon."

It took him a minute to remember.

"Is that what you're here to tell me?"

"No. But I thought we should get it out of the way. You're the one who told Gordon about seeing her, right?"

He took out his cigarettes and banged the pack against the desktop.

"Why did you do that?" I asked.

"Settles the tobacco. Makes them burn better."

That wasn't what I meant, but I was willing to let the conversation go in whatever direction he wanted. He started to smoke.

"Can I have one, too?"

His face was all these smooth planes. He must have just shaved. It looked like the outside of a hand puppet, and inside were these brainy fingers that could make it any shape, any expression. Right now they were acting out surprise, raising the forehead, pulling the tanned cheeks taut. But it's not as if you believed whatever the expression on the outside said. Or that he expected you to.

"You trying to get us both in trouble?" He smiled.

Yes, I thought. Exactly.

But he held a cigarette out anyway. I let him light it and tried not to cough. Some ash fell on the carpeting.

"No smoking allowed in county offices," he explained, using the toe of his boot to push a metal trash can around the side of the desk. "What's this all about, Eve? Aren't you people supposed to be widening the entrance ramp past Exit 193?"

"It's about Gordon," I said. "I want to talk about Gordon."

"He know you're here?"

"Of course not."

"Well, isn't that against the rules?"

I shook my head. There was plenty of betrayal in the Bible.

"You told him about seeing one of us on the back of a motorcycle in Sharon. With some guy. You must have told other people, too. Because they're all talking about it back at the Colony. Why?"

"I thought I had a responsibility."

"No, seriously," I said, leaning forward. "Why? He's your partner, isn't he? You two are in some kind of business together, right? So why'd you make trouble for him that way?"

"Did Gordon send you?"

I liked the way the cigarette tasted. Like poison. I remembered Serena saying how she didn't steal things, she just took back what belonged to her. That was kind of how I felt about drinking and, now, smoking. They just clicked into place. They were missing pieces of some puzzle. I looked down at my hand, at the smoke curling up, savored the taste in my mouth, and felt this clean, focusing shudder shake the fear from my brain.

"Nobody sent me," I said. "I just decided to come. Because I need your help."

"My help?"

"Gordon is screwing up. He's losing control of the Colony. There's people who want to make him leave. I thought you should know."

"It's no business of mine," he shrugged.

"The man who takes Gordon's place isn't going to be like him. Whatever you and Gordon are doing, you're not going to be able to do it anymore."

"We're not doing anything!" He laughed. "What are you talking about? Sure I go up to the Colony sometimes. But that's on town business. I'm the Arhat Supervisor, remember?"

"Of course I remember. It's how I got my job on the road crew. Flagman. Because Gordon told you to. Because you work for him."

He had these rimless eyes. Everything fell into them.

"I don't *work* for anybody. What exactly do you want, Eve?"

"I want him to stop this crazy stuff. I want him to stop saying he's going to marry my best friend. I want him to come down from his house and start preaching again. I want him to go back to being Gordon. That'll be good for me *and* for you, won't it?"

"Fingers," he said.

"What?"

"You're about to burn your fingers."

I looked down. It was the kind of cigarette without a filter. The glow was almost at my nails. I dropped it on the floor and he came around to stomp it out.

"I told him it was a mistake, hiring you."

"It wasn't a mistake. I'm a good worker."

"Come to think about it, that's probably the first sign that he was going off his rocker. Having me hire you. But it's too late now."

"Tell me something about him," I asked eagerly. "Something I can use. I want to be able to threaten him. If I can make him believe the whole congregation will turn on him, will stop loving him, then he'll back away from all this stuff he's doing. He'll go back to being Gordon."

"Little late for that, isn't it? From what I hear, he's already up to his eyeballs in trouble."

"He'll survive." I tried to forget last night, the meeting, everyone listening to Richard, and this morning's empty prayer service. "The Colony can't go on without Gordon. They all know that in their hearts. They're just saying he has to come back to them."

"Well, if that's true, then why should I help you? If things are going to work out anyway?"

"Because if he survives on his own, then he'll still be strong. But if he only survives because you let him . . . then he'll be weak. That's what you want, isn't it? That's why you started spreading those rumors in the first place. Because you're afraid of him."

He laughed again. He was still standing over me. He cleared a space and sat on the edge of the desk so I was staring right at his crotch.

"I'm leaving here," I said.

"So leave."

"I can't. He might come after me. I'm still a minor. And there's my mother. I can't leave her unless there's still a Colony for her to live in. Besides . . . I believe in this place."

"Except you want to get out."

He reached toward me. I flinched. But all he did was pick some ash off my shoulder.

"Too late," he said.

"What do you mean?"

"You haven't heard? That fire engine he bought himself, Camaro Z-28? Someone saw it getting onto I-80 this morning. Heading west. Word is your fearless leader already skipped town."

"No way." I shook my head. "You're wrong."

"Am I?"

In my mind I frantically went back over the morning: praying, then following the bird, the path, up past the last cabins, the gravel road, the early sun, finding Herbert . . . There had been no car. No Camaro. It was gone.

"Why don't I drop you back at the Colony so you can check out what's happening?"

I got up. He was standing too close to me. His hand was still on my shoulder.

"I'm late for work."

"How much do you make anyway?" he asked, driving me out to the site. Olney's car was a big, brand-new luxury sedan. It had adjustable seats, power windows, and a computerized dashboard that flashed Average Speed and Length of Journey. He showed them to me as if it was a toy, and he was amusing a child. Trying to make me feel like a child. I kept my hands clumped between my knees and raised my feet slightly off the floor. I didn't want to touch any part of his stupid Oldsmobile Cutlass. I was afraid it would somehow obligate me to stay in it forever. A gold tassel hung from the mirror. It was like the inside of a padded box where you would keep some dirty secret. Who *is* he? I asked. Because he definitely reminded me of someone.

"Ten an hour, right? I could look it up."

Cars passed us, going in the other direction. Was Gordon out there, heading to the Colony? Coming back to rescue us? Or was he going west, racing the sun to the Rocky Mountains, and beyond, back to the coast, back to those hilly street corners in the Castro where he would catch a crowd at the trolley stop and start telling them about Jesus. He used to make it sound so fresh. He was arriving with news. A terrible accident. Come quickly. He'll show you the way. Here! Here's what happened. Look! And all the time Mother and I pretending not to know him, part of the crowd, waiting for the wink, that rapid moment of complicity, over everyone's head. I was still waiting for that same sign, to remind me that it was all a scheme, what he was doing, part of God's plan, some holy joke.

"Because if you're stuck out here all by your lonesome . . . your mother, too . . . I could probably help out."

"We have money." Gordon had been cashing my paychecks for me. There was over two thousand dollars under my mattress. I could use a cigarette, I thought.

"Takes more than money." He drove fast. He liked to make the big car screech going around curves. But everyone knew him. So he would have to slow down and give a big exaggerated wave, as if there was this ocean of distance between them and him. Then the engine's power would push us both back in our seats. I noticed we weren't taking the most direct route to the highway.

"Smoke?"

I shook my head. But his hand stayed in front of my face, offering me the pack.

"Go on. Take 'em all."

"No."

"I own a club, you know. Well, it's more of a bar. Right here in the downtown. Maybe you've heard of it. The Number?"

I looked over. "You own the Number?"

"I'm trying to introduce a little class into this place."

"Good luck." I watched the road. We each had our own seat. It wasn't a vinyl bench, like in Joey's car. Each seat was leather, and deep. There was no danger of my tumbling against his side. Besides, he was a better driver than Joey. He seemed more in control. We got on the highway at a little access road I never knew about, farther along than the site, and headed back to it from the other direction. But how were we going to get across the median, I wondered.

"Got dancers there on Friday night. There's a stage, lights, everything. Draw a good crowd, usually."

"I've been to the Number. Not on a Friday night, but—"

"You want to be there? On a Friday night, I mean?"

He had dropped the pack of cigarettes into my lap. I picked it up and smelled the tobacco.

"Pay is a hundred. But you make a lot more than that, with tips."

"You mean, do I want to be there, *dancing*? Up on that stage? Are you out of your mind?"

"Why not up on that stage? You got a beautiful body, Eve. Why not use it?"

"Well, for one thing," I said, "I'm a Christian."

"Who was that in the Bible who danced? With all those veils?"

"God, you are sick. Get up in front of a bunch of men and . . ."

"And what? How's it different from just walking down the street? With a bunch of those same guys whistling at you? Or waving that flag on the Interstate and walking away and having a parade of cars stop to stare at your ass? That's what Victor says happens. He told me one guy almost rear-ended a Coupe de Ville. So what's the difference between getting paid ten dollars an hour for that—"

"Shut up! Just shut up!"

"—or getting a hundred dollars for about forty-five minutes' work, all told? And like I said, the tips are good. Plus there's kind of a circuit, places in some of the bigger towns. Iowa City, even. I could call people I know. You could start earning some real money."

"Just let me off here," I said. "I'll walk."

"Don't be silly. Look, if Gordon's gone, you're going to need someone. Now, maybe I can't read the Bible with you like he can, but I could help you out. You and your mother both. Colony's got a mortgage, you know. The bank would love to foreclose on it. And if that happens, where are you going to go? What are you going to do?"

"Gordon's not gone."

When we got opposite the site he went on one of those private dirt paths that had a NO U-TURNS OFFICIAL VEHICLES ONLY sign. Everyone on the crew stopped to watch.

"Well, I certainly didn't mean to offend you, Eve," he said formally. "Think about what I said, though. Only reason I made the offer is because I know you'd be good at it."

"Good at dancing?" In spite of myself, I grinned. "Mr. Olney, you don't understand. I have spent my whole life *not dancing*. That's what we do out at the Colony. We *don't dance*, all day and all night."

"It's Lyle," he said. "Lyle Olney."

Work wasn't hard anymore. Just when you got used to something, it ended. In a week and a half, school began. If Gordon was still here. If Richard and the other Elders didn't make us stay home and take Advanced Bible Study instead, along with classes in cooking and sewing and nodding meekly. If the Colony would even go on existing. I tried not to think about it. There was nothing I could do. After what Olney had told me, I hardly used the flag. I just pushed out my hand, glared at the drivers, and walked away. If they wanted to look at me, who cared? I didn't need the reflective jersey anymore. My dress alone worked fine. We had widened the road past the entrance ramp, made it two lanes instead of one. Pretty soon the rest of the crew, Victor and Walt and Big John and the others, would cross to the other side, all high up on their equipment, go to some new spot, and start over again, leaving me behind.

Love.

I vaguely remembered wanting to love. Was it only a few months ago? I had no idea what that meant anymore. I had thought there were so many kinds, now I wasn't even sure there was one. The people I wanted didn't want me. And the people who *did* want me, well, the best offer I'd gotten so far was to take off my clothes for a bunch of beer-soaked pigs down at the Number. Which left me exactly where? Far from the world of *Calling All Girls* magazine, that's for sure.

We ate with our backs to the highway, facing that no-man's-land off the shoulder, with its own atmosphere of truck exhaust and ugly, overgrown plants. I had forgotten my lunch again. Gillie always brought the same thing, a Slim Jim, one of those tubes of dried meat they sold in jars next to the cash register. He broke his in two and gave me half.

"Nice to see a girl in a dress," he said.

"You mean ruining a dress," I grumbled, looking down. It was stiff with tar smoke.

"Saw who you came out with." He didn't chew the jerky, he licked it like a Popsicle.

Well, of course you did, I thought. All of you saw who I came out with. And all of you gawked while I sat in the car, then hurried back to work when I got out, and haven't talked to me since. Not until now.

"What's it to you?" I asked.

"Nothing, I guess. You want to watch it around him, though."

"Around Olney? I remember what you said: Not worth the gunpowder it would take to blow him to Hell, right?"

The other guys grinned. Gillie looked embarrassed.

"He's my boy," he mumbled.

"Who?"

"Lyle Olney. He's my son."

"Your son? But you're . . ."

"Gilbert Olney," he introduced himself.

I tried to find the resemblance. Was that who Olney had been reminding me of? Gillie sucked on his lunch so hard his cheeks caved in even more than usual.

"So he got you this job?"

He nodded.

"Can you trust him?" I asked.

"Lyle?" He considered. "Yeah, you can trust him. He's a man of his word. Still, I'd watch it around him."

"Thanks," I said.

That whole afternoon I wondered what was going on back at the Colony. I saw Richard and the Elders climbing the hill to Gordon's house. Now they were knocking on the door, finding no one home. They opened it slowly, calling his name, exploring all the rooms, finding the home entertainment center and all the weird junk he had collected, poking the tower of Diet Coke cans, discovering the bar, the sliding piles of mail-order catalogues. Then someone came and told them about Serena. That she was gone, had disappeared! Is that what was happening? Right now? Had Gordon and Serena gone off together? Was Eulalia running around like a madwoman? And what about Mother? Were people walking right past her as if she didn't exist? As if she was already dead? Had someone thrown a rock through the window of our cabin? And what about me? Would they do the same to me? Would the light of recognition in their eyes just . . . vanish? Would we be cast out, too?

I waved cars through angrily, as if after a certain number of them I could go home. But maybe there was no home to go back to.

"OK, OK!" Walt yelled, when I kicked the side of his steam roller to make it go faster. "If we don't get done today, it's not the end of the world."

Yes, it is, I thought. It's the end of the world.

When I got back, the first thing I saw was the Camaro. My knees almost buckled, I was so relieved. So Gordon hadn't run away. He hadn't abandoned us. The red sports car sat where he had parked it before, where the Colony began, keeping watch. There was no smoke rising from the charred remains of our cabin, no clothes thrown outside on the ground. Nothing had happened, not that you could see, anyway. The work crews weren't back yet. Late in the summer they worked past dark.

Mother was cleaning. She took one look at me and put down the rag she was using to scrub the floor.

"Sorry," I said.

"You got that dress dirtier in one summer than I did in three years."

"What happened?"

"With Gordon, you mean? Nothing, so far as I could tell. Richard and the Elders went up there in the morning. After you left. Everyone was watching."

"And?"

"And they came out about an hour later." She squeezed the rag and hung it neatly over the handle of the bucket so it would dry.

"That's it?"

"Then Serena and her mother came over, in the afternoon." She sat down on the couch. She was maddeningly calm. But I knew she had something to say. She patted the cushion next to her.

"What did they come for?"

"Another fitting."

"When are you going to finish that stupid dress?"

"Well, as a matter of fact, I did."

I sat next to her. She touched my shoulder. "What is this, Eve?"

"Tar. I don't think it comes out."

"No. It certainly doesn't. They took the dress home."

"Thank God. I couldn't stand the way that thing was hanging there. It was like some kind of ghost."

"The wedding's Saturday," she announced, in that same relaxed tone. "Saturday morning."

I didn't understand. I looked at her. She was watching me.

"What happened?" I asked again. "What did he tell the Elders? How come they're letting him go ahead and marry her? I thought, after that meeting, he'd either have to back down or leave. I thought—"

"Shhh. He persuaded them, I suppose. They underestimated his power. Richard went straight into his cabin and hasn't come out since."

"Will he and Angela leave the Colony?"

"I don't think so. I haven't seen Angela."

"So what's going to happen?"

"I don't know, Eve. You tell me."

"What do you mean?"

"Well, I've done all *I* can," she said. "I let you go up there, night after night. I let him buy you things. Don't think I haven't noticed. What did you do wrong?"

"I didn't do anything wrong," I answered automatically.

"Maybe that's the problem. Maybe you didn't do anything wrong."

"What do you mean?"

"I mean, there's a time to act like a young lady and then there's a time to act like a woman. You don't seem to know the difference yet. And now it's too late."

"Too late for what?"

"You know what Gordon always says: Men will stick it anywhere. So why not you? Why not you instead of Serena?"

"Mom!"

She had that same look as when I walked in on her all those years ago, when she was with the two guys in the old apartment in San Francisco. She was putting up with this . . . unpleasantness all for me, and here I was, this ungrateful little snot-nosed kid, acting all shocked and disapproving.

"If you wanted Gordon so much, why didn't you marry him yourself?"

"Me?" She laughed. "I disgust him. Can't you see that? He knows all about my past. He used to like it. He said it helped him understand human nature. He used to have me talk about the men I'd been with and he would listen and it would get him . . . excited. But now, ever since he came out here and got so high and mighty, so *pure*, he says it just makes him sick." She took me by the shoulders. I saw this brief look of repulsion as her fingers stuck to the ruined fabric. "Don't you see? I changed when I followed him out here. I changed myself for him. But I couldn't do anything about my past. I couldn't become the girl I'd been. So instead there was you. You're me before anything happened to me. And I gave you to him. I offered you up to him. You were my ultimate gift. I let him raise you the way he wanted. I let him form you. I've been waiting all these years for when you were old enough, for when he'd take us both back into his arms. And now look how you've turned out instead."

"Stop it!" I screamed, breaking away. "I keep telling you: I haven't done anything!"

"You've sinned in your mind. It's all over the outside of you. That's why you can't stay clean. That's why you come home looking the way you do. Your guilty conscience forces you to perform these disgusting acts, forces you to . . . degrade yourself. And Gordon sees it. That's why he's turned to Serena instead."

"You *made* me go out with Joey."

"To get Gordon jealous. And it worked. You should have seen the look on his face when I told him." She smiled, remembering. She wasn't mad anymore. Her eyes were glassy, distant, the way she got at night sometimes, in her bed, staring at the patterns that reflected off the lake from his crazy TV set. "Maybe there's still time, Eve. He can do anything! He sent Richard running down the mountain with his tail between his legs. You should have seen it! Go to him. Go to him tonight! Before it's too late."

Instead, I went to see Serena. Eulalia opened the door.

"Eve," she said. "What happened?"

"Nothing," I said. Why was everyone so obsessed with my stupid dress? It wasn't that bad. In fact, it was actually kind of stylish. "Is Serena home?"

"She is. But she's already asleep. Have you heard? Saturday is her big day."

"I know."

Eulalia was holding an oil lamp, not letting me in. The light made it look as if she was peering at me from the mouth of a cave. I could just make out her eyes. They were wide and alert. You got the feeling she was going to be up all night, standing guard.

"We were so worried," she said, "after all that upset at the meeting last night. But everything turned out all right, praise God."

"Praise God," I echoed automatically. "I should have come earlier. But I was with my mother."

"That's good, child. Your mother needs companionship right now."

"I know." I waited for her to invite me in, but she didn't. Such a timid lady, but this was the one thing she had strength for. Protecting her daughter. "You sure I couldn't just crawl into bed and talk with Serena? Like we used to?"

"Yes, you did, didn't you?" She smiled. "But she's asleep now, Eve. And the next few days, well, they're going to be so busy . . ."

"I understand."

She frowned. "Is that tar?"

I said good night and walked away from the cabin, in case she was watching. I waited a few minutes, then snuck back up to Serena's window. It wasn't hard. There was a moon. Besides, I knew every inch of this tiny community. I knew it too well. I looked in and saw Serena, sleeping on her back, with her hands thrown up behind her, this graceful pose as if she was surrendering but somehow, by giving herself up so totally, winning.

I win, you lose, her quiet smile seemed to say.

She was beautiful. So perfect. I watched for a long time before I could even see her breathing. It was just this slight rise and fall.

"Serena," I whispered.

She didn't answer. I was about to whisper again, louder, when the door to the cabin opened.

"Eve?" Eulalia called softly.

"It's OK," I said. "I'm leaving."

I went down to the lake. Nobody else from the Colony ever swam. I don't know why. They were like those fishermen who spend their whole lives on the ocean but never go *in*. Did Jesus swim, I wondered, paddling away. Is that how He learned to walk on the water? By practicing really hard? The backstroke, the breaststroke, the crawl, and then, one day, the Walk? Or was I, as usual, going about things all wrong? When I came out, I just picked up my dress and carried it. So what if someone saw me naked. I wasn't real, anyway. I was just the product of someone else's nutty dream. Of Mother's. Of Gordon's. Of Herbert's. Or my own. After all, who else would be weird enough to imagine me but me?

When I got home, Mother was already in bed. I hadn't been to my room yet. There was an envelope propped on the pillow. Inside was a fancy piece of paper with just one sentence written on it:

WON'T YOU COME TO MY BACHELOR PARTY?

"What in hell is that?"

"My party dress," I said. "Remember? You paid for it. I thought you might as well get to see it."

It looked even worse than before. It was wrinkled, this cheap black rayon dress that had been stuffed behind my bottom drawer since that first night at Joey's. But actually, nothing could make it look worse. It hung where it was supposed to have shape and stretched over what it should have kept hidden. It was the kind of dress that made you want to have a drink right away. But my stockings didn't have a run in them. And I had learned some makeup tips from watching Serena. I thought I looked all right.

Gordon stared up from his BarcaLounger.

"I bought that for you?"

"Well, I said I wanted a party dress. Remember?"

"Party dress. I thought that was like . . . a Communion dress."

"It is, sort of." I looked down. "It's not that bad, is it?"

"Bad? You look beautiful. Pull up a chair. Pull up my spirits."

For someone who had just won some big important battle *and* finally set his wedding date, he looked pretty depressed. I sat on the couch, where I always did. He was watching the news. A whole city exploded. Bombs poured down on it in the middle of the night.

"Hot damn!" Gordon shouted. "Will you look at that? It's like the entire world is undergoing some . . . rite, performing some ritual self-mutilation, enacting some technological Black Mass. And these are the same clowns that have the *gall* to question my tax-exempt status."

Somehow there were cameras on the ground now, even though you'd think the men holding them would be killed. It showed the damage up close. Piles of rubble. Women screaming. Their heads were covered with scarves, which made their faces look even more terrible. The pain had nowhere to go except right out at you. Then I saw it was light, as if the bombs had turned night to day.

"What's going on?" I asked.

"We're at war, honey! Don't you read the papers?"

"No," I said, staring. There were jeeps now, speeding past, from someplace else. Someplace with tents. I began to realize these were all bits of something, that it was a story, or it was being shown like a story, even though it looked real. At least the women looked real. Their faces. "Nobody reads the papers here, Gordon. You know that. Do you read the papers now?"

Somehow that seemed worse than driving a car. More of a violation.

"Current events. It's a necessary evil. You have to act like you know what's going on when you run for public office."

"You're running for public office?"

"I'm thinking about it. Congressional seat opened up."

He handed me a bottle of Everclear. "In your honor," he said, pointing to the label. It was already half-empty.

"So how'd you do it?" I felt funny, putting my lips where his had been. I might catch some disease. But then I figured the alcohol would sterilize me. Inside and out.

"Do what?" He shook his head. "Look at that. The world's going to hell in a handbasket."

"How did you win? How did you crush Richard?"

"Oh, it's not about winning and losing, Eve. You know that. It's about encouraging constructive dissent. Bringing out the opposing point of view so you can more clearly assess the situation. Mao covers all this in his Theory of Contradictions."

"You never talk about the Bible anymore," I complained. My lips fastened around the mouth of the bottle with a sudden hunger. Immediately I felt this warmth making its way out to all my limbs, and inward, too, dissolving some hidden core, some little last pebble of . . . what? Sanity? Fear? Common sense? I couldn't tell if the direction I was heading in was good or bad. And I didn't care. All I cared about was the movement. Alcohol made me feel as if I was getting someplace. Finally. I was *getting* drunk. "I miss the Bible."

"That's nostalgia." He reached across the canyon that lay between us. His arm seemed incredibly long. And his face was both close up and far away, depending on what he did with it. He didn't have his dark glasses on, and now that I knew the people in town thought he was blind, I looked at his features differently. I saw how tender and vulnerable and . . . naked they were. Unused. They hadn't expressed that many emotions. When he smiled, it was still this shy boy's smile, but made by a man, with a man's power. He took back the Everclear. "Remember, the people in the Bible never heard of the Bible. The Bible was what was happening to them right now. It was all this knowledge they were picking up and piecing together and *figuring out*. They were flying by the seat of their pants. Some of what they believed in was popular culture and would have been scoffed at by the powers that be. It was the equivalent of that." He nodded to the TV, where a Coke commercial was playing. In the middle of a war. "Some of that knowledge was obscure and magical. Based on concepts incompletely understood. Intellectuals would have scoffed at that, too. The Bible"—he made a gesture—"is in this room, Eve."

I looked around. At all the gadgets and equipment. The mail-order catalogues. The "true mirror." The little wooden crate of a bar, a shrine. Or an altar.

"Preacher," I said.

He smiled. He took it as a compliment. I reached for the bottle.

"Where were you this morning? Early? Your car was gone."

"I was breaking in the engine. Racking up some mileage. Why? You think I'd leave you?"

He watched me. I found I could meet his gaze.

"No," I said.

"I won't be the one doing the leaving around here. You can bank on that."

"So . . . congratulations."

He took the bottle back. His fingers brushed mine and left a burn. I looked down to see if they had made a mark. That's how real the sensation was. I don't think he was aware of it, though. He had already taken another swig and gone back to watching the TV. People were talking at a big desk. You could tell, just by their tone, that it didn't mean anything, what they were saying.

I put the knuckle he'd touched in my mouth.

"Are you happy?" I asked.

"Happy," he echoed, not taking his eyes off the tube. "Well, I guess what I'm actually feeling is mixed emotions, seeing as how there's only a short time left."

"A short time?"

"Before I say goodbye to my carefree bachelor days."

Then he did something weird. He turned off the TV. He took his legs from the little footrest that rose out of the armchair but didn't shift his weight, so it stayed up there, empty, like the top end of a seesaw.

I got up. I wasn't drunk yet. I mean, not in any room-spinning, nauseous way. I just felt this flowing through my body. I was a sand dune, shifting, silently sliding over myself. I was a little girl again. I climbed up onto the footrest of the BarcaLounger, facing him. My legs were spread a little and I adjusted my dress. It was so black. I didn't like the way my hands looked against it, raw and red. I could see why women wore jewelry, rings and bracelets, anything to cover themselves, to draw attention away from the fact that they were still animals.

"You look like you're coming out of a cake," Gordon said.

"What's that supposed to mean?"

"Nothing."

He handed me the bottle. I took it very carefully, so we wouldn't touch again. He was watching me so hard I was self-conscious about drinking, except that nervousness made me want to have more, of course, so the two urges fought. I took a swallow and choked on it, coughing once. The chair, holding both of us, shook. My eyes teared. But I wasn't crying.

"So what did you do?" I asked again. "How did you get the Elders to side with you instead of Richard?"

"Why do you want to know?" he countered. "You going to turn into one of those gossiping church biddies every pastor has to put up with?"

"You said you had things to teach me," I answered. "Remember? You said I had a calling."

He nodded.

"Fair enough. If you really want to know, I gave old Richard a big coil of rope. He measured some out, swung it over a rafter, tied himself a pretty-looking noose, and then climbed up on a soapbox to deliver his little speech."

"What did he want?"

"He wanted power. The poor man. Not that he'd have the faintest idea what to do with it if he ever got it. I let him get all self-righteous, accuse me of all these heinous crimes, of letting you girls practically corrupt the entire county, from the way he put it."

"Jewell?"

He winced a little, at the pain of that.

"Jewell, and you, and Serena, even. See, the poor bastard's unnaturally excited by the thought of you young things. That's what he doesn't realize. That's what gave his talk at the Meeting Hall whatever kind of sick fire it might have possessed, from what I'm told. Anyway, then he held his own daughter up as this kind of perfect role model by comparison, like she was this little Miss Suzie Christian Homemaker."

"But she's not." The words came out of my mouth before I had a chance to stop them.

"Oh, I know." Gordon smiled. "That's exactly when I stepped in. They were practically the first words I spoke. I enlightened Richard and the rest of the Elders as to Angela's sexual shenanigans."

"Wait." I stared at him. "You know?"

"About her and this motorcycle-riding oaf named Roger Murtanski? Of course I know. His parents own a farm about ten miles outside of Altoona. I paid them a little visit this morning. That's where I was driving to. Lovely couple, although she suffers from Parkinson's disease. I said I'd pray for them. I don't think the boy will be coming around here anymore."

"You knew."

"Well, the subject of the sermon was 'Teen Unruliness.' So I gave the assembled Elders chapter and verse, names and dates, more detail than they probably wanted to hear. More than Richard wanted to hear, that's for sure. By the end, his face looked like a cross between an eggplant and a giant dog turd."

He tried to take the bottle back from me, but I wouldn't let him.

"Serena told you."

"How I found out is not important." He tugged harder. "It was the truth. I didn't make anything up."

"You threw Angela to the wolves."

"What are you talking about?"

I finally let go. He seemed surprised I was mad.

"You wanted to know how things work, honey. Well, I'm giving you a little glimpse of the inner dynamics of a Christian community. You think we all got on our knees and prayed for Divine guidance? Hell no! The man wanted a piece of my action and I let him go far enough to declare his intentions, separate himself from the others, and then I castrated him in front of his peers. I rendered him ineffective."

"He'll hurt her," I said.

He nodded and took another drink.

"I'm aware of that possibility. It's something I'll have to allow, for the time being. I have to let Richard retain his self-respect. And it will give him a useful place to channel his anger. Richard is a valuable member of the Colony. I hold his salvation near to my heart."

"What about Angela?"

"She did commit fornication," he pointed out. "And around here, missy, no sin goes unpunished. You know that."

I tried not to let my mind see what was going to happen, what might be happening already, in that creepy house with its locked door and Angela's sobs buried deep in a pillow. It was so quiet without the TV on. We both looked at each other. He held up the bottle to examine the level, which was low. I was very drunk, but I wasn't going to be sick. The night wasn't heading in that direction. I could tell. I could tell . . . everything, actually. I began to have this foresight, everything that happened just became this confirmation of what was meant to be. Gordon got sad and stared. I was his TV now. I was where the screen would be. He was giving me that same melancholy gaze.

"Mithridates." He smiled. "You remember him?"

"No."

"He was the king who drank poison, a little bit, every day, so when they tried to assassinate him he'd be immune." He watched the liquor in the bottle slosh. "But the kicker is: when his kingdom was falling apart and his enemies were knocking at the palace door, getting ready to torture him, he tried to kill himself and couldn't. He'd built up such a resistance to the stuff."

"Is that what's happened to you?"

"Huh? No. I don't think so. I was just explaining why I can't seem to get drunk anymore. I do enjoy drinking with you, though. You're the only one who understands me, Eve. I feel I'm passing the torch."

He pretended the torch was the bottle and gave it back to me. I didn't want any more. But there was no place to put it down.

"I have come a long way," he admitted. "It used to seem so much simpler, preaching the Word of God. I slept with a much cleaner conscience. I used to go to fairgrounds. Didn't even stand on a tree stump or anything. Didn't hand out flyers like the other preachers did. I just depended on my voice. I had a calling then in the truest sense of the word. Just the sound of my voice would bring people to me. And I would preach. Sometimes the Holy Ghost would descend and I would speak. I would heal."

"Speak?" I asked, looking up. "You mean you spoke in tongues? I never heard you say that before."

He looked embarrassed. I'd never been so intimate with a man. I mean, I had, of course, with Joey and Herbert, but the way I was with Gordon, both of us in the same chair, both occupying the same spot in the universe, was as if for this one moment we were the same person. Our thoughts were one.

"Calling on the Holy Ghost is dangerous," he said. "I don't do it anymore. It's no foundation on which to build a religious community."

"But you can. At least you used to."

"Oh, I still can. It's like riding a bicycle."

"Speaking in tongues?"

"That's mostly window dressing, doing the Talk. I'm not saying it's a put-on. But it's not as hard as it looks. You just do it because people expect it. They feel like they're getting their money's worth, that way. The Touch is what's important."

"You healed."

"Oh sure. Healing through Jesus' Divine intercession. It's a fundamental tenet of the faith."

"How did you do it?"

"You just reach out. If the person's ready, they're ready. If they're not, they're not."

"And what happened? They walked when they couldn't before?"

"I have made the halt walk," he said modestly. "I have made the deaf hear. I have made the dumb speak. I have made the blind see."

"No way, Gordon!"

"Oh, ye of little faith." He laughed, comfortable in his chair. It had been a long time since I heard Scripture come from his lips.

"Heal me, then."

"Heal you of what? What ails you, my child?"

"I don't know," I said. "All I know is that I need to be healed."

"Well, that's not good enough. Malaise is not a medical condition. For spiritual comfort, you need prayer."

"No," I said. "I need to be healed."

"I don't think so, Eve. Besides, I told you, it's not something I do anymore. It's serious business, not a party trick."

"Please."

He shrugged and straightened up in his chair. I don't know if he was chasing me off or not. I'll never know what he was meaning to do. What happened was, he forgot I was sitting on the footrest. The recliner folded up. I felt my seat lowering and flipping back under. Gordon reached out as I fell. He grabbed me by the back of the neck and my waist. His hands were hot. Red-hot. A ball of lightning rolled down my spine. It took forever, in this slow, deliberate, unstoppable roll. It gathered strength and smashed into my pelvis. It exploded into a million pieces between my legs, and I cried out like I had never cried before, this horrible wrenching sob that got caught somewhere and choked me before I gagged and with an effort spat it out. I let go completely, my knees, my back, my arms, my neck. I was a marionette with all my strings cut. He held me up, this limp creature. I could feel his hands sinking into me, melting into my flesh, his muscles straining to support me. I was falling. I reached out blindly and found something to hold on to and pulled myself to my feet, away from him, like he had done something horrible, although really all he had done was try to keep me up, was try to save me.

The bottle I was holding had bounced on the floor. But it wasn't broken. Anyway, it was empty. So why was I wet? I looked down at myself and at him. He was half out of his chair, crouched, as if he'd been caught in the middle of some perverted act that he himself didn't know he had been performing.

"Eve," he mumbled.

I moved. I found I could move. My damp thighs moved away from him.

"You bastard," I said. "I'm not going to let you do that to Serena."

"No," he called. "Eve! You don't understand!"

"I'm going to stop you," I promised.

I looked back once and saw him staring at his hands.

It's from that night I date my ministry, baptized in what came out of me.

9

I wore my shorts. They had unraveled even more, but with my heels they looked OK. I never really understood heels, what they were supposed to do for you, until now. Just before going on, I looked over my shoulder, twisting my neck so I could see myself from behind, and discovered how the muscles in my legs were stretched into these curves, kind of like how you saw the models in magazine ads, leading up to the little covering of frayed denim. Lyle had wanted me to wear a really ugly red sequined top with puffy velvet buttons. I just laughed.

"What?" he'd asked, offended. He must have bought it with his own money.

"I'm not getting into that," I said. Instead, I wore a clean white T-shirt. "They know me. I'm a Colony girl. That's the whole point, isn't it? Why should I dress up like a whore?"

"Got it all figured out, huh? You should see yourself," he said.

But what he didn't know was that I could, in the mirror above the bar. It was so high I could see over the piled glasses, see my face, at least. The rest of me was just this clear tower, this emptiness. I danced to the music on the jukebox. I stood four feet above every-one else on the plywood stage. It was kind of like what they used to build in the town square when they were going to hang someone. It creaked with my weight. I didn't really dance. The green, tacked-on carpeting turned out to be doormats, about ten of them. Each had a fake daisy sprouting in one corner. I stepped on the daisies. I figured as long as I stayed on the daisies I couldn't crash into the lights and burn my ankles, or go staggering over the side in my heels and flat-ten one of the poor innocent drooling lecherous scumbags who were crowded against the rail holding up money.

I hadn't been ready for the money. "Take it!" Lyle screamed, as if he was coaching me from the corner of some boxing ring. "Take the money!" I had watched the other two girls kneel down and let guys stuff it down their panties, or they grabbed it from waving sweaty hands and put it in their bra. I just danced. I watched my head float, disembodied, in time to the music and heard yells from far away. When I looked again, I saw these bills on the stage. I peeled off my shirt. They yelled some more. It was ridiculous. I wanted to stop the music and ask everyone seriously, What are you *doing*? What are you *thinking*? Then I remembered Gordon saying that when you preached, you were actually far from God, because you were so busy sensing your parishioners, trying to reach them, trying to lead them, kicking and screaming sometimes, through the eye of the needle into Paradise, that you yourself had to stay outside the gates, shov-ing the last few stragglers in. That's what it was like dancing at the Number. So I had found my calling at last: I had a body men wanted to see. I was finally preaching to my people, bringing them closer to God. Because that's what they were really lusting after. Even if they didn't know it, they craved a glimpse of the Divine, even if it was in this lowly, frail flesh. So I was doing good. And the small price I had to pay was that it left me stone cold and miles from Him.

"Holy shit!" Lyle said when I finally got away and he shepherded me into the back. "You want a drink?"

"After," I said.

"This is after."

"After everything."

Because I had to go on again. Two sets, he said. And then he'd tell me what I wanted to know. He was in a powder-blue sports jacket and a polyester shirt with a wide collar. I think it was his idea of what someone who owned a club would wear. I could see the curly black hairs of his chest. He was excited. His eyes were electric with the night and the crowd.

"You hear that? They *love* you, Eve."

"Right."

Love. At last.

I locked myself in the bathroom with a cup of coffee and waited. After a break, another girl started dancing. There were two of them, from Cedar Rapids. I had seen them, but we hadn't talked. They were older, maybe eighteen, sitting at the bar, chatting up guys, getting free drinks. Their makeup made them look like birds, with giant glittering eyes and bright lips. But their bodies were unhealthy. Pale and fat.

"Built like a pair of brick shithouses," Lyle had said admiringly.

I shook my head.

"What?"

"Nothing," I said. "It's just . . . you know how you can tell how big a puppy is going to be by the size of its paws?"

He didn't get it.

"The girls always get bitchy with each other. Why is that?"

"I'm not getting bitchy," I protested. "I'm just telling you that in a few years they're both going to be huge. Look at that one, she's eating your maraschino cherries out of the jar."

He laughed.

I massaged my calf now and pretended it was the same as taking a break from the road crew, chewing on a sandwich, listening to the traffic go by, listening to one of Gillie's soothing, not-quite-sense-making stories. Lyle had gone out, come back a minute later, and thrust this roll of money in the door. "You forgot these." I went through the bills. Mostly ones and fives. But thick. And they had a smell. Very distinctive. I sniffed at the roll and then, just to act as crazy as I felt, licked it. A big soft lingering slurp. The taste of money. It gave me a shudder. The way a minister must feel, after services, all alone with the collection plate.

The second time was even better. That's what he told me later. Apparently I got into it more. I lost myself in the music, in the yelling, which was much louder. Word must have spread through town. The place was packed. My mind traveled. The lights made it so I couldn't see anyone, just myself, above it all, but I could feel their bodies, their heat, their panting breaths. I was being slowly cooked. At the end I decided I didn't like my shorts anymore, so I took them off, too. See, I wanted to point out. No special underwear. No freakish operation. Just me. A person. So now will you finally leave me alone? I held the shorts over my head and decided it was the last time I would ever wear them. They really were too short. It was almost embarrassing. The more bored and contemptuous I was, the more they seemed to like it. Maybe they thought they were sneaking a peek at me. Some secret, interior me that didn't exist. Peering in through a cabin window. Finally finding out what really went on at the Colony. It was all too weird. There was a lot of noise. A real commotion. I didn't hear it at the time. The music was flowing through me. I was dancing now, almost in spite of myself. I threw my clothes over their heads. They turned and ran after them. I couldn't see, but I could hear this stampede of heavy shoes and shoved furniture. A fight started. I took advantage of the confusion to climb down. I felt so clumsy back on the ground again, after being up in the air so long. I had to get out. But in that short distance between the edge of the plywood railing and the doors to the pathetic kitchen, where, if you wanted, you could get a microwaved hamburger, I stopped. Herbert Biswanger was staring at me. He was sitting off to the side, against the wall, nursing a beer, and he had this hurt look. I stumbled, then moved to him. I wanted to explain, but realized I was naked. I covered myself with my hands and hurried through the swinging doors.

"Are you crazy?" Lyle asked cheerfully, following me in a few minutes later while I was changing. "All your money was in those shorts."

He tried handing them back to me. I shook my head.

"Well, take the bills at least. And here's your pay. What's that?"

"It's a dress," I said, snatching back the roll. "Did you think I was going to walk home in *those*?"

"You made out like a bandit, Eve. Here. There's more. I got it off the stage. You didn't even see it."

"That's not why I'm here and you know it."

"Well, if you don't want it . . ."

I took the money. There was still noise out front. He turned to go.

"Wait," I called. "I did my part. Now it's time for you to do yours."

"I got to close up first. Stay back there until everyone leaves. Then we'll have a drink. You could use one, I'll bet."

That was exactly right. I could *use* a drink. Use it to make me stop trembling. I opened the door a crack and looked out. Lyle had turned on the regular lights. If the Number had looked even slightly exotic before, now it was back to being exactly what it was: a dusty basement crammed with leftover furniture. Lyle's voice boomed, friendly and threatening, making sure people paid, then hustling them out. I searched in every direction for Herbert, but he must have left. Guilt welled in the pit of my stomach. Which made me mad. After all, I hadn't asked him to come. He wanted to see me naked and now he had. Now he could finish his statue. That wounded look he got, sometimes it moved me, made me want to take him in my arms. His dead wife, his ungrateful son, his sad life, all these burdens he had to bear—I wanted to gather them up and share them. But other times I got the feeling he was enjoying it all too much, that he was lingering in the lukewarm, dirty bathwater of his emotions, instead of getting up and doing something. If he didn't like me on the stage he should have taken me down, tucked me under his arm, and driven me off to San Diego, caveman style. Instead, he just stared and made me feel bad, which was too easy. I mean, I could make myself feel bad all by myself. I didn't need a man for that.

When the room cleared, we finally got our free drinks. Honey and Cherry and me. They seemed mostly concerned about getting their money. We acted as though we had all been doing something normal during the night, waiting tables or washing dishes. I saw them staring at my dress, but by now I was so used to that it wasn't a big deal. If a dress *didn't* make people look twice, then something was wrong with it, I decided. Lyle made a drink for me, gin and orange juice.

"What do you call this?"

"Breakfast."

I laughed.

We sat there while he bossed Shirley, the bartender, and this farm boy he had hired. He helped, too, emptying the ashtrays, putting the chairs on the tables, vacuuming . . . He was very neat. He looked happier cleaning up than doing anything else. In between, he came back and made us more drinks. I'd lay my face down on the bar and watch him pour almost half a glass of gin. Then as soon as the screwdriver mix hit the lake, I'd say "When!" The lake. That's what it felt like, because I was leaning up close, sloshed down onto the bar, my eye level with the glass—"When!"—and these streamers of orange would float down like a firework or a jellyfish or, as night turned into morning, as I got better, faster at telling him to stop, not like anything at all. That was the beauty of it. It was just the lake back at the Colony. And I was drinking it up.

Eventually, they all left. The girls were taking the Greyhound back to Cedar Rapids. Lyle went with them to the door. He disappeared for a few minutes, then came back.

"Just in case there are any sickos hanging around outside," he explained. "That's why it's a good idea to wait."

"Sickos," I repeated.

I had taken off my heels and sat on one stool with my feet up on another. He came over and started massaging them. My feet. I never knew they could feel so good. There was a window above the bar, high enough to reach the very bottom of the alley outside. A light patch appeared on the floor. It was just dawn.

"Mmm. Don't stop."

Who did he remind me of? It was so obvious. I squirmed a little lower into his grip. I had met this man before. I had felt this touch, but where? How? Or was it a premonition? Was this how you knew someone was right for you? Because he seemed familiar, but familiar in a spooky, unexplained way. I opened my eyes enough to confirm that he was good-looking. His hair had gone limp, which made it better, less greasy, the way it fell a little over his ice-blue eyes. He had a dark stubble from the night. His fingers were kneading each toe. He raised one to his mouth and kissed it.

"Hey," I said dreamily, pulling away.

"We got to talk."

"I did what I said I would. Didn't I?"

"You sure did. You did more." He took my empty glass away. "You damn near started a riot."

"Is that bad?"

"No. Guys liked you."

"You said if I danced here, you'd tell me about Gordon, give me something I could use to make him stop."

"Listen, you're special, Eve. Gordon and the Colony, I mean, that's small potatoes. I know these people in Iowa City, in Chicago even—"

"The wedding's tomorrow." I looked at the patch of floor where the sun was building. You could follow the tilting, glowing shaft of light, the air in here was so dusty. Some poison particles were always falling from the ceiling. "No. The wedding's *today*. So I need to know now."

"Know what?"

"Whatever it is you can tell me about Gordon."

"Who cares about Gordon?" he snapped. "I'm telling you that if you want to go places, I can get you there. Me. Not Gordon. Listen—"

I yawned. A big, unintentionally rude, jaw-cracking yawn. It made the whole night disappear, like a wet sponge passing over a blackboard. When I opened my eyes, it was morning. I felt strong. Even with the liquor inside me and the stink of smoke and the ache in my legs. Even with Lyle Olney giving me this threatening look. He'd taken off his cheap plastic-fabric jacket and had his shirt-sleeves rolled up. Hairy forearms, I noted mechanically. Men's bodies. The more you looked, the less interesting they got. It was better when there was still some sense of mystery. I got off my stool.

"You promised."

"Promised!" He laughed.

"Your dad said I could trust you."

"My dad?" He shook his head as if I'd punched him. "What've you been talking to my dad for?"

"He's on the crew."

"I know he's on the crew. But I didn't know you talked to him. That's why I got him that job, to shut him up."

"What have you got on Gordon?"

"What else did he say about me?"

"Nothing. Just that you were a man of your word . . . and that I should watch it around you."

"Dear old Dad."

"Well, was he right? Will you do what you said? Or not?"

He went behind the bar. I watched him kneel and come back up with the same leather pouch I had seen him stuff papers into before. He dried off the wooden surface with his sleeve and laid out several piles of official-looking documents.

"What are these?"

"Schedules. Affidavits. Bank statements. Tax declarations. See, your friend Gordon and I control the two ends of the labor flow here in Poweshiek County. He's got these work crews, white men, who don't need to be put up at night, who aren't on anyone's books, don't need an interpreter, aren't going to try and form some union. Hell, they don't even piss in the irrigation ditches! They hold it until they get home. They're these dream workers. You don't have to check for their temporary resident card, either. They're Americans. That's quite a commodity. It adds up, all he's taking in. So I do all the negotiating, make up the timetables, set the wages. And the money goes to Gordon and me together. To this church we set up. Well, it's not really a church. It's more like a nonprofit foundation. It's tax-exempt."

"The Tabernacle of the American Christ."

"How did you know?"

"It was on my paycheck. When I started working on the road crew."

He shook his head. "See, I told him that was a stupid idea, subcontracting you out. But Gordon hates to pay taxes. He thinks it's immoral or something."

He tried showing me some more papers, but I was pretty tired. Besides, it was boring. It wasn't what I was looking for. It was all about money.

"Well, where's the dirt?" I finally asked.

"This is it." He thumped one of the piles. "He's robbing you blind, don't you see? All the sweat of your labor, the men going out into the fields, the women cooking and cleaning and keeping house for them when they get home, all that's going into some bank account he keeps in Barbados. Only a small amount goes back to the Colony. Just enough to keep you going. That's what you can threaten him with, if you want."

"But that's nothing," I shrugged. "What he does with whatever money we make is up to him. He's an agent of God. We trust in his wisdom. That's the whole point."

He stared at me a minute.

"Well, if you people are such a bunch of suckers, then I guess that's fine." He started gathering up all the papers and putting them away. "Then you deserve to get taken. What did you expect to find?"

"Some spiritual flaw," I said numbly. "I told you, something that would make us stop loving him. Not something about money."

"*Spiritual* flaw? Now look, I held up my end of the bargain. I showed you what I had. And don't you dare tell anyone what you saw here or I'll—"

"Wait." I held on to one paper. "What's this?"

"That? That's our Letter of Incorporation. For when we set up the foundation. 'Tabernacle of the American Christ,' see? Gordon picked that."

I smiled. I had him. This was it. Not the document itself, not the evidence of the scam, of the money he was taking and using for God knows what. I had him because on this piece of heavy paper, with its deep government seal, Gordon had been forced to write down his name.

His real name.

"What is it?"

"Nothing." I didn't want Olney to know, to see how important this was. I let him take the paper back along with the others. He thought I was disappointed. He came back around the bar and began kneading my shoulders. I had to get out of there.

"Why are guys like this?" I asked.

"It's not guys. It's you," he said. "I don't know if it's your age or what, but you are putting out some powerful stuff."

"No, I'm not."

"It's probably chemical. You don't even feel it, do you? You don't feel anything."

"I have to go."

"Tonight, for example. I mean, I wish you could have seen yourself up there."

But I had. I glanced at the mirror, as if the picture of me dancing might be permanently scratched in the glass. Instead, it just reflected speckled asbestos ceiling tiles. It was light now, even down here. The electric bulbs seemed puny and stupid. He was going to try and kiss me. I hopped off the stool first and reached over to get my shoes. He caught me, kind of lazily, and pulled me toward him.

"No," I said. "It's late. I want to go home."

"I'll drive you."

"No cars in the Bible."

"Don't give me that crap. You've been in my car, remember?"

I turned my face away. But he didn't kiss me. Instead, his hand was somehow under my dress, between my legs. Like a snake. I tried to move and it coiled around, moving higher, reaching up, grabbing me.

"Lyle!"

He held me there with just his one hand, smiling, showing me how strong he was, almost lifting me off the ground. He wanted me to scream. I knew he wanted me to scream. I stared at him. My father! That's who it was. The father I'd seen in my dream. With his hideously grinning face and greasy hair, squeezing me, paralyzing me, telling me I liked it. In my dream, I remembered he had offered to make it hurt more. "If you want," he had said. But now he just looked at me, with this mocking expression, like there was nothing I could do. So I hit him. I slapped him, really, but since I happened to be holding one of my shoes the heel cut open his cheek and he backed away, spraying blood.

"Shit!"

"Don't you ever do that again," I lectured, flustered. It felt as if his disgusting sweaty hand was still there, would be there forever. There was blood on my dress, too. I brushed at it weakly. Great, first tar, now blood. I knew I was supposed to soak it in cold water, but there wasn't time. I actually wasted a few minutes putting on my shoes, which was pretty stupid, while he nursed his cut, peering in the cheap mirror behind the bar. He could have just come right back around and attacked me. But he was vain. He was worried about his face.

"I'm going," I announced, trembling, pretending it was the end of a really bad date. "I don't want a ride home from you."

I fumbled with the lock, trying to get the door open, but he still didn't come after me. I had my roll of bills. They felt good. I clutched them close to my side, as if they were a weapon.

"Cold bitch," I heard him mutter.

Cold enough, I thought.

I cut through the fields. I didn't obey the rows anymore, just pushed my way through the stalks. They fought me, this ocean of crinkly brown waves. They were top-heavy now with corn, the tassels spread out in the air. It wasn't a city. And it wasn't a maze, either. It was just an obstacle. I stuck my arms in front of me and parted the waves. My dress gave me strength. Leaves whapped against it and slid away. Tar had stiffened the front. There was a big smear of blood on the shoulder. It was my armor.

"Eve! Wait!"

There was still dew, but in a half hour the sun would burn it off. I had to get back and stop the wedding. That's all I could think about.

"I saw you from my window," Joey explained, panting. "I've been running after you. Didn't you hear?"

"No. You mean your window over the garage? How come you saw me? What were you doing there?"

"Waiting."

"Waiting for what?"

"For you!"

"Why?"

He looked out of shape. His hair was mussed. He couldn't catch his breath. He wasn't as perfect as usual, which was nice. We hadn't seen each other since that night, the night we hadn't done anything, and then the morning after, when everyone thought we had. I couldn't remember how we had parted, what I was supposed to feel.

"Well, you know." He gestured back behind us, to town. "Everyone knows. I mean, my dad told me. He came over, right after, he was so upset. He woke me up. We actually talked for about an hour. It was pretty amazing."

"He woke you up about what? What are you talking about?"

"Eve!"

There was Sunrise Service. I knew that. Morning Prayer, but with a difference. We were all going to pray for Gordon and Serena. Their happiness. It had been Gordon's brainstorm to have Richard, of all people, lead, just to show how totally under his thumb Gordon had him now. I wouldn't mind missing that. The couple themselves wouldn't be there anyway. They weren't allowed to see each other until the ceremony. So I had time, really. If I got home too early I would just get sucked into the massive preparations, all the food they were making, or cleaning up the Meeting Hall. Everything had to be spotless, to match Serena's spotless virginity. Although really, when you thought about it, thought about what she had done to Angela, she wasn't so pure. She had plenty of blood on her hands. Just not on her legs. Then I remembered that there wasn't going to be a wedding. That was the whole point. That was why I had to hurry.

"He said you were at the Number tonight. I mean, last night."

"Oh. That."

He had obviously been hoping I would say it wasn't true, that it was all some crazy hallucination of Herbert's.

"Did he tell you about our plan? That we can both go to San Diego? All three of us, I mean?"

"Yeah. He said you wanted a ride."

A ride.

"Will you do it?" I asked. "Will you go with him if I come, too? That was the deal. I could ride with you part of the way, and him the other part. I mean, if you're taking both cars."

"I can't get my car to run yet," he said uncertainly. That's why he was looking so troubled. My heart went out to him. His precious car. "Duffy and I are going to work on it all day."

"Can you fix it?"

"We have to. Dad wants to leave tonight."

"Tonight!"

"Eve, you really did that? You really stripped at the Number?"

"I took off my clothes. What's the big deal? I do that every night."

"Not in front of a bunch of guys."

"Well, I did it in front of you. You didn't seem to mind."

"That was different."

I took a deep breath. I was getting so tired of explaining myself. But I tried, one last time.

"It was part of a plan I have for getting out of here." A plan that's working, I wanted to add. If you'll just let me go now.

"Didn't it make you feel dirty?"

"Dirty? No! Why should it? I have a body. God made it. And everyone wanted to see it, so I showed them. I showed them I was normal, that I wasn't a freak. And if you and your dad have a problem with that, well, I'm sorry, but that's because you're petty and small-minded and . . . not good Christians."

He stared at me. Then he laughed.

"Dad said he was going back to his workshop and cut up your statue with a power saw."

"Of course he did. He had to say something like that to you. To act all disapproving. But he'll get over it. You told him you'd leave, right? If I came, too? I mean, we're going to San Diego, aren't we?"

He smiled. "If you want."

This excitement clicked on for me. The thought that I was finally going to get *moving*. I was billowing with power and liquor and that euphoria that comes beyond fatigue. My feet were just itching to dance again. They had this beat to them. It must have been from the jukebox. I had never heard music like that before. My pulse had been changed and was sending out different signals to my limbs. I was going to form a new world with the steps I took.

"So, where?" I asked. "The garage? Is that where your car's going to be? Tonight? You and me? Are the three of us going to drive together, or . . . ?"

"I want to be with you," he said.

We kissed. Tongues. The way he taught me. I felt his hands, so urgent, searching for a way in. He was starving. He'd never showed it before. Not like this. I wondered if it was because I had this new sleazy reputation, if that excited him. If we do it now, I reasoned, then I'll be sure of him. My head floated free, to watch from above. I was dancing again, with a stack of empty glasses where my body should be. Mother watched, from across the room, in her bed, while the boy covered her friend's mouth with his own, not kisses but a gag, so she wouldn't scream. And the little girl watched too, six years old, wide-eyed, the mattress she thought of as hers lit by a hippie candle that had layers of colored wax and was supposed to be either a sunrise or a sunset, she could never remember which, watched the two men try their best to coax some feeling from that writhing torso on the paisley sheet. But it was happening here, now, in a cornfield. I could see it from above. I had died and was just leaving my body. I could see this grunting, thudding . . . contest.

"What?" he asked.

"Nothing," I said.

I was breathing hard. I looked down and discovered I still had my clothes on, even though I could have sworn I was undressed. I had even felt a breeze and goose bumps forming on my exposed flesh. It was that dream of being naked in public, except it had invaded my waking life.

"What is it, Eve?"

"Nothing," I repeated. "It's . . . nothing. There's only one more thing I have to do, and then I'll be free."

He stood there, not backing off, waiting to see if he should start again. He couldn't read me, which made me sad, but also not. I didn't want to be read.

"So you talked with your dad," I finally got out. "That's good."

"Yeah."

"I brought you two together."

He shook his head, as if I had made some outrageous joke. But it was the simple truth.

"I should work on my car."

I'll make you so happy, I promised silently. You'll see.

"Tomorrow," I said. "Let's do it tomorrow. When I'm more awake. In the mountains. In the back seat."

"You're such a tease."

"You love it."

He laughed and turned to go.

"Tomorrow," I promised. It was a pact.

"Tomorrow's really today," he called back.

He was right. The sun was blinding us, shredding the leaves. I pushed ahead for a minute and then turned, to watch him walk away from me. That beautiful way he held himself and kind of sauntered through space. But it was too late. The stalks had closed behind Joey. There was nothing but rows of corn. It was morning. It was late. I had to hurry.

. . .

He came down the hill for me. That's how it felt. I was in the last row. The Meeting Hall doors were propped open wide. Sunshine glared in, disinfecting the space, the moldy corners, the shabby secondhand Bibles and dented folding chairs. The chairs were arranged differently than usual, not in a block, a solid wall, turning our backs on Outsiders, concealing from them our own private vision of God. They were in two sections, slanting toward the front, with a wide row in the middle missing. The aisle. I stood in back because I had come in last. Mother hadn't saved me a space. She was with the other women. They were all dressed up. They had done their hair. The men were in their Sunday outfits, stiff and embarrassed, clearing their throats, touching their sunburned necks. I had arrived a few minutes before the ceremony was supposed to start. Everyone was getting ready. Mother only had time to register my latest stain.

"Is that blood?"

"It's a style," I said.

"Aren't you going to change?"

"I don't think I have time. Besides, change into what?"

She looked back to her seat. It was with the others, not alone or off to the side. I understood the significance, and I was glad, glad to see that they had accepted her and that she was acknowledging her own drop in status. Her demotion. She wasn't the official Old Girlfriend anymore. Maybe it was a relief. The air was filled with the smell of pies, at least fifty of them, cooling along with all the other food on trestle tables down by the lake. My mouth watered. I hadn't eaten in so long. I imagined her fingers on the tender crust, pulling the covers high over my head when I was a little girl. I was so tired thoughts were cutting into each other, completing each other's image.

"You must have had a busy night."

"You too," she said dully.

"What?" At first I didn't get it. But the way she looked at me was new. Not critical anymore. Not concerned. Just sad and resigned. "You heard?"

"Everyone heard. Everyone knows. Are you happy now?"

I took in their stares again. It wasn't indifference or disapproval. I had moved beyond that.

"Where's Angela?" I asked.

She was the only one not here. But Mother didn't answer. She stepped away from me and went back to join the others. I wanted to call out to her that it was all right, that I was glad I had given her this way of doing public penance, of proving her loyalty. To give up on your own daughter, to cast her out, that was truly a worthy sacrifice. Even I was impressed.

"Mom?"

She stared past me. They all did. Gordon was standing outside his cabin. He was in a new suit, black, really well tailored, with dark glasses and shiny shoes. He even had a white carnation. How he had gotten a fresh white carnation in the middle of Iowa in late August I don't know, but it was the perfect touch. He saw us waiting and started down the hill.

He's coming for me, I thought, with this feeling of thrill and terror. For me! Whether he knows it or not.

But he did seem to know it, because he looked at me a few times, making his way around the lake. Or was I just imagining? Even through the dark glasses I thought I saw his gaze lock into mine. We were all standing. I envied how casual he made the trip seem, how his stride didn't break down into herky-jerky movements with all those eyes on it. "Praise God," several of us murmured, watching this small, smartly dressed man come toward us. It was impressive. We could feel the force of his will grow stronger with each step. He was casting a big net over us, drawing it tight. He was the fisherman. Fisherman of lost souls, come to save us. Come to haul us up, unwilling, out of the cold sea and into the sun, and then slam our heads against the side of the boat. Kill the sin. And if sin turned out to be 99 percent of who you were, if sin turned out to be your precious "personality," then so much the better. Because what did that give you but pain? What contribution did it make to the world but more suffering? Only when you were freed from your cold, flopping, scaly body of wants, only then were you left with what was pure and worthwhile. The God-in-you. The Divine spark. The unblinking fish eye that could stare straight into Heaven.

Gordon?

I snapped out of a split second's dream. I had been asleep on my feet. He had been in me, speaking to me, through me. I shook him away. He was almost at the Meeting Hall now. His eyes searched us out. It's a trick, I told myself. Everyone feels the way I do. Riveted. Accused. Unworthy. He was heading right for me. Don't be paranoid, Eve, I said. But my paranoia came true. He stopped in front of me and brought his mouth so close to mine I could see the dried, streaky, chewed surface of his lips. The skin around them was white. He was furious.

"You mocking me, girl? You think there are no limits to my patience? You think news doesn't travel fast in a hick town like this? Especially news like what I got last night?" He shook his head, disgusted. "You had to keep pushing, didn't you? Had to find a line to cross. Well, congratulations, missy. From now on you are a Colony girl in the most *literal* sense of the word. You don't set one foot outside these grounds. You don't talk to anybody who's not one of us. Not that anyone here is going to have much to say to you, either. Not for a good long time. No school this year. And no special dispensations either. You are grounded for the indefinite future.

You'll be working with the women, and when you're not doing that, you'll be doing *extra* chores, and if you ever get through with those, you'll be on your knees, praying for forgiveness, which will be damn slow in coming. You are a *girl* again, you hear me? A child. And if I hear any news, even a whisper, of you trying to pull another stunt like that, I will personally—"

"Finkelstein," I said.

I said it low. So only he could hear. I said it with my teeth. I didn't know if he had gotten it, so I said it again, a little louder.

"Finkelstein."

His mouth stayed open. There were words in there. I could see them, piled up and twisted, like when a train jumps the tracks.

"Who?" he asked, trying to brazen it out. Trying to pretend he didn't know what I was talking about. Then he gave that up. "Who you been talking to?"

"It's who I'm *going* to talk to."

Nobody could hear us. It was all in murmurs. The distance they kept from me, the Outcast, was actually the same as the distance they kept from him, the Beloved. They thought he was still chewing me out, telling me what my punishment would be. I could feel their satisfaction, their thirst for blood. She's finally getting hers, that spoiled brat. Along with her witchy mother.

Music started up. It came from his cabin. He had turned his giant speakers around again. Organ notes were flying high over the lake like a flock of Canada geese, a perfect V of sound, winging south. "Here Comes the Bride."

"Damn," he muttered.

"Nice suit," I said.

"Don't do this, Eve."

"Tell them you changed your mind. At the last minute. Tell them you came to your senses."

"I can't."

"Why not?"

He sighed and whipped his glasses off, mopped the sweat from his brow. One of those human gestures that redeem people, in my eyes, at least.

"Because I love her, OK?" he whispered. "That's why."

"Liar."

"No, it's true. Look."

He nodded to the ramshackle cabin. Eulalia must have been waiting for the music. Now she led Serena out. A lamb to the slaughter, I thought. Except . . . in her wedding dress, with her veil, she was this calm, beautiful woman. The woman I had always known she would become. She had told me she was destined to marry Gordon, and it showed in every inch of her body. Even he seemed overwhelmed. He forgot about me and started walking fast to get back on schedule. He trotted past the rest of the parishioners, then the Elders, and positioned himself at the front of the aisle, where he stood, waiting.

Don't you dare, Gordon, I called in my mind. Don't you dare go through with this after what I just told you, or I'll . . .

Or I would what? Shout out what I knew? Did I have the guts? I don't think Gordon knew himself. I could see him shift uneasily. The others probably thought it was cute, a little skittishness over getting married, just the right amount of being like them. They had no idea. He took in Serena, who was carefully climbing the hill, holding up her dress, almost at the Meeting Hall, and then he turned to me. I must have looked the part, the crazy, wild-eyed, jilted ex-, horribly dressed, the slut, "the kind they don't marry," especially when compared to this weightless piece of angel-food cake who was floating on past me down the aisle.

Could I do it?

Yes, I decided. Why not?

. . . and they'll tear you limb from limb, I stared back.

We both knew that part was true. It was the one thing they could never forgive. Stealing their money, luxuriating in the very things he had denied them, even taking his pick of their children, all that just reinforced his standing as a truly extraordinary pastor, so dedicated and special the ordinary rules didn't apply. But if these good, hardworking, God-fearing, White American Christians found out the man they had entrusted with their very salvation was really named Gordon Finkelstein, well, forget it. It wasn't fair, but it spoke to something deep inside them. Richard didn't realize how close to the truth he had come. They would never look at Gordon the same way again. I wouldn't even have to tell them the rest, what it had said under his name on the affidavit he had signed. Birthplace: Brooklyn, New York.

Serena wafted on by me as if I wasn't there. It was nothing personal. She ignored us all. She only had eyes for him. She left Eulalia behind without a word or nod and continued on up to the front. The music stopped. Birds started singing. Some even swooped into the Meeting Hall, banked in midair, and darted out again. Gordon smiled at her, at all of us, at me especially, I thought, and began.

He preached. It had been over a year. For a year we had lived on memories. And now, in a rush, it all came back. A sermon isn't made of words. It's a taking in, an all-embracing gesture, gathering the flock and leading it to the very gates of Heaven. Then it gets personal again and you need prayer. But Gordon standing in front of us, as he had not for so long, was all the stained glass, organ music, smoke, robes, fancy carvings, and marble floors you could imagine. He was the whole *show* most people call Religion, all that in the simplicity of a single man, speaking in a normal voice. He reminded us of our strange fate, to be alive on this earth, here, of all places, together, at the very darkest of times; of what we had created, a New Eden, the spiritual equivalent of America itself, a starting over. And now a turning point had come. It was time for the Colony to move forward. To break out of our self-imposed exile and bring the Word of God to all. Our lives would become the subject of a new Gospel. Words would come later. Words were afterthoughts, what clung to our actions, dirt or dust; but our actions themselves, how we lived, would become the story that a new millennium of worshippers would pore over for clues and signs. Scripture flew from his lips. And it was us, all of us! As if the Bible prophesied our very existence. We started where it left off. He proved us to ourselves. Chapter and verse. That's why we loved him.

Then he started reciting the marriage vows. My body gave a start. I had been so mesmerized by his sermon, by its hypnotic, unexpected message, and then he had slipped so seamlessly and quietly into the ceremony itself, as if one led naturally into the other, that I had forgotten to jump up and testify. To unmask him. I saw what he had done. He had blown it up into something more grand and meaningful; he had made his marriage a symbol for healing the Colony, taking it to this new level, mending the rift that had grown between him and us, uniting us all through this spiritual bond and signaling the start of a New Covenant. Without waiting, he looked into Serena's eyes and asked her if she would have him as her husband. He knew the vows by heart, like he knew everything else. We all stopped breathing and strained to hear. And she spoke for all of us when she said yes. Then he tilted his head as if listening to some inner voice and answered—repeated, really—that he took Serena as his wife, to love, honor, and cherish, for richer or for poorer, in sickness and in health, for as long as they both shall live. Amen.

He turned to the congregation and asked if any of us objected. It was a typical shrewd Gordon move. He had tied up the big and small, so it wasn't clear what we were sanctioning. He waited.

People looked to Richard, of course. He was the obvious person, the leader of the opposition. I was no one. Just some girl who had strayed and been destroyed, casually, in passing. But Richard was the one who was broken. Not me. He would object all right, tonight, with Angela, in the privacy of their own home. But for now he pretended not to notice. I opened my mouth. Gordon was looking straight at me. Are you sincere? I wondered. That was the question you could ask forever with Gordon and never really get an answer. He had preached again, for the first time in a year. And with a new message. He was here among us, as he had not been for so long. I was grateful for that. And he said he loved Serena. He had never said that before. Not about Mother. Not about me. Did he? I hadn't even considered the possibility. Because if he loved Serena . . . then I had to give him up. It came to me: All this time I had been looking to fall in love, but maybe what I really had to do was *stop* loving, before the rest of my life could happen. Stop loving Gordon. Stop loving this place. I stood there, not saying anything, just being another dumb female, while the congregation waited and the birds sang. Inside, I was dying.

"I *will* kiss the bride," he warned.

Everyone laughed.

Music came on right after. It was magic. He glanced up to his house, nodded, and these notes exploded in the air. "The Wedding

March." I asked him later how he did it. He grinned. He was very proud.

"It was all a tape," he explained. "First I recorded 'Here Comes the Bride,' then I recorded twenty-five minutes of silence. So while I was preaching, I was preaching over the silence, so to speak. I allowed time for the ceremony and for our responses . . . so all I had to do was make sure we ended right on cue. Pretty slick, huh?"

"And this is still a tape, what's happening now?"

"It's all a tape, Eve. Our very thoughts are prerecorded."

The speakers were blasting hymns. Down below there was a party. It had been going on for hours. We were hysterical with happiness. We were so relieved. The shadow that had lain over the Colony for so long had finally been lifted. And the future had been revealed. Praise Him. I could still feel what I was supposed to feel, what everyone else felt, even though I was no longer part of it. I sat under the willow, inside its branches, alone, and thought about how I was the only one left. Jewell, Angela, Serena, one by one they had made their choices and disappeared, abandoned our secret hideaway, our refuge. Now the green was turning yellow.

"Figured I'd find you here."

He had come with meat, potatoes, corn, and a big wedge of peach pie. I smiled at the pie, but couldn't eat. Even though I was starving. I stared at the paper plate.

"Persephone."

"Who?" he asked.

"She went to Hell and ate a pomegranate," I remembered, thinking of Herbert's dead wife. "With six seeds. So she had to go back every year for six months. That's why we have winter."

"Well, you've eaten a lot more than six seeds here," he pointed out. "Over the years."

He looked good. His body was at ease. He sat on the ground. He had a big smile. The carnation was still fresh and perfect. He was almost handsome.

"Those things I said," he began, "about punishing you and all. I hope you realize that was mostly for show. I had to tough up on you in front of the congregation. Otherwise there'd be talk. We can work something out, just you and me. Something less drastic. Maybe—"

"Gordon Finkelstein."

"Yeah, yeah." He tried to be casual, but I saw it still made him cringe. "The only other person who says it that way is my mother."

"So you're . . . ?"

"All the original Christians were really something else, Eve. Think about it."

"Then how did you become a Tertiary Baptist?"

"Well, I started out doing stand-up and—"

"Doing what?"

"Never mind." He speared a baby potato and examined it. "Put it this way: I found where my talent lay."

"And where was that?"

"Here. In the heartland. In America."

"But do you believe?"

"I don't have to believe. That's not my job. I don't think about believing. It gets in the way, makes you self-conscious. It gums up the works. Did Jesus believe? I don't think so. He was too busy walking on the water. That's a tricky stunt, you know. It requires incredible powers of concentration. *It is not easy.* You're the ones who have to believe. You, out there. The audience. All I think about is turning in a good performance. The Lord is my spotlight, I shall not want. You saw it today, the way He shone on me."

"But then it's an act. The way you talk, the way you dress, everything! You're ashamed of who you are."

"We're all ashamed. That's why we're here. Anyone with half a lick of sense is ashamed."

"Not me," I said.

"Then you are my most perfect disciple." He cleared his throat and looked embarrassed. "Though wiggling your rear end for a bunch of yahoos down at the Number is not the most accepted path to Christian enlightenment. You didn't let Olney keep a cut of your tips, did you?"

"I want to leave here."

"Of course you do. Don't you think I want to leave here from time to time? But wanting to leave is the most compelling reason to stay on. You got to fight your desires, Eve. Every step of the way."

"I don't think so, Gordon. I think I want to go with my desires for a while. I mean, I'm sixteen. Desires are pretty much all I have."

"You're sixteen?"

"My birthday was last week."

He shook his head.

"I remember when you were just a little slip of a thing. Aw, come on, Eve. Let me make it right. I'll take back all that stuff I said to you. I'll take it back publicly. How about that? Serena needs you here. And what about your mother?"

"I'm going to San Diego."

"With Herbert Biswanger and his moron son?"

"Joey's not a moron."

"Upper body type," Gordon said dismissively. "It's like they *want* to strengthen their minds but they only get as far as their necks. It's a bad move, Eve. Those two are mediocrities. They're not worthy of you. And San Diego!"

"What's wrong with San Diego?"

"Nothing. Very pretty place. I just have this theory that New York City is where the smart people live, and then, as you cross the country, from east to west, the population seems to grow progressively more ignorant."

I reached to him. I put my fingers to his troubled face. He took off his glasses.

"That New Covenant you preached. You believe in it?"

"Sure. Why not? Can't just sit around here and wait for the Second Coming."

"I thought that was exactly what we were supposed to do."

"Expansion is a logical step," he shrugged. "Like in a business. First you solidify your base, then—"

"What about all that money in Barbados?"

"You know about that, too, huh? I guess you do know too much to stay. That's my nest egg. In case things go wrong. Nothing sadder than a preacher without a pension." He shook his head. "I got to go up there soon."

"To the house?"

"Yeah. Serena already left the party. She's . . . changing, I guess."

"You scared?"

"Surprisingly, yes. Didn't think I would be."

"I'd be scared, too."

He laughed.

"What do you want, Eve?"

"I want to leave tonight, with Herbert and Joey. And I don't want any trouble. I don't want you sending anyone after us."

"Done," he said promptly. "That it?"

"No. I want you to do something about Angela."

"Angela?"

"I want you to take her away from Richard. She can move into our cabin. Mother will take care of her. They'll be good for each other."

He rubbed his eyes. "That's not going to be easy. Stepping on Richard again so soon. It'll cost me with the Elders. Cost me some of my precious credit."

"There you go, talking like a Jew."

"Don't you get crude," he warned, wagging his finger. "I never preached any of that White American Christian crap and I never will. As for Angela, OK, I'll save her sorry ass for you. Not that she'll appreciate it."

"One other thing."

It had come to me, this sudden burst of inspiration.

"Don't push it, Eve."

"I want the Camaro."

"What?!"

"It's for the best, Gordon. That car's too flashy. What are you? Forty? Forty-five? You're not going anyplace. You're a married man now."

"Son of a bitch."

"And don't forget to keep up the leasing payments."

"I taught you too well," he grumbled, fishing around for the keys.

I'd like to think that, when he gave them to me, he felt a great weight being lifted. Actually, he looked as if he was being robbed.

"It's a beautiful suit." I tried cheering him up. "And I love the carnation. That was the perfect touch. It's amazing it hasn't wilted."

"You're still a sucker. It's fake. Look."

He turned back the lapel. A thin rubber tube ran down his shirt to his pants pocket. "Couldn't get the real article in that weed patch that passes for a flower shop here. I found this baby at a novelty store, of all places."

"You mean it squirts?"

"I guess." He played with the rubber squeeze ball. "It's not loaded or anything. Should be. I should fill it with holy water. Make it into a kind of practical-joke baptism. Hey, that's not a bad idea! The element of surprise, of hilarity even, in being reborn. I like that. Maybe I can work it into something . . ."

By evening I had been up for almost two days. It took me a while to figure out how to turn on the Camaro's headlights. I sort of got what Gordon had explained to me about gears, though I felt as if I was creating a few of my own, careening down the county highway. I couldn't wait to see Joey's face when I brought him this bright red love offering, plus all the money I had taken from under my mattress. We would break 100 miles per hour on our way out of town.

When I got to the garage, he was still working on his old car. His body was bent far over the engine, with that same light hanging from the hood. It was getting dark earlier, so it lit him very beautifully. His muscles stretched. He had lost weight. His jumpsuit wasn't new anymore. So much had happened. It was tighter than I remembered, and worn in places. Almost worn through. I snuck up and lovingly ran my fingers down his sides. His hips straightened. He didn't hit his head this time. He stood up and I saw it wasn't him at all. It wasn't Joey. I jumped back.

"Hello," he said.

"Who are you?" My hands tried rubbing off whatever it was they had just touched. There was no name over the breast pocket, just DUFFY'S AUTOMOTIVE.

"I'm the owner," he said. "Can I help you?"

"You're Duffy?"

He couldn't have been more than thirty. Tall and thin. He had a slightly open mouth, as if he was permanently surprised. His light curly hair and complexion were both sandy. He must have had

freckles when he was younger. Now they were just this kind of tex-
ture to his skin. His eyes were light brown, too. He had unzipped his
overalls enough to free a big Adam's apple. His face was long and
stretched out, like a dog's.

"Can I help you with something?"

"But this is Joey's car."

"It *was* Joey Biswanger's car. I bought it off him."

"When?"

"This afternoon."

I wanted to sit. But there was no place. I felt my knees getting
weak.

"Joey left town," he said carefully. "A couple of hours ago. His
father came by to get him. They were all packed up. This thing
wouldn't have made it over the mountains, anyway. Is that yours?"

He nodded to the Camaro.

"Yeah."

"You want me to turn off the engine?"

While he did, I went around to Joey's car, opened the door, and
sat on the passenger side. Where I had ridden around for the first
time. Where I had first been kissed.

"You OK?" He was kneeling on the asphalt, trying to find my
eyes.

"You're Duffy," I said again, as if it was news to him. "I didn't
think you were a real person."

Mediocrities. That's what Gordon called them. Not worthy of
me. But apparently I wasn't worthy of them, either. I swallowed
hard. It's not easy being cast out twice in one day. At least the
Colony had done it to my face. I looked up at the room above the
garage, the little window. Was my love still there? I remembered
throwing it, the beautiful curve it made in the air, and the trail it
left, all colors, like a rainbow. Where was it now? My love. Lying on

the floor with all the other junk Joey hadn't taken with him, hadn't had room for? Or was it with the sawdust and wood shavings Herbert made after sacrificing my likeness to whatever cheap suburban god he worshipped?

"Well, I am," he said.

I looked back down. He was still kneeling, watching me. Duffy.

"I'm sorry. What did you say?"

"I'm a real person." He grinned.

I had forgotten all about him. I tried to figure out what he was talking about. His eyes weren't really brown. They glittered in a funny way, as if they had copper in them. Or gold. It must have been the light. Except there wasn't any. It was night. He was wiping his hands on a rag. Very slowly. The rag looked soft. I was staring.

"I'm Eve."

"I know who you are."

He'll do, I thought.

The next morning I got up early. The Camaro was waiting. I didn't go past the speed sign. I didn't try to break 100. I was through playing games. I headed out of town in the other direction, over the entrance ramp I helped build. I headed east, to New York City, where the smart people live.